Lilith Whispers Back

a novel

KAREN STEUR

ARCHWAY PUBLISHING

Archway Publishing books may be ordered through booksellers or by contacting:

Archway Publishing
1663 Liberty Drive
Bloomington, IN 47403
www.archwaypublishing.com
1-(888)-242-5904

ISBN: 978-1-4808-1282-6 (sc)
ISBN: 978-1-4808-1283-3 (e)

Library of Congress Control Number: 2014919143

Printed in the United States of America.

Archway Publishing rev. date: 12/08/2014

DEDICATION

THIS BOOK AND THE AUTHOR'S PROCEEDS are dedicated to education for the prevention of childhood sexual abuse. May we protect the children and never ignore their cries for help.

Author's Note

THIS IS A WORK OF FICTION. With two exceptions, all names, places, and situations are fictional and in no way a correlation with actual people or facts. The exceptions are Michele Anderson, who is an animal communicator and whose insight and expertise facilitated one of the stories, and Paula Vaughn, my spiritual mentor.

ACKNOWLEDGEMENTS

I WANT TO THANK MY WRITER'S group, Louisville's Writers on the Range, (Lyla Hamilton, Paula Karen and Leslie Myers), for their support and superb editing. I give a huge thanks to Leslie Myers for her beautiful painting which is the cover of this book. I give humble gratitude to my editor, Ruth Feiertag of PenKnife Writing and Editorial Services, for her expertise and gentle guidance. And thank you to all the folks at Archway for making this possible. Any flaws or errors remain my own.

I want to thank my children, Sabrina and Tara, for your support, praise, and honesty. I love you, your husbands, and my grandchildren with all my heart.

TABLE OF CONTENTS

Whispers

On the wind they come
Gentle, unconcerning
She might take notice
Or dismiss and continue on

Sometimes they nag
Thoughts drift in
Voices but no one there
Dismiss again as if imagined

But in her quiet
A message comes
She listens
It makes sense

An awakening
She understands
The gift
Of whispers in her quiet

Karen J. Steur. "Whispers". *Palimpsest A Creative Journal of the Humanities*.CU Literaria Society: 8 Days a Week. Boulder, CO. 2012. p.36.

Whispers in Her Quiet

THROUGH THE OPEN WINDOW ON WARM summer nights the sounds of crickets, cicadas, owls and coyotes are heard. It was the crickets that held her attention. Crickets make their sound by running the top of one wing along the other. That was what she heard in her ears: an orchestra of changing notes and pitches. The sound was initially disturbing until she understood that the sound was whispers that became comforting, soothing, and rhythmic. But it was never quiet.

As far back as she could remember Lilith had a sense, a gut feeling, or an awareness of something, something she could not see. Her mother, Julia, said she had an overactive imagination.

When Lilith was seven her friend Sara was killed in a car accident. While traveling on vacation Sara's family car was hit by another car that ran through a red light. Sara and her mother, who were not wearing seatbelts, were thrown from the spinning car and died. Lilith heard the words her teacher spoke as she gently notified the class, but these words were hard to absorb. Lilith had never known anyone that had died. That night Sara appeared in Lilith's dreams. Lilith and Sara played together as they did last week at the park behind the school. Being with Sara felt in some ways the same, in other ways different. Sara was lighter, wispy, and almost transparent. Lilith would see her waiting at the park, leaning against a picnic table or tree. They would laugh and run. After they played Sara would wave and go off in the opposite direction from which they used to travel. Lilith called out asking Sara where she was going. Sara just turned, smiled and waved. Sometimes Lilith was sure she saw Sara when she looked out the school window toward the park.

The dreams continued for several months. Then one day Sara was gone. It was as if she had moved away or moved to another space in time. Lilith did not share this experience with anyone. She did not want anyone to tell her it wasn't true. It was hers.

When Lilith was 15, an accident affected her hearing. She was on a small plane with friends and a school counselor going to a conference on career aptitudes and opportunities. As the plane took off it had trouble pressurizing and once pressurized, there was an explosive sound to the right of Lilith's seat. Screams were heard from the passengers as oxygen masks dropped from the upper compartment above their seats. Lilith quickly put on her mask and motioned for her friends to do the same.

The pilot's voice was heard over the intercom. He spoke calmly, "This is Captain Taylor. The plane is safe. Please remain in your seats with seatbelts fastened. There was a problem with pressurizing the aircraft that caused that loud noise. We are flying low in oxygen rich air. You do not need the oxygen masks. We are returning to the airport." He repeated, "The plane is safe, you are in no danger. We will be landing soon. Please remain in your seats. Flight attendant prepare for landing. Thank you for your cooperation."

Lilith looked around at her friends and saw that Fabian and Tasha, the ones closest to her, were holding their ears and crying.

She reached over and touched them gently and said, "Are you OK?"

Fabian answered, "My ears. They hurt."

Lilith said, "It was from the loud noise. We'll have you checked out when we land."

Tasha called out, "Lilith, you are bleeding! Look at your shoulder."

Lilith looked at her shoulder and then put her hand to her right ear feeling the trickle of blood. She smiled at her friends, "I guess I'll be checked out as well."

Lilith had not noticed the ringing and throbbing in her ears. She tried to keep her panic to herself. She took in slow deep breaths and let them out slow. She felt a calm come over her and knew she and her friends would be all right. She wasn't sure where this knowing came from, but she was grateful.

The plane landed safely, but Lilith had extreme barotrauma to her ears, especially the right one. The other passengers seated at the back of the plane with Lilith, including Fabian and Tasha, had pain to their ears, but it resolved with no damage. The explosive noise damaged Lilith's hearing in that it heightened her sensitivity to sound. Ballgames, concerts, and church organ music became intolerable. Ear plugs were her constant companion to help muffle the loud sounds of the world around her. Her ears were permanently sensitive to sound, and her world was never quiet. Lying in bed at night, she heard a sound like crickets in her head. If she concentrated, it almost sounded like whispers. There were changes in tones. She would silently speak to the whisperers and heard a response.

Lilith's Mom, Julia, felt sure it was tinnitus and took her to a specialist. The doctor found no physiologic reason for the ringing in Lilith's ears. Julia, remembering that Lilith had always been able to sense events before they happened, came to realize that Lilith's intuitive gifts were heightened by the accident and the ringing in her ears.

It took a couple of years for Lilith to adjust to the sound sensitivity and whispers in her ears. And she mourned the loss of joining her friends at concerts and ballgames. But she was delighted to find that she could tolerate organ music in church with the use of ear plugs. Her challenges made her aware of her blessings, and she found she was interested in helping others with loss. She decided she wanted to study to be a nurse.

Lilith sought out psychics and read everything she could get her hands on to help her understand her gifts. She met some good gifted people as well as some who had the wish but not the gift. She was surprised to find she had angels with her. They spoke and assisted her in weeding out the psychics that would be of no help to her. She came to realize she was on a life-long growing journey.

One moonless night when Lilith was a senior in high school, she stepped out the door of Shady Hills Nursing Home where she worked as a nursing aide and got into her Jeep. She turned onto the freeway to head home. Suddenly a swish of sound ran through her ears. It was so powerful that her body swayed. It captured her attention and she became more vigilant. In her heightened awareness, she spotted a stalled car ahead in her lane. She had just enough time to maneuver into the other lane and barely miss the car. Lilith felt she had been warned. Lilith called 911 to report the car and gave thanks to God and her angels.

Lilith believed she had a gift, the gift of clairaudience. This gift allowed her to communicate with the spirits of those who had died as well as with the angels who surround her. After a friend or family member died she felt blessed to be able to converse with them before they departed this place. It was reassuring to her to know that death was not simply the end.

Thoughts, messages and answers whirled around Lilith. It was sometimes hard for her to distinguish which thoughts were hers. But she learned to pay attention.

Lilith became accustomed to her whispers. She felt guidance, reassurance, and shared joy, and on an occasion she received a warning or advisement. Lilith felt comfort in the whispers in her quiet.

Baby Lilith

JOHN STANSON WAVED HIS LONG LEAN arm at his friends still on the slope after he took off his skiis. He looked around at the beautiful mountains. It had been a great day of skiing, but his legs were tired. Even though he worked out constantly in the army, he hadn't skied since college. He entered the lodge to get some food and something warm to drink. He looked around as he headed toward the snack bar. He couldn't help notice the blue ski suit that he had spotted on the slope. She was sitting near the fire.

Boy, could she ski! John said to himself as he remembered admiring her as she easily passed him on the slope.

John was surprised that she looked up at him through long dark eye-lashes and smiled. He had not been interested in any woman for a long time, so he headed toward her.

Julia's heart beat faster. This ruggedly handsome man was heading toward her. His stride was without hesitation, very confident. Julia rose from her seat where she was warming her cold feet against the stones of the fireplace hearth.

John approached Julia as she stood and said, "Hi, my name is John Stanson." He extended his hand to her.

Julia took his hand in hers. Although her hand was small next to his, she gave him a strong hand shake and said, "Hi, my name is Julia Montgomery."

"Can I buy you some hot chocolate?" John asked.

Julia noticed his warm smile. "No, thank you, I have some right here. But would you like to join me?"

John forgot that he was hungry and thirsty and sat down next to her. "Are you from here or on vacation?"

Julia answered, "I'm from Denver. I came up for a long weekend with some friends from work."

What kind of work do you do?" John asked.

"I work for Stonewell Homes. I manage the office accounts," Julia answered.

John removed his ski hat revealing his short cropped blond hair. He ran his hand through his hair as if he was combing it back in place. He caught Julia smiling at him. John laughed, "Yes, I'm in the service. This is the style of my job."

"Which branch of the service are you in?" Julia asked with a smile.

"I'm a sergeant in the US army. I've been with the army for about five years. This is the first leave that I have taken. Some old friends from college invited me to come skiing here in Breckenridge for the week."

"Are you having a good time?" Julia asked.

"Yes, I am. I haven't skied in years. It's fun. Some of my friends have been taking me down the black slopes. I'm sure I'll feel my sore muscles tomorrow." John smiled as he looked at Julia.

"Would you and your friends like to join me and my friends at the Steakhouse for dinner tonight, say 7pm?" John asked.

Julia was about to answer when she saw her friend Kate enter the lodge and head toward her. "Here comes my friend, Kate, now. I will check with her," Julia answered with a smile.

"I figured you were hiding out in here." Kate said with a laugh as she looked from Julia to John.

"Kate, this is John Stanson. He invited us to join his friends for dinner at the Steakhouse. What do you think?"

Kate shook hands with John and replied, "I've wanted to try that place, sounds good to me."

John said, "Well, I better get some water and rejoin my friends. How many in your group? I'll make a reservation. And it was nice to meet you both." He smiled at them both, but his eyes lingered on Julia.

Julia said, "There are four of us. We will see you later."

The two women watched John leave. Kate turned to Julia.

"Cute! About time you showed some interest in a guy."

"Cut it out. We just met," Julia laughed. "But he sure is cute. And those blue eyes, I could swim in them."

John and Julia started skiing together, enjoying each other's friends, and time alone just the two of them. John's friends were happy he met Julia, and Julia's friends were delighted as well. Julia's time in the mountains flew by and it was time to leave. John still had three more days, but he cut it short and drove down to Denver with Julia and Kate.

Julia invited John to stay with her for the rest of his leave, which was two and a half weeks. John toured the city and spent time in the library reading while Julia was at work. He prepared dinner for her when she arrived home. They played games with questions to get to know each other better.

One of Julia's questions for John was, "What was your most embarrassing moment?"

John thought for a moment and said, "I am sure there are others. But I am remembering one from college."

Julia laughed. "Share!"

John took a deep breath in and let it out dramatically with a smile. "When I was a pledge for a fraternity in college, all the pledges were taken camping. They gave us some red hot chili that was very spicy. I had eaten my share of hot food, but something in it upset my intestinal tract. I found an outhouse and thought I had snuck away quietly. While inside the outhouse, I heard a noise and all of a sudden the roof and walls were lifted up. There was a flash of light from a camera, and laughter as I sat with my pants down. I was embarrassed. It was so stupid. I then decided fraternities were not for me. Oh, and my friends in Breckenridge had nothing to do with this group."

"How awful for you!" Julia said, holding back a laugh. Then after collecting herself she said, "I hope those boys matured before they graduated."

John laughed and replied, "Probably not. Now it's your turn. Any regrets in your college years?"

Julia's breath caught and she hesitated. John, sensing her pain, took her in his arms and said, "You can tell me anything."

Julia cringed as she remembered. She began, "I was so in love with Paul, my fiancée. We planned a life together after college. He took me home to meet his parents. It was to be a lovely weekend. When we arrived at the family ranch, Paul's dad, Richard, asked if we would like to take a ride on horseback around the property. I was amazed how much Paul and his dad resembled each other. Martha, Paul's mom, settled us into our separate rooms. Paul was to sleep in his childhood bedroom, and I had the guest room. Paul winked at me, and I smiled remembering that he had told me how old fashion his mom was. It was a great ride, and the rolling hills were beautiful. Fall provided a painted picture of yellow, red and gold. I could tell Paul was pleased to see how well I rode. We galloped home and cooled the horses before cleaning up for dinner. The dinner gathering was full of good food, laughter, and stories."

Julia paused, got up and got a drink of water. John waited patiently on the couch.

"Would you like some water?" Julia asked.

"No, I'm good. Thanks," John responded and patted the cushion of the couch next to him.

Julia put down her glass and joined him. She leaned into John and felt his warmth. After a few minutes she began again.

"I was tired from the traveling, riding and a bit of wine, so I went to bed and fell fast asleep. I was awoken by the creak of the door opening.

With sleepy eyes I saw Paul sneaking into my room. He dropped his clothes and snuggled in bed behind me. His touch was soft and gentle. He kissed my neck. As I turned to him, I found in horror that it was not Paul at all but his father. I jumped away and started to scream. He pulled me back and covered my mouth. I struggled and fought as he grabbed at my breasts and between my legs. I continued to struggle, and our bodies fell off the bed. Richard grabbed his clothes and ran from the room. I curled in a ball, trembling and crying. I couldn't believe this had happened. I pulled a robe on and tied it tightly around myself. Peeking out the door to see if anyone was in the hall, I ran to Paul's room. I shook him out of a deep sleep. 'Hey babe, something wrong?' Paul asked. I cried, 'I need to leave now. We need to leave this house now.' Sitting up quickly, Paul asked, 'Are you sick?' 'No! Yes! I will meet you in the car.' I ran from the room, dressed, and waited in the car when Paul entered. My bags were in the back seat. I looked at Paul. 'Where are your bags?' I asked. 'What do you mean? I am just taking you to the hospital,' Paul responded. 'No, we are going home,' I cried. 'What is the matter with you?' Paul yelled. I cried out through sobs, 'Your dad came into my room and tried to rape me!' I was devastated and wanted to leave with Paul. But he did not believe me and we broke up. Going back to college was tough. Paul told stories about me to our friends and I was shunned from the group."

John held Julia tight as she cried. When she stopped crying he asked, "Did you notify the police?"

Julia's red eyes looked at John, "No, I was too ashamed."

John took Julia's hands and looked deep into her eyes, "You had nothing to be ashamed of. You did nothing wrong." John took a deep breath and let it out fast. "I wish I could get my hands on those bastards!" he yelled out a bit louder than he meant to.

Julia smiled through tears, "I wish you could too."

Julia sighed, "My roommates believed me. So I didn't feel as lonely. My parents died my first year of college in a car accident. So I was so glad to have my three roommates, one was Kate.

John sighed, "My parents died when I was graduating from college. There was an electrical fire in their old house that started while they were sleeping. I was told the smoke killed them. They never had a chance to save themselves. I was so distraught and angry I didn't know what to do with myself. Before I left school, I was notified that I was drafted, so off I went to Vietnam. I had no family to come home to, so I didn't take any of my leaves. I just kept working."

Julia cupped John's face in her hands. "I'm so sorry for your loss. I found that I had to make a new family. Perhaps that is what you did with the guys you serve with."

John leaned into Julia's touch and pulled her into his arms. "You are right about that. And you know, I hadn't thought about family until I met you. I love you, Julia. What would you think about marrying me?"

Julia gasped and her mouth hung open, then she smiled and threw her arms around John's neck. "Yes, I will marry you today, tomorrow, or when you get back. I love you too!"

They both cried and held each other. Then John said, "I want to get married today and not waste a moment. Life is precious and we never know what lies ahead."

Julia said, "I would be honored to be your wife."

They went to the court house and got a license and found a justice of the peace who agreed to stay late in his office to marry them. Kate and her boyfriend Dan stood up for them as they exchanged vows. John had his parent's wedding bands that he always kept with him. The rings fit perfectly.

After the service John announced to Julia, Kate and Dan, "I have a picnic reception planned in Boulder County."

Julia laughed, "You're kidding, right? It's winter and forty-two degrees out!"

John's face lit up with mischief, "Trust me, you will like it."

They piled into Julia's Toyota while John put supplies in the back. It was a thirty minute drive. They began passing small farm houses.

John pulled into a long drive that was fenced on both sides. The remains of a building appeared into view.

Julia asked, "Was that your parent's house?"

John responded, "Yes, this was their property which is ours now." He stopped the car in front of a big fire pit that overlooked the mountain range. "You guys can stay in the car while I make a fire. I am going to cook you up a burger feast with schmoores for dessert."

Julia hopped out of the car followed by Kate and Dan. "That sounds yummy. But we don't need to sit in the car. We want to look around. This is beautiful," Julia replied.

John smiled at his new wife, "I want to build us a home here someday."

Julia and John were just starting their lives together when John's unit was called back to Vietnam. They wrote letters for three months. Then Julia's doorbell rang. She opened the door to find two men in uniform, one and officer and the other a chaplain. They told her that John was killed in action fighting for his country.

Julia wailed, "Not my John!"

Julia felt as if her chest had been crushed. Moving day by day was excruciating. She couldn't eat or sleep. She returned to work three weeks after the memorial. But weakness and fatigue overtook her and she collapsed at work. Kate took her to the hospital.

A doctor entered the room and greeted Julia and Kate and then turned to Julia. "Julia, my name is Jason Schmidt. I'll be caring for you while you are in the emergency room. We're giving you fluid and electrolytes. You were very dehydrated." After getting a history and hearing about Julia's husband, Dr. Schmidt said, "I'm so sorry for your loss. I can give you some names of grief counselors in the area." He rolled his chair closer to Julia and touched her hand. "Julia, your blood work indicates that you are pregnant."

"I'm pregnant?" Julia exclaimed in surprise.

"Yes. When was your last period? I want to determine how far along you are now," Dr. Schmidt added.

"OK, Oh my God, John's baby!" Julia cried out with tears streaming down her face. Kate rushed to Julia's side and took her hand.

Kate said, "Don't worry, I will help you. I'm going to be an auntie!"

Julia's mind wandered back to the last time she saw John. He had held her close and whispered, *"Never forget this beautiful time we have had together. We are and will continue to be blessed."*

Julia wondered if John sensed that he wouldn't be back and knew she was pregnant. The months before his death he had kept a journal titled "For Julia". In it he wrote about his life before her and how it had become richer after meeting her. After his death she received the journal, found that he had taken out a life insurance policy, and titled the land, which had been his parents, in her name. He made sure that his family was taken care of in the event of his death.

Six months later a baby girl was born. She was six pounds, eleven ounces, with light blond/brown hair and big blue eyes like her father. Julia gazed down at her baby nestled inside the wooden cradle she had bought in a second hand store. The baby stirred and she picked her up.

Julia held her close and whispered. *"I will call you Lilith. You will grow to be strong, brave, and stand on your own. You are my warrior princess. I will teach you to be wise, compassionate, and happy. Perhaps, like your father, you will have a sensing, a knowing. And with your gifts and talents, you will know how to take care of yourself in this uncertain world."*

Julia leaned down and kissed Lilith's soft head, breathing in the intoxicating baby smell. Her eyes filled with tears. She knew she was speaking for herself as well.

Julia realized that her tears were spilling over onto baby Lilith. She quickly brushed them off, and took a deep breath in and let it out.

She whispered, *Someday, I will tell you about my happiness with your dear father. But for now Lilith, my warrior princess, you sleep while I take care of you until you can take care of yourself.*

Young Lilith

LILITH WOKE AND SMILED. THE REUNION this past weekend at Lake Dillon with her suite mates from college had been memorable. Lilith, Angie, Rebecca and Samantha had filled their time with memories of their support, fun pranks and love. Even though it had been two years since they graduated, the young women would regress to acting like college kids. They would laugh and tease each other. It was a relaxing step back in time, and they got to share their lives since graduating. Samantha had just finished her second year of law school, and was interning for a handsome Texas attorney who was smitten with her. Angie had introduced her partner Sue to her parents and was pleasantly surprised at their warmth and acceptance. And Rebecca was assistant editor of a local newspaper, and was working on her first novel. Lilith had shared some of her nursing stories and her amazing opportunity to fly with a flight nurse on the hospital helicopter. That was a job she aspired to do someday when she had more experience than just two years.

Lilith stretched and yawned. It had been a great weekend, but Monday meant back to work. As she climbed out of bed her mind started anticipating her day in the ICU. She wondered what kind of patients she would have, and she got excited. It was the challenge that fueled her. She learned something new every day. She loved the adrenalin rush when alarms went off, and she had to jump into action. Her job was very satisfying and often humbling as she experienced the love, hope and sometimes loss with her patients and their families. It was a Sunday morning and it could be quiet, or wild with the aftermath of the Saturday celebrations.

Today was Fathers' Day. Lilith would travel to her mom's house after work for dinner. It was their tradition to celebrate with Julia telling Lilith stories of her dad, who died before she was born. She never tired of hearing her mom's exciting tales. Even now at twenty-three, Lilith still got an ache in her heart thinking about how she had never known her dad, and how her mom raised her on her own. As Lilith shook off the sadness, she smiled as she thought of her amazing mom.

Her ears buzzed and she heard her angels whisper, *She is thinking of you, too.*

Lilith silently said, *I'm sure of it.* She added, *Send my love to Dad.* Lilith heard, *We will.*

Once in the hospital, Lilith stopped by the chapel. She touched the holy water at the door and made the sign of the cross.

She looked toward the empty altar and said to herself, *I guess we are both working today, Lord. May I heal and do no harm.*

As Lilith approached the ICU her ears buzzed and she heard, *We send you love.* She knew from experience that her angels were warning her that something was going to happen. It made her a bit pensive, but she knew she was not alone in handling whatever presented itself.

It had taken Lilith years to realize she didn't always get clear messages from her angels. Sometimes she had to interpret the meaning. And sometimes it was not the time for her to know, but they wanted her to be aware that something was coming. If not knowing made her anxious, Lilith would pray for all her loved ones and pray that she handled the situation in the best way possible.

She whispered silently to her angels, *Thank you. I love you, too.*

Entering the ICU, Lilith checked the assignment board and saw that she had been assigned patients in rooms 2 and 3, the ICU nurse to patient ratio. Lilith was to receive report from Sandy. Taking out a pen and paper, she joined Sandy at the nurses' desk.

Sandy began: "Tom Clancy, in ICU 2, is a twenty-seven year old male. We are unable to get a medical history on him due to his condition, except for the mom's report of his alcohol abuse. He drinks a pint of Vodka a day and occasionally goes on binges as he did last night. He lives with his mom who took him back in after he repeatedly lost jobs and his apartment. She came home from work and found him unconscious on the floor of his room. There was vomit on his mouth and floor. Mom called 911."

Sandy explained what EMS did for the patient. Once in the emergency room, the patient's alcohol level was found to be high, he needed electrolytes, and required oxygen. Chest x-ray showed atelectasis. Patient was admitted to rule out aspiration pneumonia with high oxygen demand, for electrolyte replacement, and to sleep off his alcohol. Sandy warned that he was confused and aggressive when awake.

Lilith knew that she needed to look for signs of rhabdomyolysis in patients who had fallen and remained in one position for a period of time. It was a breakdown of muscle fibers that entered the bloodstream and could cause kidney damage.

"Has his mom been in to see him?" Lilith asked.

"No, she called and gave her number. She said to call if any change, but that she would not be in to see him. Sounds like she might have been through this before," Sandy added. She continued: "In ICU 3 is a nineteen year old female named Robin Jones. She is in her first year of college. She has a history of anxiety and depression, on amitriptyline since age twelve. Roommate reported that Robin got a phone call from her mom demanding her presence for a Fathers' Day dinner. After the phone call Robin was anxious, tearful, pacing and excused herself to the bathroom saying she felt sick. Her roommate heard the bath water running and shut off and figured Robin was soaking in the tub to relax. She became worried when Robin did not come out of the bathroom after an hour. She banged on the locked door and got no response. She opened the door with a screwdriver and found Robin in a tub of bloody water, her wrists sliced and bleeding and an empty pill bottle on the floor. Robin's head was above the water and she was breathing but unconscious. Her roommate called 911. In the emergency room they evacuated her stomach for some pill fragments and gave her charcoal. Her toxicology was positive for tricyclics. The empty bottle was her amitriptyline and the prescription was dated yesterday so she took a full bottle. At this time she is lethargic, flat affect, answers questions appropriately, refuses to let parents visit her and gives no reason. Something happened! Hopefully when she is medically cleared, the psychiatric team can help her. Her heart rate is low sinus tachycardia, afebrile, two peripheral IVs and normal saline at 125cc an hour, respirations 12-20, lungs clear, urinary catheter with clear yellow urine, abdomen soft, nontender with positive bowel sounds. Last bowel movement yesterday. Her wrist lacerations were mostly superficial. She required three sutures each wrist and the wrists are wrapped with the dressings dry and intact. Otherwise her skin is intact. She is on a mental health hold with a security officer named John at the bedside. Oh, no sign of arrhythmias at this time and no prolonged QT segment. Remember the patient that was an overdose like Robin and the QT on his EKG got wider and wider becoming Ventricular tachycardia. We coded him for what seemed like hours, but he didn't survive. These kids don't realize what they are doing to themselves. Too sad." Sandy shook her head and breathed out a sigh before asking, "Any questions?"

"Poor kid, there must be more to this story," Lilith said, shaking her head as her ears buzzed.

She heard, *There is, and you will know soon.*

"I am sure glad you have Robin today. You have a way about you that gets patients talking. Have a good day," Sandy added.

"You too and thanks," Lilith answered.

Lilith checked her patients' medications, labs and orders. She took a thermometer and her stethoscope into ICU 2. The patient was sleeping. Lilith knew she had to wake him in order to do her assessment of his condition. Lilith turned on the lights and moved closer to the bed to do her assessment and neurological exam.

Lilith called out, "Tom?" There was no response, so she spoke louder and shook Tom's shoulder. "Tom?"

"Cut it out!" Tom yelled, and he swung at Lilith.

Seeing Tom's arm move, Lilith stepped back to miss the swing. "No, you don't hit." Lilith said firmly. "Tom, my name is Lilith. I am your nurse today. Do you know where you are?"

Lilith knew from experience that patients under the influence of drugs or alcohol can be unreasonable, act out, and often may not know what they are doing or saying.

"Leave me alone bitch! I'll hit you where it hurts!" Tom yelled with eyes still shut.

Lilith called out to the nurses' station, "Can I get some help in here?"

Three nurses joined Lilith: one brought restraints. Lilith began again, "Tom, you are in the hospital. You had a lot to drink and you were found unconscious. We are trying to help you get well." Only Lilith spoke, the other nurses knew that the patient in his condition could not focus on more than one voice.

Tom interrupted, "Shut up, bitch. Get out of here. I want to sleep." Tom swung at Lilith again and kicked out at Dan, one of the other nurses.

The four nurses approached Tom and each took hold of an extremity. They worked quickly as they applied soft restraints to his wrists and ankles and secured them to the bed frame. Lilith continued to tell Tom what they were doing and why. Tom fought against them, spitting and screaming profanities. Once he was secured, Lilith thanked her coworkers, and got a dose of 2mg Ativan to sedate Tom and help him relax. Once he relaxed she listened to his heart, lungs and abdomen. His lung sounds were coarse and diminished. His oxygen demand had increased while he was anxious. He was now 93% on 6 liters of oxygen. Lilith saw the bruising on his left side where he had been lying on the floor. His urine output was greater than 100cc an hour. Lilith knew that meant his kidneys were still working, and no sign of rhabdomyolysis, the sign that muscle breakdown was clogging the kidneys. Tom's temperature was normal.

Lilith got a flashlight and approached Tom again. "Tom, my name is Lilith. I am your nurse. I am going to look in your eyes with a bright light." Lilith repeated herself knowing that patients who are under the influence of medication, alcohol, or who are critically ill don't remember words spoken to them.

Tom resisted and squeezed his eye lids shut against Lilith's hand. She waited for him to relax, and then she was able to open his eyes to see that his pupils were equal and reactive, though sluggish from the alcohol consumption. Lilith checked his skin color and temperature at the restraints to make sure he had good circulation. Once she finished her assessment she went out to the nurses' desk and called the doctor to alert her that the patient had become combative, violent, and had to be restrained. She received the doctor's order for restraints, and again thanked her coworkers for their help.

Dan smiled and replied, "You're welcome. That's what we do: teamwork."

Lilith returned his smile. "Is it the same as when you round up your cattle on the ranch?"

"No, the cattle are more reasonable." Dan said with a laugh.

Lilith laughed and then entered ICU 3. Robin had her eyes shut as if she was sleeping. Lilith turned on the lights and approached the bed.

"Robin?" There was no response, but Lilith heard a sharp intake of air. Again Lilith said, "Robin, my name is Lilith. I am going to be your nurse."

With eyes still closed Robin said, "What kind of a name is Lilith?"

Startled, Lilith responded, "Oh, it has many meanings. My mom named me Lilith because she thought it a strong name. She said that it would help me in life."

"Has it helped?" Robin asked, now looking at Lilith.

"I guess. Maybe it is too soon to tell." Lilith smiled at Robin. "Robin, how are you feeling?"

"Sad, embarrassed, and really sick to my stomach with cramping," Robin responded.

Just then, Robin grabbed her abdomen and curled forward. "Ouch!" she called out.

"Robin you were given a substance called charcoal to absorb the pills you took. The charcoal will cause cramping and diarrhea. I'll get you some medication for nausea. Here's a basin if you need it," Lilith said as she handed her the basin.

Just as Lilith was about to leave the room, Robin retched black grey charcoal into the basin. Lilith got her a cold rag for her neck and one to wipe her mouth. She hurried to the medication room to get an antiemetic to stop the nausea. Back in Robin's room, Lilith double-checked the medication with the medication record and the patient's arm band; then gave it to her.

"Robin, this is Phenergan and it'll help with the nausea, and could make you sleepy." Lilith explained.

"That's all right with me. I'd prefer to sleep." Robin closed her eyes and settled into the pillow.

"Robin I'm going to listen to your heart, lungs and belly. I'm watching your heart rhythm closely to make sure that the drugs you took have not affected your heart." Lilith said.

After Lilith did her assessment she said, "Robin, I will be back later to check on you. Officer John will be sitting in the room with you. Do you have any questions about anything?" Lilith waited for a response.

"No, no one can help me." Robin turned her back to Lilith and curled in a ball.

"Robin, I hope you'll let us try to help you. You rest now." Lilith gave John a nod as she left the room.

Lilith went in to check on Tom. She noticed his breathing was labored and his oxygen saturation read 88%. To increase his oxygen she placed a simple mask on him. Listening to his chest she heard scattered rhonchi and wheezes indicating that his lungs were compromised.

Lilith said, "Tom?" There was no response. She shook his shoulder. "Tom, open your eyes." There was still no response. She rubbed his sternum with her knuckles to try to see if he responded to painful stimulus. There was still no response. Lilith knew that this was a bad sign and Tom's breathing was compromised.

Lilith thought to herself, *Oh no, Tom. You probably aspirated your stomach contents into your lungs when you threw up at home while unconscious. Now you probably have pneumonia, will be on a respiratory, and go into withdrawal from alcohol. We will support you with medication and you will be a patient with us for a while. Hope you won't go back to drinking when you get home. But sadly, you probably will.*

Lilith called respiratory therapist Ken to do an arterial blood gas. When he arrived he drew the blood. The results showed that Tom was acidotic. Lilith knew that Tom was producing too much acid and not breathing well enough to oxygenate his lungs. Lilith phoned the in-house physician, Dr. Maner, and with the help of Ken they prepared the intubation tray to place a tube in Tom's mouth and down his trachea to assist his breathing. Once Tom was intubated, his breathing was assisted by a respirator. He was given sedation to keep him comfortable and help prevent the severe alcohol withdrawal symptoms of seizures, tremors, and hallucinations. A chest x-ray was taken to confirm placement of the airway and it confirmed placement and the presence of pneumonia. Tom's temperature was now 102 degrees Fahrenheit. Blood cultures, sputum culture, repeat electrolytes and arterial blood were drawn and sent to lab. Tom's electrolytes were normal, his white blood cell count was elevated consistent with an infection and his arterial blood gas was within normal limits. The patient was started on antibiotics. The blood and sputum cultures were still pending. Lilith knew that the antibiotics might be changed depending on the culture results. Tom was now resting comfortably, sedated and on the respirator.

Lilith checked in with Robin and found her sleeping. She went out to the desk to catch up on her charting. The doorbell, notifying the staff that visitors were waiting outside the ICU door, rang. Lilith pushed the button to allow them to come forward to the nurses' desk. A man and woman in tailored dark suits approached the nurses' station.

"Can I help you?" Lilith asked with a smile.

"We're here to see our daughter, Robin Jones, who was brought in last night. Show us to her room." The woman spoke as she leaned toward Lilith.

Lilith's ears buzzed a warning. She heard, *This is trouble.*

Lilith, remembering that Robin had preferred to not see her parents, responded to the woman, "She's been sleeping. Wait right here. I'll check."

Lilith entered Robin's room and pulled the curtain closed.

"Robin?" Lilith said softly.

"Yes?" Robin responded.

Lilith approached Robin's bed and said softly. "Your parents are here. Wou..."

"No! Don't let them near me!" Robin screamed.

John the security guard stood. "Do you need me to do something?"

"Please stand in the doorway. I will tell her parents that they can't visit," Lilith said.

Lilith exited the room. John was close behind as he stood in the doorway. "Robin does not want visitors at this time," Lilith said.

"But — we're her parents. What happened to her? I demand to see her!" Robin's mom yelled as her dad stood silently behind.

"Robin is an adult. Her medical information is private and she can decide who visits," Lilith said calmly.

"This is unheard of! We are her parents. This is Fathers' Day. You can't prevent us from seeing our daughter!" Robin's mom got close to Lilith.

Lilith backed up and nodded to Susan, a nurse behind the nurses' desk. Susan quickly picked up the phone and called for security backup.

Lilith, with heart pounding and palms sweaty, held her ground and spoke firmly. "Mrs. Jones, you and your husband need to leave now. Robin is not seeing visitors."

Two security guards entered the ICU. Seeing the guards, the parents backed away, shaking their heads, and exited the ICU. Lilith took a deep breath in and let it out slowly. She thanked the guards and headed back into Robin's room.

Her ears buzzed and she heard her angels, *Nice job!*

She answered silently, *There is more to this story.*

She heard, *Robin appreciates what you did.*

Lilith passed John who was seated just inside the door. She touched his shoulder and whispered, "thanks". He nodded and smiled at her. She saw Robin was curled in a ball facing away from the door. She could hear Robin crying.

Lilith pulled up a chair. "Robin, may I sit with you for a while?"

Robin nodded between sobs and blew her nose with a tissue from her bedside table. "Thank you, no one has ever stood up for me."

Lilith sat down and said, "You're welcome. I want to help," Lilith said softly. "Do you feel like talking about what happened?" Lilith moved her chair closer to Robin so they could talk privately.

Tears rolled down Robin's cheeks. In a quivering voice she said, "My father sexually abused me my whole childhood. I suppressed the memories and was living in some kind of dark fog. When I went away to college I started having nightmares. This summer I stayed at school and continued my studies. I didn't want to go home. I felt more comfortable at school. But the nightmares continued. They got so bad they disturbed my sleep and my roommate's. I didn't understand it. I would wake up screaming or crying. So I went to the campus doctor who referred me to a therapist. After several sessions my memories cracked open and I remembered the horror, my dad had been raping me for years. I also remembered trying to tell my mother and her yelling at me that I was making it up." Robin stopped and sobbed. When she looked up she saw Lilith's eyes flooded with tears.

Robin paused. Lilith waited patiently, not touching Robin but leaning in close. She reached for a cup of ice water for her. Robin took a few sips followed by some deep breathing in and out.

Robin leaned back with eyes closed and began again. "My therapist taught me this relaxation breathing. Sometimes it works. It didn't last night."

"What happened last night?" Lilith asked.

Robin began again, "I haven't confronted my parents since I realized what had happened to me. I don't want to ever see them again. Mom called last night and *demanded* that I come home for Fathers' Day dinner. I told her that I couldn't. She became so angry and said that I would be there. I still haven't figured out how to talk or not talk to them. It's too painful, too much pressure. I feel so alone. I just want the pain to go away. My choice wasn't very smart; it was cowardly." Robin looked away.

"But you survived. You were strong enough to get help. I am so glad you had someone to talk to at college. We'll help you, too. This was not your fault. There is a lot of help available when you are ready. You are not alone." Lilith touched Robin's hand and she squeezed Lilith's, as tears rolled down both their cheeks.

"I go through so many emotions: guilt, disbelief, anger, loneliness, disgust and sadness. I don't know how or if I want to talk to my parents. They could deny it all and cut me out of their lives." Robin cried into her hands. "That probably sounds pathetic, but I am scared of losing them, scared they won't acknowledge what they did, and scared they won't be sorry for scarring my life. I didn't really mean to end my life. I just didn't know what to do. I wanted the pain to stop."

Lilith, trying to collect herself, took a slow breath in and let it out. "Robin, those are natural emotions and fears. Remember you survived and are willing to help yourself."

Lilith waited to see if Robin wanted to say anything else. After a silence, Lilith said, "Now you rest. We need to get you feeling better. I'll be right outside the door if you need me. When I go to lunch, another nurse will be available if you need anything."

Lilith went into Tom's room to check his heart, lung sounds, and temperature. He was comfortable on the respirator. His heart rate, respirations, temperature, and blood pressure were normal. She returned to the desk to do some charting. At lunch time Lilith gave her report to Diana who would watch her patients while she ate in the lounge. John, the security guard for Robin, would have a lunch break when Bill came to relieve him. Bill would get an update and information that the parents were not allowed to visit.

After Lilith entered the lounge, a man rang the bell outside the ICU and was buzzed in. Diana watched as he approached. He wore a ball cap, jeans and a shirt that had paint spots. He carried a *People* magazine and a couple of paperback books.

"Hey, I'm a friend of Robin Jones. I'd like to visit her, please," he said. Diana pointed to the room. On entering the room, the man said, "Hi baby, looks like you're feeling better. How about a hug?"

Robin turned quickly toward the man as he approached. She glanced at the new guard and yelled at the visitor, "Get out of here! You're never touching me again! Leave me alone!"

Bill rose and stood between the man and Robin. "You need to leave now," he said.

Robin's father tried to stand taller than the officer and asked, "What's wrong with my baby? Why's she so upset?"

Bill repeated firmly as he approached Robin's father causing him to back out of the room, "You need to leave now."

Lilith heard Robin scream and ran for her room. She passed Bill and a casually dressed man outside Robin's room. As she entered the room she saw Robin sitting up in bed facing the door with fists clinched smiling through tears that were pouring down her face.

Two more security guards arrived and escorted Robin's father out of the hospital.

Lilith asked as she approached Robin, "Are you OK?"

Through tears Robin responded, "Yes, I believe I am. I stood up to my father and told him he was never going to touch me again."

"Wow. That's a big step. I'm proud of you. And I'm so sorry that no one prevented him from coming in here." Lilith sighed.

"Oh, I figured he would find a way. He's used to getting what he wants," Robin added as she fluffed her pillows and pulled her side table across her lap. "I think I'm ready to have some of my lunch."

"Looks like *YOU* were in charge this time." Lilith gave Robin's hand a squeeze and with a smile she left the room.

The rest of Lilith's shift was uneventful. She monitored, assessed, medicated and charted on her patients. The dinner trays arrived so Lilith took Robin's tray in to her.

"Knock, knock? Robin, are you hungry?" Lilith asked as she brought in the tray.

"I am. Thank you," Robin answered.

Lilith added, "The night crew will be arriving soon so I'll introduce you after I give them my report. Do you need anything before I go?"

"No. But Lilith, thank you for everything," Robin said.

"You are going to be fine. And you are welcome." Lilith smiled, turned and left the room.

After reporting to Jim, showing him the patients and introducing him to Robin, Lilith left the ICU. She stopped by the chapel. Lilith sat in a pew and sighed. She knew she needed to head to her Mom's house. But how would she release herself from this day? At home she went for a run and then took a long shower and let the stress flow down the drain. She couldn't talk to her dear friends and coworkers, Linnhe and

Karen Steur

Judy. They were not working today. Lilith smiled as she thought of all the hours the three of them stood in the parking lot talking, crying, and releasing the tensions of the day.

Practicing her relaxation breaths, she found herself sobbing. She cried for both her patients. When she felt she had no more tears to cry she headed for her car. It had been an emotionally draining day, and she looked forward to seeing her mom.

As she drove, Lilith's ears buzzed and she heard words of admiration and support.

She silently said, *Thanks.*

Turning into her mom's drive she parked near the front door. As she stepped out of her car she could smell the summer flowers. There was an array of roses, peonies, and geraniums. She opened the door and her senses became alive with the smell of cinnamon, her mom's favorite and the smell that was always lingering in her house.

"Hi Mom, it's me," Lilith called as she rounded the corner into the kitchen and found her mom preparing dinner.

Smiling, Julia approached her daughter and said, "I'm so glad to see you."

Lilith hugged her mom and could smell the cinnamon even more strongly. "I swear, Mom, it smells like you dab cinnamon behind your ears. You smell delicious," Lilith laughed.

"Maybe I do." Julia laughed. "Now, why don't you set the table? Dinner is just about ready. We're having roast pork, potatoes and peas."

"And strawberry short cake for dessert?" Lilith asked.

"Of course! All the food your dad loved." Julia smiled proudly.

"Mom, before we talk about Dad, can I tell you about one of my patients?" Lilith asked.

"Sure, honey," Julia responded.

Lilith told her Mom about the young woman who didn't see a way out from an abusive father. She shared the interaction in the hospital.

Lilith was careful not to give details so as to protect the privacy of her patient.

"Mom, it was so awful. How could a father do something so horrific to his child? And the mother, how did she not know, or did she?" Lilith wiped tears from her eyes.

Julia came over next to her daughter and put her arm around her shoulder. "Honey, it is sadly more common than you know. But, that does not make it right."

"It is just horrible to think about," Lilith said.

"Honey, I know it is hard to imagine being able to recover from sexual assault, especially from a parent. But maybe I can help you understand that with help, someone can recover," Julia said. Julia told Lilith the story of her boyfriend Paul from college, and how his father had tried to rape her.

Lilith responded in shocked disbelief, "Oh Mom, that's terrible."

"It was awful. I didn't think I would ever let a man get close to me again. It took therapy and some excellent books that I read to pull me out of my darkness. And then one day I met your father. Once we got to know each other I told him about Paul." Julia sighed. "He wanted to go and beat him up. It felt good to have someone believe me."

Lilith hugged her mom. "I love you Mom."

"I love you too," Julia answered.

The evening turned to stories about Lilith's dad and his courtship with her mom. Lilith never tired of hearing the romantic sweet stories. Her mom's eyes lit up as she talked of their love for each other while reading passages from the journal he had left for her. It was a beautiful way to keep him alive in their hearts.

Mud

THE QUIET OF THE MORNING PLEASED Lilith as she drove to one of her familiar trails. The sky was blue and clear of clouds. She parked at the trailhead, exited her car and stretched her muscles before starting her warming walk that would progress to a run. Colored leaves covered the path making soft landings and takeoffs as Lilith pressed on, enjoying her early morning run. The air was crisp with a hint of warmth as the sun rose. Her long curly blond hair pulled back in a ponytail swung with each step as her feet kept rhythm with her breath.

As the path crossed a road, she heard a scream. Picking up speed, she came across a woman kneeling in the street.

"No, no! Someone help us!" the woman screamed.

As Lilith approached she saw that the woman, probably in her early thirties, was kneeling next to a lifeless dog. A car was in the ditch nearby. Lilith knelt down by the woman.

She gently said, "My name is Lilith. I'm a nurse. Let me help you up and out of the street."

The woman held out her arms, palms up. "I pulled her from the burning car."

Lilith's ears became full of whispers, as Lilith started to listen, the woman cried out.

"I tried to save her!" And louder, "I tried to save her!"

Tears were flooding her face. Lilith looked around and saw no other person. Lilith glanced over at the car and saw no sign of fire or smell of smoke. She looked at the woman's outstretched arms. Her experienced nurse's eyes saw skin grafts and scarring. Lilith knew these scars must run deep.

"What's your name?" Lilith asked.

"Mary Sims," she sobbed.

"Where do you live?" Lilith continued.

"Springfield," Mary pointed to the right.

Confused, Lilith looked over at the car banked in the ditch. It had Massachusetts plates. Lilith asked, "Are you from out of town?"

"Yes, no. Oh, that's right. I'm from Springfield. Live here now," Mary explained.

"Do you have any pain?" Lilith asked.

"No," Mary responded.

"Did your airbag deploy?" Lilith asked.

"Yes, when I hit the ditch," Mary added quietly.

"Did you lose consciousness?" Lilith asked.

"Did I what?" Mary startled as if she had not been listening.

"Do you remember waking up as if you had been knocked out?" Lilith tried to explain.

"No, I remember everything. I got right out of the car after it hit the ditch. It just took me a moment because of the airbag," Mary explained.

"Mary, I am just going to check you over to see if you have any injuries. Is that OK?" Lilith asked.

Mary answered as she stared off at her car, "Yes."

Lilith went into nurse mode and did a quick assessment exam which included Mary's neck and spine. She found Mary unharmed physically.

"I was just taking a morning drive with my cup of coffee when....," Mary stopped talking and started screaming and sobbing.

Lilith pulled Mary to her and hugged her tightly. She said, "Take it easy. Your safe."

Mary sobbed and yelled, "No, no!"

Lilith coaxed Mary to move out of the road and to sit in the grass facing away from the road. She pulled a bottle of water from her backpack and handed it to Mary. Mary tried to drink but she was breathing so rapidly that she swayed. Lilith eased her down so she was lying flat. Lilith's fingers went to Mary's wrist. Mary's pulse was rapid.

"Mary, relax. Slow your breathing. Slow in through your nose, slow out through your mouth. That's right. Slow in through your nose, slow out through your mouth," Lilith softly directed.

Mary's breathing was now slow and steady. Lilith, feeling Mary's pulse at her wrist, found her heart rate was also beginning to slow down.

"Mary, you are doing a great job with your breathing. How do you feel?" Lilith asked, trying to assess if Mary needed an ambulance or just a ride home.

"OK." Mary paused and then asked, "What happened?"

Calmly Lilith explained, knowing that Mary's reaction was about more than just the dog. "You were very upset about the dog on the road."

Mary exclaimed, "Oh, the dog came out of nowhere. I tried to miss her but the poor thing ran right in front of me. It was so awful. Is she OK?" Mary pleaded as she looked at Lilith.

Lilith softly touched Mary's arm. "I'm sorry but the dog is dead. Looks like it happened instantly and she didn't suffer. It was an accident." Lilith wondered why Mary was calling the dog a female.

"No! She can't be dead." Mary sat straight up and started rocking as she sobbed.

Lilith took Mary in her arms, and they rocked together. Then Lilith heard whispers. She asked silently, *Are you familiar to me?*

She heard, *No.*

She asked silently, *Are you familiar to Mary?*

She heard, *Yes, I am her sister Jamie. Please let her know it was not her fault. She risked her life to save me. But I was already gone. Please tell her I am doing well. And I send her love all the time.*

Lilith whispered back, *I will. I will try to tell her.*

Lilith thought carefully about what to say to Mary. Lilith suspected that Mary was suffering from PTSD, post-traumatic stress disorder, and that Mary might be reacting to the dog's death with emotions she felt when her sister had died.

Lilith asked, "Mary, is there someone I can call for you?"

"What? Oh, yes, my boyfriend. Oh, and my car. I'll have to have it towed," Mary said as she stared at the ground.

Lilith pulled her phone out of her pocket. "What is his name?" she asked.

"Travis." Mary said and gave Lilith the phone number.

Lilith called the number. "This is Travis."

Lilith answered, "Hi, Travis. My name is Lilith Montgomery. I'm here with your girlfriend, Mary. She's fine."

Travis interrupted, "Is she OK? What's this about?"

Lilith began again. "Travis, she's OK. There was an accident and her car went into a ditch. She is not physically hurt, just shook up. She needs someone to pick her up, and her car needs to be towed."

"Give me the location, tell her I'll be right there, I'll call AAA to get her car," Travis said without taking a breath.

Lilith gave Travis directions and said, "Travis, Mary's not hurt. She's safe. Please drive carefully. We'll see you when you get here."

Lilith turned to Mary and told her that Travis was coming to get her and would take care of her car.

Mary looked up at Lilith and asked, "It was a dog that died today, not my sister?"

"Yes, it was a dog." Lilith took Mary's hand in hers and touched the scars of her arm. "What happened to your sister?"

Mary squeezed Lilith's hand. She spoke in a monotone as she stared out at the road. "Ten years ago we were driving back from

Christmas shopping. Jamie was driving the car. It was snowing and the car slid on some black ice. Jamie tried to get control of the car. It spun out of control, went off the edge of the road, and down into the ravine. We were screaming as the car rolled over and over. I was knocked out, and when I awoke we were upside down. I was coughing and realized there was smoke. I called for Jamie. Her eyes were open but she didn't say anything and didn't move. The windshield was broken so I crawled out. The car was hot, so hot, and there were flames. I pulled Jamie out and dragged her away from the car before it exploded."

"That was very brave of you," Lilith said softly.

Mary sobbed loudly, "I tried to save her. I tried. And I tried. She shouldn't have died. I pulled her out of the car."

Lilith took both of Mary's hands and looked her in the eyes. "Mary, you did everything you could have done. I believe Jamie was already gone."

Mary sobbed, "That's what the doctor said. But why did I survive and not her?"

"I don't know why. Sometimes things just happen," Lilith said, hugging Mary.

"I still feel her with me." Mary tried to smile through her tears.

"I'm sure that she is. And I am sure she is sending you her love," Lilith said.

"I feel her love." Mary's smile brightened her face.

"Mary, do you have anyone to talk to about your loss?" Lilith inquired.

Mary was quiet for a moment and then answered, "No, but I know of someone. I'll contact her on Monday."

Travis's car pulled up and parked. He got out of the car, came over to Mary and knelt down next to her.

"Are you OK honey?" Travis kissed Mary's forehead. "I'm glad I was only ten minutes away."

"Yes, thanks to Lilith. But my car will need a bit of work." Mary leaned into Travis.

Travis helped Mary up. "Let's get you home."

They both called out, "Thanks, Lilith!"

"My pleasure. Take care." Lilith waved as she took off to continue her run.

Lilith said to herself, *Life is muddy.*

She shook her arms and shoulders to help her move out of the stress of the encounter.

She heard, *Thanks.*

You're welcome, Jamie, Lilith responded silently as her eyes welled with tears.

Lilith breathed in a quivering breath, shook her head, and picked up speed as she circled back toward her car.

Vacation

IT WAS A COOL MORNING AS Lilith put the final items in her suitcase before closing it and heading out the door to the airport. The eastern sky was lavender and orange. The stars and crescent moon shone down on Lilith as she drove. It had been months since she had had a vacation. She was looking forward to some rest and relaxation. When Mark and Jen suggested she come visit their family in Massachusetts and see the fall foliage, it sounded perfect and relaxing. Mark and his wife Jen had known each other since high school. Lilith met them in college and the three became friends who had kept up with each other through the years. Both Mark and Jen were CPAs. They had been blessed with twin daughters. Lilith smiled to herself as she thought of the funny family Christmas photo on her refrigerator with Mark as an elf.

On board the American Airlines flight headed to Boston with one stop at the Dallas Fort Worth airport, Lilith settled into her seat to read one of her many historical romance novels that she brought with her. As the plane ascended there was some turbulence moving up and out of the Rocky Mountains. Lilith heard a swoosh in her ears.

She whispered silently to her angels, *Do you have a message for me?*

She heard, *Yes.*

Lilith asked, *Is there trouble with the plane?*

She heard, *No.*

She asked, *Is it someone on the flight?*

She heard, *Yes.*

Lilith scanned the passengers and crew and saw nothing out of order. Lilith had learned not to worry. She would get information when she needed it. The rocking of the plane relaxed Lilith, and she fell fast asleep.

Lilith was awakened from a sound sleep by an announcement. "Are there any medical passengers on board? Could you please come to the forward cabin?"

Lilith jumped up and went forward. She gave a flight attendant her name and told her she was an ICU nurse. She explained that one of the crew was ill. Lilith saw a man in uniform lying on the floor, curled up in a ball. The flight attendant handed Lilith a medical first aid kit.

In the small space, Lilith knelt down next to the man and said calmly, "My name is Lilith. I'm a nurse. What's your name?"

"Jason," he moaned.

Lilith asked, "Can you tell me what happened? I want to help you."

Jason replied, "I came to work, felt a bit of indigestion, a burning in my chest and stomach before I got on the airplane. Once we were airborne, I had cramping and sharp pains in my belly. They came on suddenly."

Lilith's mind was racing. She thought of all the possibilities these symptoms could indicate; cardiac, stomach, intestines, bleeding, aneurysm, infection, etc.... Lilith put on a pair of latex free gloves.

Lilith asked, "Do you have any allergies?"

Jason replied, "No."

Lilith asked, "Are you on any medication?"

Jason answered, "Vitamins and Tums."

Lilith asked, "Have you had any medical problems with you heart, lungs or belly?"

"No," Jason responded.

Lilith explained, "I'm going to take your blood pressure and heart rate and listen to your chest and belly."

Lilith took the stethoscope and blood pressure monitor out of the medical kit. Jason's pulse rate was elevated at 120 beats per minute; she thought: could be due to pain or bleeding. Respiratory rate was 28 breaths per minute; possibly due to pain. She took his blood pressure in both arms to see if there was a disparity. Both arms were close to 180/98; so low probability of aneurysm. With the stethoscope she listened to his lungs, heart and abdomen. His lungs were clear and heart strong. Jason's color was pale and his skin was diaphoretic, sweaty.

Lilith said, "I'm going to palpate your abdomen." As she pressed the upper and lower quadrants of his belly she said, "Does this hurt?"

When Lilith palpated Jason's abdomen in the right upper quadrant he yelled, "Ouch!!"

Lilith asked, "On a scale of 1 to 10 with 10 being the worst, what would you score your pain?"

Jason replied, "20!"

Lilith asked, "Does the pain increase when you take a deep breath?"

Jason responded, "No."

Lilith knew that Jason could have one of a variety of problems in his abdomen: intestinal gas, infection, obstruction, bleeding or involvement of large organs like the liver or pancreas. And she couldn't rule out cardiac involvement. Lilith updated the flight attendant who was on the phone with the airport medical personnel.

Lilith explained, "Jason, I'm going to put a catheter in your vein so that I can give you some fluid. I will give you some oxygen through a tube in your nose. An ambulance will meet the plane in Dallas."

Lilith looked through the first aid box to get supplies. She placed an oxygen tube in Jason's nose and hooked it to the oxygen bottle the flight attendant handed her. She placed a catheter in a vein in Jason's arm, and started giving him fluid from a bag of Normal Saline that she hung from a hook on the wall next to where Jason lay. The first aid kit did not contain any narcotics for pain.

Just then. Jason said, "I feel sick to my stomach."

Lilith found an antiemetic in the box. "I'll give you some Phenergan for your nausea. It may make you sleepy."

Lilith positioned Jason on his left side with his knees bent. She knew he would be more comfortable in that position because of the pain on the right side of his abdomen.

Lilith asked, "Jason, how would you rate your pain?"

Jason yawned and said, "It aches, but is not as sharp. Maybe a 5."

Lilith said, "We will be landing soon."

The pilot announced that the plane was descending into Dallas. And he said, "All passengers must remain in their seats once we arrive at the gate so the medical crew can board and attend to a patient."

Lilith stayed sitting on the floor next to Jason as the plane landed and taxied to the gait. When the door was opened the medical crew entered the plane. Lilith gave them report on Jason. As she got ready to stand up, Jason grabbed her hand and gave it a squeeze.

Lilith smiled and said, "Jason, they will take good care of you. I hope you feel better."

Jason nodded and said, "Me too."

Lilith returned to her seat to await take off to Boston. She was glad her four years in the ICU had prepared her to handle an emergency.

Lilith's ears buzzed and she heard, *We are proud of you.*

Lilith answered, *Thanks.*

Once en route to Boston, Lilith fell fast asleep. She was dreaming when she was awakened by one of the flight attendants touching her shoulder.

The flight attendant asked, "Can you come look at one of the passengers? She's acting funny."

Lilith nodded as she blinked her eyes to make sure she was fully awake. Coming out of her seat, she followed the flight attendant up five rows. A passenger got up to make room for Lilith. Lilith sat down and saw that the woman in the seat next to her was babbling and weaving in her seat.

Lilith said, "My name is Lilith. I'm a nurse. What's your name?"

The woman tried to talk but her speech was garbled. Lilith felt for a pulse at the woman's left wrist. Her heart rate was 107 and weak. The flight attendant brought Lilith the first aid kit. Lilith found the woman's blood pressure was 80/48. Lilith gently laid the woman down in the two seats with her head resting in Lilith's lap. Lilith knew that lowering her head would assist her blood pressure to normalize and perhaps help her mentation. The woman was pale and her skin tight with not much elasticity. Her pupils, however, were equal and reactive, a normal sign.

Within a few minutes the woman opened her eyes and looked at Lilith. She said, "What happened?"

Lilith softly explained, "My name is Lilith. I'm a nurse. You were not feeling well. What's your name?"

The woman answered, "Susan."

"Do you have any allergies?"

Susan responded, "No, I don't think so."

Lilith asked, "Are you taking any medication?"

Susan answered, "No."

"Do you have diabetes?"

Susan answered, "No."

Lilith questioned, "Do you have any medical problems of your heart, lungs, blood pressure, or circulation? Have you ever had a stroke?"

To all questions Susan responded, "No."

Lilith was unable to check Susan's blood sugar to rule out hypoglycemia or low blood sugar. She knew that could have caused her symptoms. Lilith wanted to give her something to drink that contained sugar.

Lilith asked, "Do you think that you could drink some juice?"

Susan responded, "I can try."

Lilith touched the call button and requested an orange juice and 2 bags of sugar from the flight attendant. Lilith took hold of both of Susan's hands.

Lilith asked, "Can you squeeze my hands hard?"

Susan squeezed Lilith's hands. Her squeeze was equal. Lilith knew that an unequal squeeze could be a symptom of a stroke. She retook Susan's blood pressure and found it to be 112/62; normal. Once the juice arrived, she mixed in the sugar. Susan sat up long enough to drink. Lilith felt for her pulse and found it was weakening.

Lilith asked, "How are you feeling?"

Susan looked at Lilith, but did not answer. Lilith knew Susan was probably dropping her blood pressure again so she laid her back down. Her blood pressure measured 80/50. Lilith reached for the first aid box sitting on the floor next to her. She saw that it had been restocked by the medical crew in Dallas. She put on some gloves and spoke to Susan.

Lilith explained, "Susan, your blood pressure is very low. I'm going to put a catheter in your vein and give you some fluid."

Susan responded in a meek voice, "OK."

Once the fluid was running, Lilith asked, "Where do you live, Susan?"

Susan responded, "Boston."

Lilith asked, "Where are you traveling from?"

Susan answered, "I was in Colorado visiting my Mom. She was in the hospital."

Lilith said, "I'm so sorry. She must have been glad to see you."

Susan wiped away her tears. "She was very ill, but is recovering. I cleaned her house, shopped for food and got her back home. She has a friend checking on her so I was able to return to my home."

Lilith asked, "Susan, were you drinking extra water while in Colorado's dry climate?"

Susan answered, "No, I hardly thought to eat or drink anything."

Lilith added, "You're probably dehydrated. The IV fluid will help and a medical crew will meet the plane when it lands in Boston. Do you have any pain or burning with urination?" Lilith was trying to rule out a bladder infection.

Susan answered, "No."

Just then, the pilot's voice came over the intercom. "We are starting our descent into Boston. Please return to your seats and secure your seat belts. Once we are at the gate, please remain seated so that the medical crew can board and take off one of the passengers. Thank you for your cooperation."

Lilith buckled Susan's belt around her as she lay across the two seats. She then secured her own belt. Lilith had no place to hang the bag and allow gravity to help it flow so she used what she had at hand. She put the blood pressure bag around the IV fluid and pumped it up. The fluid was flowing easily into Susan's vein.

Once the plane landed and the forward door was opened, two medical crew members entered the plane and made their way down the aisle. Lilith gave them Susan's history and an update on her condition. She stepped up and away so that the crew could assess the patient. Susan was feeling stronger and felt she could walk with the medical crew to exit the plane.

Susan stopped and said, "Thank you Lilith for being so kind."

Lilith answered, "It was my pleasure, Susan. Hope you feel better."

Lilith sat back in the seat to await her turn to leave the plane. She took a deep breath in and then let it out. She stretched and rubbed her neck muscles.

Lilith heard a buzz in her ears and heard, *Well done.*

Lilith answered silently, *Thanks.*

Lilith let out a deep long sigh as she left the gate. She stopped by the restroom and splashed some water on her face. Then she headed to baggage with the other passengers. Just as she arrived, she spotted Mark, Jen, and the twins waving. Lilith was swallowed up with big hugs. Closing her eyes, she took in the love.

Mark grabbed her bags off the turning belt. "Hope you got some sleep on the plane. We're going on a bike ride, then picnic and concert in the park with dancing! Sound good?" he asked.

Lilith smiled and said, "Can't wait.

TORNADO

It is a day of routine.
Then a twister appears
Full of color, whirling
On her blank flat screen TV.

She looks for reflections
Tries to wipe it off
Check that the TV still works
It does.

How could this be?
What can it mean?
In contrast, she feels comfort.
Love is all around her.

Then the phone rings.
She is sucked in,
Whirling upside down, inside out
Hours, days without stopping

Occasionally, she is tossed out.
Frightened, bruised, breathless,
She prays, bargains, pleads for an end.
Then, she is sucked back in.

Calm
She moves in slow motion.
The world is spinning around her.
Is this the eye or shock?

The tornado lifts
Up into the sky
Leaving her
Exhausted, disoriented.

The storm passes.
Raw wounds begin to heal.
Those who came to help
Return home.

She picks up the pieces.
Mourns, cries, breathes
Breathes, cries
Gives thanks, gives thanks.

Saying Goodbye

THE ROAD WAS SLICK AND DARK as rain pelted down on Lilith's car. The wipers, moving rapidly, failed to clear the windshield sufficiently. Lilith wished she had wipers for her eyes as they filled with tears. She had just gotten off work and was driving home when she got the call.

A voice said, "Lilith Montgomery?"

Lilith answered, "Yes, this is Lilith Montgomery."

The voice said, "Lilith, this is Margaret Wright. I'm a nurse at Platt County Hospital. Your mom, Julia Montgomery, was just brought in by ambulance."

As her breathing became rapid, Lilith asked, "What happened? I just spoke with her this morning. I'm an ICU nurse. How is she?" Lilith noticed that she was yelling.

Margaret said softly, "Lilith, your mom complained of a headache at her office and then was found on the floor. She was brought here with diagnosis of a possible stroke. We're still doing tests. She's in CAT Scan now."

Lilith asked, "Is she awake?"

Margaret answered, "She was unconscious when the paramedics arrived at her work. They intubated her and placed her on a ventilator. She has not awakened yet."

Lilith said, "I am on my way. I will be there in forty-five minutes. Take care of my mom. And thanks for calling me."

Margaret responded, "Be careful driving. We are doing everything we can for her."

Lilith's mind raced through memories. She loved to hear the stories of how her mom and dad had met. Mom had such touching sweet stories of their time together. Lilith felt she knew her father through her mom's stories. Mom had hinted that her father had a knowing, an insightfulness, that made him special. Her mom had told her that he knew things before they happened. Once her parents were in a restaurant and her father became anxious. He said that they needed to leave now. Her mom thought he was ill, so she got the check and paid so they could hurry out. John had been looking around and continued to do so as they left. Once they were in the car the restaurant filled with smoke, the fire alarm went off, and the sprinklers covered the guests with water. There was a fire in the kitchen. Fortunately, everyone got out, and no one was hurt. Her mom held onto her dad in disbelief and relief. Her mom told her that she realized after Lilith was born that her dad had known she was pregnant. He had whispered to her mom, *We will continue to be blessed.* As Lilith grew to understand her empathic gift, she realized her father probably had a similar gift. How she wished she could talk to him. She had experienced no spiritual encounters with him. He must have moved on and chosen or couldn't make visits back to her.

"I can't lose you, Mom," Lilith cried aloud. Lilith shook her head and chided herself, "Calm yourself Lilith. You have to stay focused on the drive."

Lilith's thoughts went to happier times with her horse Rosie. On her horse-themed eleventh birthday, Julia gave her horse-crazed daughter a beautiful red mare. Lilith always felt carefree without a worry in the world when she was with Rosie. She smiled as she remembered there was no fence or body of water that could stop Rosie. They jumped over everything. Lilith felt a closeness with Rosie that she never felt with any other horse. Each anticipated what the other was thinking. Lilith would just think about a fence, and Rosie would head for it and the two would fly over it as if they had wings. When Rosie retired from jumping, because of a painful arthritic back leg, swimming and trail rides were still a source of joy for them both. Rosie loved to swim. Eventually, x-rays showed an old injury that was becoming more arthritic with time. She remembered Rosie's decline. She tried all kinds of medicines and healing treatments. Some would work for a while.

One day Lilith was brushing Rosie, and she began to cry. "I need to find something to help you. I don't want you to be in pain. I love you so much."

Rosie turned her head to Lilith and said, *I love you too. You have done all that you can.*

Lilith answered, "But I want to do more." Then Lilith stopped and stared at her beloved horse looking at her. She took Rosie's head in her arms. "You spoke to me. I could hear you."

Rosie leaned against Lilith and Lilith heard, *It's time to let me go. I don't want to hurt anymore.*

Lilith had the vet assist Rosie's death. When Rosie died, Lilith stayed in bed all day crying. When she finally slept she had dreams of riding Rosie at full gallop, legs flying without pain. When she awoke, she realized it was a dream and burst into tears. Then, Rosie appeared to her. She was frisky, beautiful and, most importantly, free of pain. Lilith tried to reach out to her, but Rosie pranced away playfully, gave a big buck, and reared up on her back legs. For a few days she saw Rosie and then she just felt her presence. Rosie became one of Lilith's angels that watched over her. Lilith knew she was watching over her now.

Lilith's thoughts drifted to her first night at college. In the morning the alarm had sounded on the bed-side table. Lilith had reached over and turned it off. As she opened her eyes, she was shocked at her surroundings. Then she remembered it was her first morning in her dorm room. Clair lay, still sleeping, in the bed beside the window. Clair had not heard the alarm. Lilith laughed to herself as she remembered all the times of waking the sleepy Clair because she never heard her alarm. Then she remembered when she and her mom arrived on the campus, her mom frantically helped her get settled into the dorm, she was busying herself so she would not break down and cry. That had been an important milestone and an adjustment for both of them. It had been just the two of them together since Lilith was born.

Lilith smiled and said out loud, "We did adjust, Mom. I became an independent adult, and you starting enjoying your friends more. But you always remained a proud, supportive mom.

Lilith was brought back to the present as her car pulled up in front of the Platt Valley Hospital. She parked, ran into the hospital and stopped at the information desk.

Lilith said, "I'm looking for my mom, Julia Montgomery, who was brought into the emergency room."

The receptionist woke up her computer screen. "Yes, your mom is in the ICU. It's down the hall and to your right."

Lilith called out thanks as she quickly headed to the Intensive Care Unit. Lilith entered the ICU, inquired at the nurses' station and was directed to room 3.

After seeing that family had arrived, a man in blue scrubs approached and said, "Hi, I'm Dr. Darin Wilson your mother's neurologist."

Lilith shook his outstretched hand and said, "I'm Lilith. I'm an ICU nurse. Please tell me what happened. How's she doing? Do we need to transfer her to a stroke center?" Lilith was talking as fast as her heart was pounding.

Dr. Wilson motioned for Lilith to sit in a chair outside Julia's room. "When the paramedics found your mother unresponsive they thought she might have had a stroke. Her heart rate was normal, her blood pressure was elevated and one of her pupils was sluggish. They intubated her to protect her airway. She was taken to Cat Scan as soon as she arrived at the hospital. Your mother has a cerebral hemorrhagic aneurysm. It has filled her brain with blood and is now tamponading the tear in the vessel."

Lilith face flushed and she felt her skin dampen as she asked, "If the blood is pushing up against the vessel that was torn and has stopped it from bleeding, when are you going to repair the vessel and evacuate the blood?"

Dr. Wilson spoke softly, "Lilith, your mom was deprived of some blood flow to her brain. At this time her pupils are fixed and dilated, and she's completely dependent on the respirator.

Lilith asked louder than she meant to, "So she has some brain damage? Oh, my God!"

Dr. Wilson touched Lilith's hand, "Yes. And her blood pressure dropped so she is being supported by two medications, Levophed and Dopamine to help bring up her blood pressure. Dr. Wilson paused and rubbed his chin before continuing, "We could try to put a coil around the vessel to stop the bleeding and then evacuate the blood. But she might not survive the procedure, and if she did, there is no guarantee that she will ever wake up."

Tears streamed down Lilith's cheeks. She said to herself, *How could this be happening? Why did I not know? Maybe I could have done something. What should I do?*

"What do you recommend?" she asked Dr. Wilson.

"It won't unduly harm your Mom if we try the procedure. She has a slim chance of survival either way. I'm so sorry. Please let me know soon what you decide."

Lilith went into her mom's room. It was a familiar site to her with the monitoring devices, but that wasn't supposed to be her mom in the bed. She moved close to Julia and took her hand while scanning her heart rate, blood pressure and ventilator rate. As she gently touched Julia's pale face, the room filled with the smell of cinnamon, mom's smell.

"Mom, it's me, Lilith. I love you so much. You have to get better. I can't lose you." Tears spilled over onto Julia.

Lilith heard, *Oh Honey, don't cry. I'm all right. And you'll be all right too.*

"Mom, stay with me. You're not dead. Why didn't I know? Please tell me how I can help you." Lilith checked a pulse at her Mom's right wrist.

Lilith heard, *Honey, I'm here but not quite in my body. I see that my body is tired and I'm not sure that it can be saved. Sometimes you aren't supposed to know everything. You do what you have to do. I love you. And I'm with you. I'm so thankful that your gift allows you to hear me.*

Lilith looked out of the room and saw Dr. Wilson at the desk. She headed toward him. "Please have the coiling done on my mom as soon as possible. I can't lose my mom!"

"I've already alerted the team. I'll just give them a call. They can probably start in less than an hour." Dr. Wilson picked up the phone.

Lilith returned to her Mom's room. "Mom, they're going to do surgery to coil the bleeding vessel in your head and take out the blood. You hang in there. There are things that we still need to do together."

Lilith heard, *Lilith my sweetheart, do not be sad. You are an amazing woman, and you have a wonderful life ahead. I will be fine.*

Lilith pleaded, "Mom, stay with me. I love you."

A tall nurse with long black hair pulled back in a clip entered Julia's room. "Hi, my name is Mandy. I have been caring for your mother. Do you have any questions for me?" Mandy extended her hand to Lilith.

Lilith shook her hand. "No, but I might later. I think they are taking her to surgery soon."

"Yes, and I need to get her ready. I will be busy around her, but let me know if you have questions," Mandy said as she disconnected monitors from the wall and set them on a table at the foot of Julia's bed.

A team of technicians and nurses came to transport Julia, the only parent Lilith has ever known, to the operating room. Lilith gave her a kiss and then collapsed into a chair. Mandy came back into the Julia's room after an hour and gave Lilith an update on the surgery. After three long hours, a tall, thin man approached Lilith.

"How's she doing?" Lilith asked.

The man pulled up a chair next to Lilith and spoke. "I'm Dr. Miles Lamb. I'm the neurosurgeon who operated on your mother. We coiled the aneurysm with the help of fluoroscopy; then I opened her skull enough to evacuate the blood. She didn't have any ill effects from the procedure. However, her pupils remain fixed and dilated. The next twenty-four to forty-eight hours will give us an idea if she can recover. Do you have any questions?" He paused.

Lilith spoke slowly, "No, thank you for all that you did." She stared at the empty place where her mom's bed had been just hours ago. Dr. Lamb squeezed Lilith's hand before standing and leaving the room.

Soon Julia was brought back into her ICU room. Her head was wrapped with a white bandage. The nurse in charge of her care in the operating room gave report to Mandy, Julia's nurse. Mandy was busy setting up the monitors and adjusting Julia's medications. She answered Lilith's questions and went back to work monitoring Julia.

Lilith felt dizzy, the room was a blur of activity, words and sounds that were so familiar yet she was detached in her whirl of fear. Lilith stood and then sank back into the chair. There wasn't anything she could do but pray.

Lilith leaned forward with hands clasped and prayed, *Please Lord, may it be Thy will that Mom is all right. We still have things to do together. I don't know what I'd do without her. Please be with her, Lord, may she not be in pain, may she not suffer. May I have the courage to do what's best for her.*

Lilith felt a swoosh in her ears. The room filled with the smell of cinnamon. The monitor alarms were sounding. Her mom's heart rate and blood pressure were dropping. Nurses rushed into the room to adjust IV drips and give medication to increase her heart rate and blood pressure. One nurse brought in the code cart.

Lilith felt a pressure on her shoulder. *Lilith, sweetheart, It's time. My body won't support me anymore. Your dad is here to escort me on my journey. He's even more handsome than I remember. We both love you so much. It's time for you to let me go. A part of me will always be with you. I love you.*

Lilith stepped forward and told the nurses that her mom wouldn't want any more heroics. She laid her head on her mom's chest and wept.

Mandy touched Lilith's shoulder and gave it a gentle squeeze. She left the room to consult with the doctor.

Lilith heard, *Honey, you're doing the right thing. This is what I want. I love you.*

Mandy returned to Julia's room and turned off the ventilator, medications and monitor. Lilith climbed up on the bed next to her mom, and held her in her arms.

Mandy asked, "Can I call anyone for you?"

Lilith responded, "No, thank you."

Mandy asked, "Can I get anything for you?"

"I want my mom back!" Lilith cried.

Mandy said, "I'm so sorry for your loss. I will call the chaplain."

Lilith asked, "Could you call Mom's priest? His phone number should be in her chart."

Mandy answered, "I'll do that right now. I'll close the curtains on my way out. Let me know if you need anything."

Lilith responded, "Thanks. I need to be alone with Mom now."

"I'll be right outside the door if you need me." Mandy touched Lilith's arm gently and left the room.

Lilith snuggled into her mom and whispered, "Mom, I love you always. It's OK to go. I'll be all right. Go and be with Dad. I'll see you both someday at another time."

Julia's body took its last breath and Lilith felt her spirit leave the room. Lilith kissed her mom's forehead.

Lilith whispered, "Mom, God bless you, and may you be at peace." Lilith made the sign of the cross over her mom.

Lilith's ears buzzed and she heard, *She is. And we are with you always.*

Lilith answered silently as tears streamed down from her eyes, *Thank you. I need all of you right now.*

Lost

THE DEATH OF HER MOM LEFT a huge emptiness within Lilith. During the four months after her mom's death, Lilith went through the motions of working, eating, sleeping, and going on runs, but she felt nothing. She couldn't even taste her food. Lilith knew she was grieving. After a long day at the hospital she would begin to call her mom's number to check in and hash out the day. Then she would remember that she was gone.

Lilith said to herself, *How could she be gone? How could I have not known? Why couldn't I have done something to help her? Hey, you, my angels! You are always with me, talking, talking. Where were you? Where was my God? Now it's too late. Mom is dead. Stop talking to me. I don't want to hear it. Leave me alone. What good is this gift? You are white noise to me now.*

Lilith listened, but there was silence. She knew her angels were still there. They never left her. They were being quiet at her request. They would forgive her outburst. She was angry at her loss. And she just didn't have the energy to talk with them.

Lilith pulled into her garage, turned off the car and shut the garage door. She laid her head against the headrest and cried, hard racking sobs, louder and louder. The garage light went out leaving her in darkness. There was a stillness. She had no sound in her ears. Her angels were quiet. Exhausted, she relaxed into the darkness and fell asleep.

Lilith awoke and was startled to find that she was still in her car. She got out and went into the house. The clock read 11:00 p.m. She made herself a salad and thought about the next day. She had signed up to take a pharmacology workshop to earn some more continuing education credits for her critical care certification. The topic was FDA-approved pharmacology medications versus homeopathic remedies, pros and cons and interactions. Lilith knew that this was always a burning topic, but could also be a boring sleeper. However, the location and time worked for her. She had heard of the speaker. He was a pharmacist from Texas who now worked in southern Colorado at a trauma hospital. His name was Ken Richardson.

Lilith put out a pair of jeans and one of her favorite purple and blue blouses. She was getting to bed late and wanted the morning to go smoothly. She reached into the freezer for an eye mask. She hoped it would sooth her swollen, inflamed eyes.

The alarm sounded too early. Lilith dressed and grabbed a cup of coffee before heading out the door. It was a short drive to the Marriott Hotel. She was surprised to find the conference room was packed. She found her way to an empty seat in the front row. Ken Richardson walked out onto the small elevated platform.

Lilith smiled to herself and said silently, *Mr. Richardson is wearing a cowboy hat and cowboy boots. It's the west, but really. If he weren't so handsome, he would look ridiculous.*

Then Richardson introduced himself with the deepest Texas accent that Lilith had ever heard. And he was theatrical. Never had pharmacology been so entertaining. At one point Lilith found herself laughing hard, and she realized that she hadn't laughed in quite a long time. She caught Mr. Richardson looking at her, and saw him wink.

After the workshop concluded, Lilith viewed the drug books on the display table at the back of the conference room. She picked up a book and thumbed through it.

Ken Richardson approached the table. "See anything that looks interesting to you?"

Lilith turned and smiled. "Just checking to see if there are any good resources for my unit."

Ken asked, "Where do you work?"

Lilith responded, "In the ICU at Denver Memorial."

In his smooth, sensuous, southern drawl, Ken asked, "Would you like to get a cup of coffee? I want to wait out the traffic before heading home."

Lilith paused and then said, "Sure. I think there's a restaurant off the lobby."

Ken and Lilith walked to the restaurant, and took a seat at a table in the bar. They started with coffee and easily talked into dinner time, so they ordered a meal. Lilith tried to pay for her portion of the bill, but Ken insisted on picking up the bill.

"Would you like to do this again?" Ken asked.

"Sure. I would like that." Lilith smiled, trying to contain her excitement. She wrote down her phone number, and handed it to Ken.

As they walked to their cars, Ken tipped his hat and said, "Until next time."

Lilith found she was smiling as she drove home. It felt good to smile. It had been a while. She was going to Google-search Ken Richardson when she got home.

With an hour and a half distance between them and two busy schedules, it took creativity to make a date happen. In two months they had a handful of dates, and many phone calls. Their last date ended with the sweetest kiss that lingered and lingered until they were both breathless, and their lips were raw.

As Ken held Lilith close in his arms, he asked, "Would you like to go to the mountains for the weekend?"

Lilith smiled and kissed him. "Let's see what we can work out."

The next day was busy at work in the ICU for Lilith. The operator called "Trauma 1, ten minutes by air" over the intercom, which meant a severe accident was being flown into the hospital by helicopter, and the crew needed to be met on the helipad. Lilith had been assigned the patient. The patient was a female in her thirties who had been thrown from her car in a rollover accident. She had a severe head injury and massive internal injuries. She was taken into the operating room after a brief stop in the emergency room. After the removal of her spleen and one kidney; 5 chest tubes were placed to reinflate her damaged lungs. A piece of skull was removed to give her damaged and bruised brain space to swell, and then she was taken to the recovery room. The young woman remained in the recovery room for an hour before being transferred to the ICU.

After her patient arrived in the ICU, Lilith worked about an hour getting her stabilized. Lilith heard and felt a familiar swoosh. She then heard familiar whispers. It had been 6 months since her mom had died, and she had turned away from her gift and her angels.

Lilith asked silently, *Why am I hearing you now? I thought you were gone. Do you have messages for me?*

Lilith heard, *Yes. And we never left you.*

Lilith answered, *I knew you really didn't leave me.*

Lilith heard an unfamiliar voice and she asked silently, *Are you familiar to me?*

She heard, *No.*

Lilith asked, *Are you Linda, the patient I'm caring for?*

She heard, *Yes. What happened? Where am I? Oh, God, where is my daughter? I have to find my daughter. Is she all right? I have to find her.*

Lilith took a deep breath and answered silently, *Linda, you had an accident. You were thrown from your car, and you have a head injury and other injuries to your body. You had surgery and are now in the intensive care unit. I will give you pain medication to keep you comfortable.*

Lilith heard, *My body isn't moving. How do you hear me? Where is my daughter?*

Lilith answered silently, *Linda, your daughter is fine. She was in her car seat unharmed. She was taken to Children's Hospital. Your husband is with her. She is safe. You have a bad head injury. We have put you in a chemical coma to let your brain rest. Linda, I can hear you, because I have the gift of clairaudience. This gift allows me to hear your spirit. You need to rest, and know that your daughter is fine.*

At the end of her shift, Lilith drove home. Her mind was racing. Her ears were alive with voices. Her gift was back and she realized she was glad. She had missed her angels and her gift. The phone rang and it was Ken.

"Do you have your schedule? Do you want to plan our weekend away?" Ken asked.

Lilith sighed. "Ken, can we get together first? I had a difficult shift at work and I want to talk to you about it."

Ken responded, "Sure, honey. How about tomorrow?"

"Sounds good. Come by my place and I'll make dinner about 6 p.m. Bye for now." Lilith took a deep breath.

"I'll bring the wine. See you soon." Ken ended the call.

Lilith's mind went into planning mode. Her mom acknowledged her gift. But as she thought back to her childhood and college, she realized that the few people she shared her gift with didn't believe her. Her only adult friends she shared with were Michele and her mentor Paula. Paula had helped mentor, and validate Lilith's gifts as she grew to understand them. Lilith had met Michele at a spiritual conference. Michele had the gift of communicating with animals. Lilith felt support and camaraderie with the joint sharing of gifts with her friends.

Lilith said silently, *Oh, Mom. I miss you. Wish you were here. You would give me some advice.*

In the past 10 years her gift and understanding had grown. The voices were part of her everyday life. Her angels talked with her throughout the day and night. She sometimes forgot that not everyone had these experiences. But when her mom died, and she shut out the gift, she thought she would be satisfied to live and have relationships like most people. But the experience in the hospital made her realize that the gift was part of who she was as a person, and whoever shared her life needed to know and accept all of her.

Tears rolled down her checks as she thought of her gifts. Was it unrealistic to think that a lover could accept such an intangible belief system? What she did know within her being was that she wouldn't get close to someone who didn't.

The next day after work, Lilith made dinner, set the table, and then took a shower. She picked out a feminine, flowing shirt to wear with her favorite black jeans. She sprayed on her favorite lavender perfume.

At 6 p.m. she looked out the kitchen window and saw Ken pull up. She smiled to herself as she caught him checking his hair in the rearview mirror.

He is such a handsome guy, Lilith said to herself.

She went to the door and opened it as Ken approached. He had wine and flowers in hand. They kissed each other, a sweet passionate kiss full of longing. Lilith clung to him a bit longer than she meant to.

"You OK?" Ken asked, sounding worried.

"Yes," Lilith said and tried to hide her doubt. "Let's get to eating. Dinner is ready."

After dinner Lilith and Ken moved to the couch with their wine. They snuggled next to each other.

"Now what is it you wanted to share with me?" Ken asked, looking compassionately into Lilith's eyes.

Lilith turned toward Ken and said, "Ken, I had a spiritual experience at work. We have not talked about our spirituality, and I feel it's very important to share."

"Well, I'm a Christian. And I think you are as well, because of the cross you wear around your neck." Ken grinned.

"Well... I believe in an afterlife and spirit guides or angels," Lilith said, breathing in deeply.

"And I believe there is probably life on other planets," Ken said as he laughed and smiled.

He's not taking this seriously, Lilith said to herself.

"Ken, I have a gift. I can hear spirits. They give me messages. Some are my angels, and some are the recent or soon-to-be-recent dead. I can talk to them and help them understand what has happened in their death, and move them on in their journeys." Lilith sat back breathing rapidly and waited for Ken to respond. She felt her heart pounding in her chest.

Ken responded in a loud voice as he moved his arms around to demonstrate his point, "Oh, Lilith, the only spiritual voices I know about are God and Satan. And it doesn't sound like you're talking to God."

Lilith responded just as loudly, "It's not Satan. My mom talked to me in her coma, and just before she died. I've had this gift all my life."

Ken took Lilith's hand and softly said, "Lilith, honey. I can get you help. I know you believe this, but it can't be so. The devil can be sneaky. He can talk in all kinds of voices to lure you in. My minister has dealt with possessions."

Tears of sadness and loneliness flooded Lilith's eyes. "Ken, I have enjoyed our time together. But we are very different. Please go now."

With a look of shock, Ken said, "But, Lilith, I can help you."

"No, please go." Lilith said firmly.

"No, I will not go. It is my Christian responsibility to help banish Satan from unsuspecting Christians who have let him in." Ken pulled out his phone and started to make a call.

Lilith stood and said, "I appreciate your belief and concern, but I do not need your help."

Ken ignored her and continued to dial and said into his phone, "Pastor Frank, this is Ken Richardson. Can you call me back? I have a possession that I need your help with. Thanks." Ken put his phone back in his pocket and turned toward Lilith.

Lilith's face was flushed red. She said, "Ken, you have a different belief system from me. I will respect yours, but you have to respect mine."

Ken responded loudly, "Help is what you need! I'm going to help you! We need to banish Satan!"

Lilith opened the door and said firmly, "Ken, you need to leave now!"

"Lilith, you're making a mistake. I'll pray for you." Ken walked through the doorway and down the walk without looking back.

Lilith closed the door, turned, and felt the soft texture of the door against her back as she slid down onto the floor. She cried hard, body racking sobs. She felt pain in her chest.

She cried out loud, "Why didn't Ken believe me? I feel so lonely! Is this my fate?"

Lilith's ears buzzed and she heard, *You are never alone. Good things are coming.*

Lilith answered out loud, "I know you're with me. I don't mean to seem ungrateful. I'm grateful. But sometimes, I'm lonely for a man to share my life."

Lilith realized she wasn't crying anymore. She felt relief as she breathed out her sadness. She knew she'd been true to herself.

As she got up off the floor and stretched, she said to herself, *Maybe someday. Yes, maybe someday.*

Down by the River

"DAD, LOOK AT THE SUN," SAM said as he pointed out the front window of their red Cherokee Jeep.

"Wow, the colors of orange and pink are beautiful. The sun will be setting soon. Keep a look out for animals along the road," Brad said as he smiled at his 7 year-old son who held onto the dash as he peered out the window.

"Dad, wait till Mom sees the fish I caught!" Sam exclaimed excitedly.

"You brought it in like a champ," Brad responded.

"Dad, thanks for letting me sit up front. So far I have seen 4 deer, 2 antelope, and that one big elk," Sam added.

With the road now dark and Sam dozing, Brad reached down to scan for a radio station. In that instant an elk jumped in front of the Jeep, hit the front corner, and sent the vehicle into the ditch. Brad, not badly hurt, called out to Sam. The boy was against the dash, unconscious.

The ambulance, that Brad had called, arrived and transported the still-unmoving-yet-breathing child to a nearby clinic. A trauma fixed-wing plane, and crew had been requested, and were en route to them. On board the air-flight plane were the pilot, Joshua, the flight nurse, Lilith, and the paramedic, Ron. Joshua was an experienced pilot of ten years. Ron had been a paramedic with the fire department for five years, and with the flight team for two years. Lilith had been a flight nurse for two years now. It had become her dream after she got some ICU, and emergency room experience. She found the job always exciting, challenging, and very humbling. She knew she would be dealing with some of the worst experiences of her patients' lives. She felt blessed to be a part of their experiences, and to try to heal, comfort, relieve pain, and get them to a hospital as soon as possible.

"We've got a 7 year-old male, 24 kilograms, car versus elk, with severe head injuries to be transported back to Children's Hospital in Denver," Lilith reported to Ron.

"I'll calculate the ventilator settings while you do the medication plan," Ron said as he checked to see that they had all necessary equipment secured on the stretcher.

An ambulance was waiting at the airport to transport the flight team to the clinic. On arrival to the clinic, the child, Sam, had a secured airway supporting his breathing, but his heart rate and blood pressure were elevated. Lilith gave sedation, pain medication for comfort, and diuretics to reduce brain swelling.

Lilith leaned close and spoke into Sam's ear, "Sam, my name is Lilith. You hit your head, and we are going to take you to the hospital. I will give you medicine for pain. You will not be able to talk because you have a tube in your mouth helping you breathe. Your mom and dad will be going with us. You are safe."

Lilith and Ron moved quickly to stabilize Sam and prepare him for transport. Lilith, knowing that a head injury, and medication could affect the short-term memory, kept repeating information to Sam every ten to fifteen minutes during the transport.

"Sam, my name is Lilith. You hit your head; we are taking you to a hospital; a machine is helping you breathe; I'm giving you medication to help you rest; your mom and dad are with us; you are safe."

Sam's mom sat up front with the pilot Joshua, and his dad sat in the back with Lilith and Ron. Sam was loaded onto the plane on his stretcher with the respirator and multiple monitoring devices. When all was secured the plane took off for Denver. Lilith and Ron continued to monitor, and treat Sam.

Lilith repeated again, "Sam, my name is Lilith; you hit your head; we're taking you to a hospital; a machine is helping you breathe; I'm giving you medication to help you rest; your mom and dad are with us; you are safe."

Sam's heart rate and blood pressure stabilized. Lilith and Ron started catching up on their medical documentation. The flight was smooth, the skies were clear, and no storms were expected.

Music interrupted Lilith's thoughts. "Ron, where's that music coming from?"

"What are you hearing this time?" Ron smiled.

Ron knew Lilith said crazy stuff, but sometimes she was right on. He tended to pay attention to what she was saying.

Lilith looked up front and saw Sam's mom talking with Joshua. His dad, exhausted from worry and remorse, was asleep in his seat. Lilith and Ron exchanged worried glances. For a moment they worried that Sam was in danger, but everything indicated that he was stable.

"What kind of music do you hear?" Ron asked.

Lilith listened closely and spoke the words,

"Down by the river,

-Down by the sea,

-Johnny broke a bottle

-and blamed it on me.

-I told ma, ma told pa,

-Johnny got a spanking

-so ha ha ha.

-How many spankings did

-Johnny get?

-1, 2, 3..."

Lilith smiled, "He keeps repeating it over and over. It's a jumping rope rhyme."

"Who's 'he'? Do you mean the boy?" Ron asked.

"Yes, Sam's singing. He must be comfortable." Lilith smiled.

She continued to whisper in Sam's ear, "Sam, my name is Lilith. You hit your head; we're taking you to a hospital; a machine is helping you breathe; I'm giving you medication to help you rest; your mom and dad are with us; you are safe."

The team safely arrived at the airport and took their helicopter, flown by pilot Ralph, to the Children's Hospital. Report was given to the physician and nurses, and Sam's care was relinquished to them. Lilith and Ron took their equipment up to the helipad where Ralph waited with the helicopter.

As the helicopter lifted off, Ron padded Lilith's knee, smiled, and spoke into his microphone that was attached to his helmet, "Interesting trip!"

Lilith smiled and nodded. She was careful not to divulge too much. She didn't want to risk her credibility. Experience had shown her that she couldn't share her gift with just anyone. But sometimes she just couldn't help herself when things happened that surprised her. This was the first time she'd heard a child's voice, when the child was unconscious.

Weeks later the flight team got word that Sam had recovered from his injuries, and was back at home with his parents.

Rowing

She lives on a raft of hope
Rowing through the sea of life
An unpredictable journey

Storms and turbulence rock her
Tossed into the dangers of the unknown
She swims with all her strength

Bruised and exhausted
She pulls herself back onto the raft
And evaluates her loss and gain

She prays for days of calm and sun
Nights of moon and stars
Across the glassy seas of time

Now to recover, rebuild
Thoughts, plans and wishes
She gratefully relaxes and enjoys

Then the sky darkens, the wind howls
She grabs her oar and rows
Will she escape?

Yes, she chooses to ride
Hanging on by fingernails
Rather than surrender to the sea

Jeremy

LILITH ROSE ON A BEAUTIFUL AUTUMN morning with the sun streaming in her window. The leaves on the oak tree outside were a burgundy orange. Lilith leaned on the window sill and breathed in the crisp air with eyes closed. Moments like these reminded her of the blessings of life.

She put on her shorts, tee shirt, and shoes and closed the door behind her as she started out for a run. After the first mile, her muscles were warmed and relaxed. Her breathing became more rhythmic.

Her thoughts drifted to the surprise phone call from Jeremy. She hadn't heard from him since the note in his Christmas card. She smiled as she remembered his clever funny words. Lilith had known Jeremy since they were kids. He lived next door. They were best friends, confidants, mischief makers, and first-time lovers up in his childhood tree house. Jeremy was a sensitive, ardent lover. It seemed only fitting that you would try out your firsts with your best friend, the one that you trusted with your secrets and dreams. Lilith shared almost everything with Jeremy. He knew she had a sense or knowing about things, but she never told him about her angels and spirits.

She remembered his freckles and wild, curly, red hair. She laughed to herself as she remembered how his ears grew red when he was embarrassed. And her eyes welled with tears at the memory of her mom's memorial when she looked up and saw this handsome, older, red-haired man approaching with the familiar smile and warm, comforting hug. She hid herself in his arms for moments, or maybe hours.

Lilith slowed to a walk. The cool air felt good on her skin as she tried to shake off the sadness. She thought again of Jeremy. He was taking a vacation from his active and often intense law practice. He would be back in town in a few days. They'd have a great time catching up on each other's lives.

Her mind now drifted to her lists. She needed to plan a dinner, shop for food, and clean her house. Jeremy was going to stay in her guest room. His dad had died before Jeremy was born. Lilith and Jeremy shared that emptiness together. And now his mom lived in a nursing home that specialized in the care and treatment of Alzheimer's.

"Friends 'til the end," Jeremy would say. And Lilith would add, "And beyond." It always made them both smile.

Lilith was busy all day preparing food, cleaning, and thinking of the fun they would have together. A hike in the mountains to see the golden aspens would be fun; maybe they could lease a boat, and sail on Lake Dillon.

The day flew and it was now time to climb into bed and rest before her work day tomorrow. Lilith checked to see if she had a message from Jeremy. No message, so she still was unsure when he would arrive. She read for a few minutes, set her alarm, and drifted off to sleep.

Lilith's alarm sounded. She reached over and turned it off. She slipped on her flight uniform, and headed toward the kitchen for coffee and a bowl of cereal. It was her experience that told her to eat before going to work. She could have a flight when she got there, and never have a chance to eat. Lilith finished getting ready, exited her house, slid into her car, and was off to the hospital. After five years flying she still got excited about what the day would bring. The helicopter was an amazing machine that could quickly get a patient from a terrible accident to a hospital, and into an operating room.

As Lilith parked her car she noticed the helicopter blades were turning. She took off at a run hoping she had time to jump on so the night shift folks wouldn't have to take this flight just as they were supposed to get off work. As she reached the helicopter Jack, the night nurse, handed her a flight helmet, and gave her a thankful smile.

Lilith climbed in and secured her seatbelt. The pilot was Hans, an experienced Vietnam pilot who had been flying with the team for ten years. Lilith's partner, Robert, had been a paramedic with the flight team for five years. He had long black hair, pulled back, and big broad shoulders.

She spoke into her mic to her partner Robert, "What do we have?"

"Motorcycle versus car, 3 minutes out," Robert replied and then said, "I got here early and checked our equipment."

"Good man!" Lilith said, and smiled.

Lilith and her partner put on gloves, grabbed their bags, and a couple of chest tubes and exited the helicopter after it landed. They ducked under the turning blades and headed for the crash site. The emergency response team, who had gotten to the scene first, and had decided that a helicopter was needed, were surrounding the patient, doing chest compressions, and pushing oxygen into his airway using a mask attached to a pressure bag. They looked up as Lilith and Robert approached.

"Unhelmeted motorcyclist traveling at high speed hit turning car on hill; he was thrown head first into the side of the car. Pulseless and not breathing on our arrival. He has normal saline wide open, asystole on monitor, compressions continue, unable to get an airway due to his facial injuries," the emergency medic reported.

Lilith had the highest level of expertise, and was in charge. She grabbed the open medic's bag with an airway kit, splashed some betadine on the patient's neck, stabilized the trachea with one hand, and used the other to slice through the skin and trachea with a scalpel, and inserted an airway. She bagged the airway with oxygen, ventilating the lungs. Robert listened for breath sounds: first left then right chest. He nodded to Lilith that both lungs were getting oxygen. They continued CPR with three rounds of emergency drugs to try and restart the man's heart. Two liters of normal saline fluid flowed into his veins. The monitor still showed asystole, a flat line with no heart rhythm or pulse, and there were no spontaneous respirations.

Lilith asked, "How long have we been resuscitating?"

One of the emergency crew yelled, "twenty minutes."

Lilith responded, "Twenty minutes of CPR, severe head injury, no other obvious injuries. Any other ideas?" She waited for a response. She saw the crew sadly shaking their heads. "Time of death, 6:55 a. m.," Lilith stated.

Lilith said a silent prayer, and made the sign of the cross over the patient. The team covered him and gathered their supplies. An officer would stay with the body until the coroner arrived.

Lilith thanked the ground crew and checked to see if they had any questions or concerns. They talked about the accident, the horror of his mangled face and why an airway was difficult to locate.

Lilith said, "No matter how long we do this job, it's never easy to have a call like this one. You guys did a great job."

One of the crew members said, "Thanks. And thanks for coming. See you the next time."

"You bet," Robert answered.

Lilith and Robert put on their helmets and belted into the aircraft. The helicopter lifted off for home base.

As they headed back, the pilot, Hans, spoke to Lilith and Robert though their headsets. "We have another call. Do we need to return for supplies? We have plenty of fuel."

Lilith spoke, "No, we used the EMS supplies. But do we need blood? What does dispatch have for us?"

"7 year-old female with liver failure on transplant list. She's at a small hospital south of Colorado Springs. The Colorado Springs helicopter is out, and she needs to come to Denver for a transplant. A match has been found for her. She needs to be in Denver before noon," Hans stated.

Lilith said to herself, *A happy transport.*

She heard a swoosh warning. She said silently, *Is it the patient?* She heard, *No.*

She asked silently, *Is it the weather?*

She heard, *Yes.*

Lilith spoke into her mic, "Hans, do we have any weather issues?"

"I checked before we left; only scattered clouds to the south. No big storms," Hans reported.

Lilith sighed to herself, awaiting what would come. She finished her charting on her previous patient as they flew south. Just past Colorado Springs, they saw the scattered grey clouds ahead.

"Looks like we have some thickening of the clouds. I'll try to go around them," Hans said.

Lilith and Robert looked out at the approaching clouds. If they couldn't find a way around, they'd have to turn back. The helicopter couldn't fly unless it had a mile out and three miles up of visibility. They would need the radar-equipped fixed wing plane crew to go get the patient.

Hans got on the mic and said, "Look at that, guys."

"Oh, my gosh. What kind of miracle is this? Looks like the clouds are parting for us," Robert said.

Lilith and Robert gazed in amazement at the wall of clouds beside and above them. The ground was visible below. The wall gave them plenty of room to continue on to the hospital.

Lilith silently said, *Thanks!*

On arrival at the hospital Lilith and Robert got report on Megan, and lifted her onto their stretcher. They wheeled her to the aircraft with the help of the hospital staff and loaded her stretcher.

Megan said, "This is my second helicopter ride. Can I sit up so I can see? And I have my camera. Can you take a picture of me before you close the door?" Megan waited excitedly for an answer.

Lilith smiled and said, "Of course you can sit up, just like you're doing right now on the stretcher. I'll put ear protectors on you to shield your ears from the loud helicopter sounds. And I'm sure one of the hospital staff would be happy to take your picture."

Megan held out her camera, and one of the emergency room nurses took her picture. Once Megan received her camera back, her door was closed. Lilith and Robert climbed into the aircraft, put on their helmets, and secured their seat-belt harnesses.

As the aircraft lifted Robert said through his mic, "Will you look at that? The clouds have cleared. We have blue sky ahead."

The crew landed at Children's Hospital, and off-loaded Megan. Hans lifted off to get fuel, and then return for the crew. Lilith and Robert gave report to the nurses, and finished their charting. When they were done they said goodbye to Megan and the staff, and headed back to the helipad to meet Hans.

Hans was waiting when they returned. They loaded the stretcher, and climbed in just as their hand-held radio went off. "We have another flight for you. A forty-five year-old male with an acute Myocardial Infarction who needs to go from Payton Hospital to Smith's catheterization lab," dispatch reported.

Robert clicked his phone. "Got it. We're on our way."

Lilith and Robert secured themselves in the aircraft, and nodded to Hans that they were ready. The aircraft lifted off, and headed for Payton Hospital. Within five minutes they landed at the hospital, unloaded the stretcher and equipment, and hurried in before the blades had even stopped beating.

Lilith's ears buzzed with chatter. She heard, *They're waiting for you.*

Lilith was in a hurry and didn't have time to ask what her angels meant, so she just replied silently, *OK.*

Screams could be heard from inside the emergency room. As they approached the patient he was yelling in pain. Lilith looked at the monitor, and saw large peaked t-waves, an elevation in the EKG, indicative of a myocardial infarction. Robert and Lilith got report on the patient as they checked his fluid and drew up some morphine sulfate.

Lilith explained, "Johnathan, my name is Lilith. I'm going to give you some morphine for pain. I will keep medicating you until your pain is gone. My partner Robert and I will be working quickly to load you on our stretcher, and fly you to the lab at Smith Hospital. In the catheterization lab a large catheter will be placed in an artery of your leg, and through that catheter a small catheter will be threaded up toward your heart. Dye will be injected and the physician will see if you have any blockages in the arteries of your heart. If you do they will open them," Lilith said.

Just before rolling Johnathan's stretcher out of the emergency room, Lilith noticed a calm had come over him. Lilith asked, "Johnathan, are you having any pain?"

Johnathan responded, "No, I'm going."

Lilith looked at Robert as her ears buzzed. She said, "Johnathan, we will be loading you on our helicopter to fly to the hospital."

"No, I'm going with them." Johnathan pointed to the corner of the room.

Lilith's ears buzzed and she heard, *His angels are here for him.*

Robert leaned down close to Johnathan's face and said, "Johnathan, you're going with us. Hang in there."

Johnathan said, "You'd better hurry. They're waiting."

Lilith and Robert quickly loaded Johnathan into the aircraft and secured themselves with their seatbelt harnesses. The helicopter lifted off for the 3-minute flight to the hospital. On arrival, they off-loaded Johnathan, and quickly headed to the cath lab.

Lilith said, "Johnathan, we're almost there. How are you doing?"

Johnathan said, "Fine. They're with us."

Once in the catheterization lab, Johnathan was moved over to the table just as he lost consciousness. Lilith quickly placed an endotracheal tube to secure his airway, and he was given oxygen and artificially ventilated. Johnathan had no pulse. First-line cardiac advanced life support drugs were given, and chest compressions were done to try and restart his heart. He was shocked three times due to ventricular fibrillation, a quivering of the heart that produces no pulse. His heart didn't restart. Lilith knew he'd gone with his angels, and she saw that Robert was visibly upset.

Giving Robert a hug, Lilith said softly, "He went with his angels."

Robert sniffed and said, "I know, but that was the first time a patient told me they were going to die, and that someone was waiting for them." Robert sighed, "It kind of gives me hope." He attempted a smile.

Lilith squeezed Robert's hand, and said with a smile, "It sure does!"

Lilith finished her charting as Robert remade the stretcher with clean sheets, and cleaned and secured their equipment. They slowly walked back to the helipad, and loaded the stretcher on board.

As they lifted off, Hans said, "How about some food?"

"Great idea," Lilith and Robert said together.

Back at base, Hans refueled the aircraft so it would be ready when they might need it. Lilith and Robert restocked their equipment. Then all three went to the cafeteria for lunch with pagers and phones on. They knew they needed nourishment, and had to get it as soon as possible.

Lilith checked her cell phone and saw that Jeremy had called that morning. His message said he thought he would be at her house sometime late afternoon or evening. Lilith had left a key under the stone angel to the right of her front door. Jeremy could let himself in, and relax if he got there before she got off work. After a day like today she knew she would be exhausted, but she would still stay up late into the night visiting with her friend.

After eating, Lilith and Robert walked to all the units in the hospital to see if anyone needed help with their patients. They started a couple of intravenous lines in the emergency room.

Robert and Lilith's radio beeped. Lilith answered, "Yes?"

"Got a call for you, motorcycle versus semi," dispatch reported.

Lilith ran for the helipad as Robert grabbed two units of O-negative blood from the refrigerator. They climbed in the aircraft with its rotors spinning. The aircraft landed on the freeway between two fire trucks. Lilith and Robert grabbed their bags, exited, ducked below the turning blades, and headed to the accident scene.

Lilith's ears buzzed a warning that she couldn't make out.

Her ears buzzed again and she heard, *We are with you.*

One of the firemen approached. "Semi apparently blew a tire weaving into a motorcyclist throwing him under the rig. He's helmeted and trapped under the tires. We have some equipment to lift the rig off him. He's unconscious with a weak pulse."

Lilith and Robert got on their knees as they assessed the patient. The patient still had his helmet on which couldn't be easily removed until he was freed from the rig's tires. Knowing that he probably had massive trauma to his body, Robert placed a large bore IV into both arms with normal saline fluid flowing wide open. Lilith placed an airway and bagged the patient as Robert listened for breath sounds.

"No breath sounds on the right and I feel crepitus," Robert reported. Robert knew that the patient probably had broken ribs that had punctured his lung. That would cause air and possibly blood to escape into the tissue making a popping sound and feel which is crepitus. "Possibly a hemopneumothorax; I will needle it to see if we get breath sounds in the right lung." Robert placed a needle between the ribs. Blood and air escaped through the needle allowing the lung to expand. "I hear bilateral breath sounds," Robert exclaimed.

Lilith and Robert saw that the tire was crushing the patient's lower abdomen and pelvis. The fluid was running in and they still had a weak pulse. The fire crew asked them to be prepared to pull him out as they lifted the rig up. Lilith held the airway securely while Robert kept the patient's head in alignment. Five of them waited to the count of three and pulled him out as a unit. They placed him on a backboard to support his spine in case of injury. Lilith continued to bag oxygen into his lungs as Robert felt for a pulse.

"No pulse. Start CPR," Robert shouted. One of the fire crew started compressions and Lilith bagged the patient. There was no time to remove the helmet. The patient needed to get to the hospital.

Lilith noticed that the once flat abdomen was becoming distended. "He's bleeding into his belly. Hang the blood."

Robert hung both units of blood with pressure bags to push the blood in fast. The patient was loaded onto the aircraft, and it lifted as they continued CPR and pumping in blood. Lilith bagged the patient and Robert did compressions. Lilith and Robert knew the patient's only chance was to get him to an operating room. They called a "trauma alert" and landed within three minutes. Both units of blood had infused and CPR continued. The monitor showed a tachycardia, fast rhythm, but there was still no pulse; pulseless electrical activity. The trauma team met the flight team on the helipad, and helped transport the patient to the OR.

Once in the operating room, Lilith gave report about the patient to the trauma team as they all moved the patient to the operating table. His abdomen was exposed, covered with betadine and opened. The team was busy removing his helmet and clothes, putting in arterial lines for blood pressure and central venous lines. CPR continued as the surgeons tried to find the source of the bleeding and repair it. Robert had given over compressions to one of the OR techs.

One of the nurses handed Lilith a wallet and said, "Lilith, can you give his wallet to the chaplain so she can locate the family?"

Lilith took the wallet and said, "Sure, and I need the name for my chart."

Lilith opened up the wallet and there was Jeremy's picture on the driver's license. She let out a scream, and fell against the wall. Robert was quickly at her side.

Lilith screamed, "No Jeremy. Not you. Please Jeremy, no."

Robert put his arms around Lilith. "Oh Lilith, he's your friend who was coming to visit?"

Lilith grabbed at Robert, "Yes, they have to save him."

Robert held Lilith and tried to help her up. "Let me take you out of here to wait."

Lilith straightened up and took a long look at Jeremy's body lying helplessly on the trauma table as the surgical team worked on him.

"Jeremy, come back to me," she called out.

Then she heard, *Lilith, I'm right here.*

Lilith called out, "No, Jeremy come back!" She saw his vital signs were still at zero.

The team surgeon looked up at Lilith and said, "He had a third degree tear to his liver, his liver was bleeding beyond repair, and a tear to his mesenteric artery, so no blood flow to his intestines. He bled into his abdomen and his heart was empty. All of his organs are ischemic, lacking in blood and oxygen due to the blood loss into his belly. We did everything we could. I'm so sorry Lilith."

Lilith collapsed in a heap, crying loudly.

She heard, *What do they mean? I'm right here!*

Lilith cried, "Not my Jeremy!"

The trauma team closed Jeremy's abdomen and covered his body with a sheet. Robert and Chaplain Susan helped Lilith stand, and move slowly over to Jeremy. Lilith laid her head across Jeremy, soaking the sheet with her tears.

She heard, *Lilith what's happening? Why are you crying?*

Jer, you died!

She heard, *No, I'm right here! You're talking to me.*

Jer, I have the gift of speaking and hearing the dead. Your motorcycle collided with a semi-truck.

She heard, *No, I'm here. Look at me. That's not my body. It's here.*

Jeremy, look closely. It's you.

Robert said, "Lilith, take your time. I'll be outside if you need me."

"No, wait. I just need to say goodbye." Lilith moved up to Jeremy and stroked his face with her hand. She leaned down and kissed his forehead and whispered in his ear knowing that Jeremy could hear her. "I'll try to help your mom understand. I love you and will help you through this."

Lilith picked up Jeremy's helmet and his personal effects. She remembered that she and Jeremy had signed papers designating each other as the next of kin when her mom died and his mom became ill.

She heard, *Lil, I don't understand?*

Come with me, Jer. I'll help you understand.

Lilith left the trauma room and collapsed into Robert's embrace. The two walked back to the helipad to return to base. Lilith knew that Jeremy would follow.

Three Months Later

As LILITH DROVE HOME FROM A long, tiring day at work, she realized it had been three months since Jeremy's accident. He had remained with her since that terrible day. She wondered if she had been selfish, keeping him to herself. She knew he needed her in the weeks following the accident to help him come to understand about his death. He kept forgetting what happened to him. Then he needed to deal with the loss, pain, anger, and denial. His funeral was beautiful with his friends and coworkers from Oregon, and his poor mom who lived in a nursing home nearby. Lilith had tried to help her understand what happened, but her advanced Alzheimer's shielded her from the traumatic pain and realization. Lilith had felt spirits pass through her and sometimes linger a while in her body. She had learned how to prevent it from happening; it was intrusive and exhausting. But she told Jeremy that he could come into her body to say goodbye to his friends and his mom. It was at that moment that Lilith felt there was some recognition from his mom. She held Lilith (and Jeremy) tight for a long time.

Since his death, Jeremy had been in Lilith's house. She felt she hadn't really lost *him*, just his human form. He was with her laughing, sharing, and keeping her company. Lilith had missed her friend. She wondered sometimes why he was still here. Lilith hadn't asked her angels about it. She really didn't want to know.

Lilith's ears buzzed. It was the familiar chatter of her angels. They had been quiet for a while. She heard, *You know what to do. We are with you.*

She said silently, *I know,* as tears rolled down her cheeks.

Lilith slowly entered her house, dropping her keys in the silver bowl near the door. She walked pensively toward the living room and kitchen.

She said out loud, "Are you here, Jer?"

She heard, *Where else would I be, silly? I would never follow you to work. What you do makes me queasy.*

Lilith laughed, "You never liked blood. I remember when you fainted after I cut my leg on barbed wire."

She heard, *No, I didn't,* said Jeremy, *snickering.*

"Jer, we need to talk," Lilith said.

Isn't that what we're doing? she heard.

"Jer, this is serious. You aren't supposed to stay here with me. As much as I love it, you need to move on to the next place." Lilith sighed.

She heard, *But, I want to stay with you.*

"Jeremy, you have exciting adventures ahead of you," Lilith encouraged.

Lilith and Jeremy stayed up most of the night talking about their lives and reminiscing about their childhood. It was unbearable to Lilith to think of never talking to Jeremy again. She was becoming fatigued, but fought it so she wouldn't miss a minute with him. Sometime before morning her body and mind betrayed her and she slept.

When Lilith awoke she called out, "Jer, are you still here?" She called out again louder, "Jer!!!!!!"

There was no answer. He was gone. Lilith wept into her pillow. She stayed in bed most of the day watching old movies, crying, and dozing.

The next morning she dragged herself out of bed and went to work. As she started her drive to work she noticed the dark sky. It opened up and poured rain. The wind blew leaves and debris across her windshield. It felt as if the world was reacting to the loss of Jeremy. The storm lasted through the day, grounding the helicopter. Lilith was glad to have a chance to help in the hospital and catch up on some projects. The day flew by, much to her relief.

Then it was time to return home. Her heart was heavy. She decided to visit Ruth, Jeremy's mom. When she entered the Alzheimer's unit, she didn't see Ruth in the living room. She asked one of the staff about her, and was surprised to find that Ruth was staying in bed a lot of the day.

Betty, one of Ruth's nurse aides, shared with Lilith, "She is so sleepy. The smallest activity, like eating, exhausts her. I don't know if she'll be with us much longer."

Lilith's ears buzzed and she heard her familiar voices. *Her angels are coming for her. It won't be much longer.*

Lilith asked silently, *Is she in pain?*

Lilith heard, *No.*

Lilith peeked in on Ruth, and found her sleeping. She asked Betty to call her if there was any change. She made sure that she was on the emergency contact list. She planned to take care of the funeral arrangements when it was time.

Lilith drove home slowly. She didn't want to go home to an empty house. She grabbed some Chinese takeout and couldn't think of any other errand, so she went home. Setting her food on the table, she showered, put on her pajamas and settled into the dining chair for her dinner.

Her ears buzzed and she heard, *You're not alone.*

I know. I appreciate that you're with me, Lilith responded back silently. *Please help Jeremy in his travels.*

Lilith heard, *You will have to save that wish.*

Recognizing the voice, Lilith said out loud, "Jer, what are you still doing here?"

Lilith heard, *I don't know. I tried to leave, but I'm still here. I guess I don't know the rules.* Jeremy laughed.

Lilith responded out loud, "Selfishly, I'm glad you are here. But, I might have an idea as to why you're here."

Lilith told Jeremy about his Mom's change in condition. "You should go and see her. Perhaps you're waiting for her?"

Tell you what. Let's spend tonight together and once you fall asleep, I'll go see Mom, Jeremy suggested.

Lilith smiled, "I would like that."

Lilith and Jeremy talked and laughed most of the night. Just before Lilith drifted off to sleep she said out loud, "I love you, Jer."

She heard a whisper, *I love you too, Lil.*

The phone rang, startling Lilith awake. She knew who it was before she heard Betty's voice. Tears spilled from her eyes as she thought of Jeremy with his mom. He would make sure she was comfortable with her journey until her mind returned, and they could enjoy the experience together.

Lilith had learned from her deceased patients when she helped them understand their passing. She found that the departed were very similar in death as in life for a short time until they evolved and became aware and sometimes younger. Lilith knew that it wouldn't be long before Jeremy's mom got her memory back.

Hard Decisions

LILITH ARRIVED EARLY AT 6:30 A.M., as she always did, for her shift at the hospital. She stopped by the chapel to say her prayer-wish.

Please Lord, may I heal and do no harm.

She walked down the long hall which was decorated with beautiful hanging works of art: landscapes in oils and pastels. They hung right up to the entrance of the Intensive Care Unit. It had been a year since Lilith had stopped flying, and had rejoined the ICU. She had loved flying with the challenge, autonomy, and constant variety of patients. It humbled her to be a part of one of the worst days of someone's life, and be able to give them nursing care, comfort and fast transport to a hospital. But her love was the ICU. In the ICU she could still use all of her critical thinking skills, plus work with the patient, family, and physicians to plan the care. It was satisfying to see a patient go from so critically ill to a resolution of healing and discharge, or comfort and an ease into a peaceful death. Sudden deaths didn't have a peaceful process, but Lilith felt blessed that she could talk with the deceased and help them understanding what happened and what to expect.

As Lilith entered the ICU, she saw the circular nurses' station packed full of the day and night shift nurses ready to give, and receive report on their patients. Lilith received report from night nurse, Judy.

Judy was an accomplished nurse of 15 years, and a long-time coworker of Lilith's. Her reading glasses sat low on her nose, and her salt and pepper hair was pulled back tight in a bun.

Judy began, "You will have just one patient today, because she is so unstable. The patient, Marie, is 32 years old, married, with a 1-year-old child. Last night she had drinks with some friends and was driving home on an apparently dark, windy road when she hit a 25-year-old male bicyclist, and then flipped her car down an embankment. She was seat-belted, and her air bags deployed."

Lilith asked, "What time did the accident happen?"

"The ground crew estimated about 11:00 p.m. A motorist found the man near his bicycle, called 911 and started CPR. When EMS arrived the man was pronounced dead, and they found Marie unconscious in her car. She arrived at the hospital about 1 a.m.," Judy added.

"Marie was lucky someone drove by that late at night," Lilith said.

Judy continued, "She received a cardiac contusion, a spleen hematoma from the seatbelt, and severe head injury with swelling. Her brain has no bleeds or tears. Pupils are fixed and dilated. She went to surgery, had a skull flap removed for brain swelling and an intracranial pressure monitor placed, you know, the ICP. She arrived in the ICU at 5 a.m. Her ICP was elevated so we placed her in a chemical coma, paralyzed and medicated for pain. She has a bandage at her left temporal area with minimal drainage. I marked the drainage on the bandage when she arrived. Be careful with that side of her head. She has no protective skull at the bandage site. Isn't it amazing that a piece of your skull can be removed to allow the injured brain to swell and heal. That is why I love medicine! Oh, and the patient's husband, David, was in to see her, but he had to go home to take care of their daughter."

Judy went through her physical assessment of Marie. After report Judy and Lilith went into Marie's room to view her ventilator settings, and all the intravenous fluids that were pumping into her veins. The

ICP reading was normal. Lilith knew that the medication was working to keep the pressure in her brain within normal limits so that the brain tissue could heal.

Judy added, "Any stimulus, including suctioning her airway, turning her or loud noises, causes her ICP to rise. She is on a rotating bed, thank goodness. The gentle turn of the bed does not affect her ICP. I spaced out her care and procedures throughout the shift. Her husband was instructed to not stimulate her, and keep his voice low." Judy took in a tired breath. "Any questions Lilith?"

"No. Have a good sleep."

"Thanks." Judy looked over at Marie. "She has a long road ahead of her."

Lilith knew she was not just talking about her physical healing. "You got that right," Lilith, added.

Lilith started her physical assessment of Marie. She spoke softly, and touched gently so as not to stimulate Marie, increase her ICP, and cause further brain injury. The room was dimly lit, and quiet except for the sound of the monitoring devices.

Lilith began, "Marie, my name is Lilith. I'm your nurse today. You were in an accident and had surgery. You are now in the intensive care unit. You have a tube in your throat helping you breathe. I'm giving you pain medication and a medication that prevents you from moving so that your brain can rest and heal. You're safe. David was just here, and went home to take care of your daughter."

Lilith retrieved a pen light from her pocket. "I'm going to look into your eyes with a bright light." Lilith shone her pen light into Marie's eyes, and saw that the pupils were fixed and dilated, the desired reaction of no response to light when a patient is in a chemical coma.

"I will now listen to your lungs, heart and belly." Lilith placed her stethoscope on Marie.

Lilith continued, "I'll check your skin and pulses. I'll straighten out your sheets so that they won't cause wrinkles on your skin. You have a tube that goes into your belly. I'll check to see that it is still in place."

Lilith noticed that Marie's ICP was elevated. She adjusted the sedation and pain medication. She silently watched as the ICP normalized. Just as Lilith was leaving Marie's room, she heard an unfamiliar voice.

Where am I? What happened? I can't move.

Lilith inquired, *Are you Marie?*

Lilith heard, *Yes. What happened?*

Marie, you had an accident in your car, and hit your head. You have a brain injury. You can't move because we placed you in a chemical coma. You are breathing with the help of a ventilator. I will keep you safe and free of pain. Your brain needs to rest and heal.

Lilith heard Marie cry out, *Am I paralyzed?*

Lilith answered, *No, it's a temporary due to the medication.*

Lilith heard, *How can I talk to you? How can you hear me?*

Lilith answered, *You are in an altered state due to your injury. I have the gift of hearing you in this state.*

Lilith heard, *My daughter? My husband?*

"They are at home. Your husband will come and see you later today." Lilith said as she viewed the ICP, and was relieved that Marie's anxious questions had not caused it to elevate.

Marie cried out. *What happened? How can you hear me?*

Lilith knew that Marie was confused and it would take her a while to grasp what had happened to her. Lilith repeated what she had told her.

Lilith said, *You need to rest now, Marie.*

Lilith went out to the nurses' station to chart on the computer. Marie's spirit came with Lilith, and she asked her questions over and over again. Lilith answered the questions silently as she tried to do her charting.

At 10:00 a.m. David, Marie's husband came in to see her. After getting an update from Lilith he entered his wife's room, and took a seat next to her bed. Lilith saw him as he looked up at all of the monitors and then down at his bandaged, swollen wife with tubes coming out of everywhere.

David gently kissed his wife's hand and lay his head down next to it. He cried. "Oh, Marie, I wish you hadn't driven. Why didn't you take a cab or call me? How will we deal with all of this? I need you, baby."

Then Lilith heard, *Lilith, why is David crying? What is he talking about? Was I drinking and driving? Why can't I remember anything?*

Lilith spoke silently, *Marie, you were driving after you had drinks with some friends. You had an accident and hit your head.*

Lilith heard, *What does David mean? Am I in trouble?*

Lilith let out a long breath. *Marie, you were seriously injured in the accident. Your important job is to rest, and heal so that you can get back to your daughter and your husband. David misses you and he is just scared.*

Lilith went into Marie's room and checked the monitoring devices. She saw David crying and approached him. "David, is there anything I can do for you?"

David looked up at Lilith. "How can I help Marie?"

Lilith went over to the bed. She touched David's shoulder and said, "You are doing it. Just talk to her. She can hear you even though she can't respond due to the chemical coma."

Lilith gave report to Judy as she finished her shift. Marie was silent. The conversation between Lilith and Marie remained their secret.

When Lilith got home, she showered. She let the warm water roll off her, and willed her stresses down the drain. When she went to bed she tossed and turned.

She called out, "My angels, how do I handle this? I took an oath to heal, and do no harm. I can't jeopardize Marie's recovery by telling her everything that happened. I feel caught between my work job, and my spiritual job or gift or whatever you call it."

Lilith lay still as whispers whirled around in her head.

Lilith heard, *Trust yourself. You will know what to say or not say.*

The room became quiet and Lilith fell fast asleep. Lilith dreamt of riding her horse, Rosie, through fields of colored flowers. She could smell their fragrance. There were majestic mountains, and fluffy clouds against the bluest sky. The wind whipped her hair and she laughed. Then there was a ringing noise that was out of place in all the beauty. She wondered what it could be. Lilith was pulled away from her beautiful dream back into wakefulness as her alarm clock invaded the darkness. She hit the button, climbed out of bed, and back into her world.

"What a great dream. I need to plan a vacation. Perhaps a reunion with my girlfriends, someplace where we can ride horses," Lilith said aloud with a smile on her face.

After coffee, breakfast, and putting on her scrubs, Lilith drove in to work. When she entered the hospital she stopped by the chapel, and prayed her prayer wish.

Please Lord, may I heal and do no harm. May the words I say to Marie be full of truth and cause no damage. Please guide me.

Lilith dipped her finger in the holy water at the chapel door, made the sign of the cross, and headed for the ICU. She got an updated report from Judy. There were no changes. Days turned into weeks and Marie's husband held vigil at her bedside whenever he could. Marie repeated her questions and Lilith answered. There were no more questions about the accident. All questions were about her condition and her family.

Marie would say, *I miss my daughter. I want to see her.*

Lilith would respond silently, *Go and be with her. Just close your eyes and think of her; your energy will take you there. Feel her love, and give her your love.*

Marie would later respond, *Oh, Lilith, she is so precious. I love her so much.*

In week three Marie's condition changed. She had a normal ICP, and it no longer elevated with stimulus. Lilith was continuing her assessment of Marie when her ears started buzzing.

Lilith heard, *Lilith, I need your help. I don't understand what is happening. Please help me.*

Lilith responded silently, *Marie, I need to check on your body and give you medicine. When I am finished; I will answer your questions.*

Thanks. Marie fell silent.

Lilith did her assessment, charted, and gave Marie her medications. Dr. Amy Waltz came into Marie's room. She was short with brown hair swept up high on her head, and small dark rimmed glasses hanging from a chain around her neck. Lilith was glad to be working with Amy. She was a talented neurologist.

"Hi Lilith, any changes?" she smiled.

"It appears that Marie's ICP has stabilized. She does not have spikes with stimulus. Do you want to start weaning her from the paralyzing agent and sedation?"

"This is good news. Let's do a repeat Cat Scan. If there is improvement, we can start the medication wean."

"Sounds great." Lilith ordered the Cat Scan.

Lilith heard, *What does that mean? Tell me everything.*

Lilith spoke silently, *Marie, remember you had a car accident, and hit your head. We have had you in a chemical coma to let your brain rest. You are getting better. We will get a picture of your head. If it looks better we will start to wake you up from the chemical coma.*

David arrived just as Lilith was returning from Cat Scan pushing Marie's hospital bed back into her room in the ICU.

"How's she doing?" David's brow was furrowed.

"Better today. We rescanned her head, and will have the results soon. The monitor in her head has shown improvement. If the scan is better, we will start weaning her from the medication, and allow her to wake up."

David gasped, "I don't know how I'm going to tell her what happened."

Lilith gently patted his arm. "David, just take one step at a time."

Lilith went out to the nurses' station and left David sitting next to Marie.

Lilith's ears started buzzing. *Lilith what did he mean? What happened?*

Lilith took a deep breath, and let it out slow. She felt it was important for Marie's recovery to be honest with her. She hoped that she was making the right decision.

Marie, your car accident involved a bicyclist. It was a dark road, and your car hit a man on a bicycle, Lilith explained silently.

Lilith heard, *Is he all right? Is he here in this hospital?*

No, he's not here. He died in the accident. Lilith explained silently.

Lilith heard, *No. It can't be. No. Was it my fault?*

Lilith paused, trying to hide her own worry, and breathed in deeply. *Marie, I don't know the circumstances. Please try to focus on getting better.*

Lilith heard Marie say, *How can I live with myself if I killed someone? What kind of example will that be for my daughter? Will David be able to forgive me? This is too much. I should just die.*

This was what Lilith feared. Silently she spoke to Marie firmly. *Now Marie, you go see your daughter right now. Give her love and give your husband love. Hold onto them.*

Kathy, the unit secretary, said, "Lilith, you have a phone call."

Lilith answered the phone. "This is Lilith."

Dr. Waltz responded, "Lilith, Marie's scan shows decreased swelling. Why don't we let her rest tonight, and start the weaning tomorrow."

"Sounds good to me. We'll start the medication wean tomorrow." Lilith hung up the phone. She was relieved to have some extra time to talk with Marie.

When Lilith got home she put on her sweats and went for a run. Her body was fatigued, but her mind was racing. The twelve-hour shift was tiring physically and emotionally for Lilith. She ran faster than she thought she could. She was running and running, trying to outrun her anguish, and the dilemma that lay ahead. When she returned home, she showered, had a strawberry-orange protein smoothie, and went to bed.

The next morning Lilith headed to work thinking about what she might say to Marie.

She prayed, *Please Lord, guide me to say the right thing. Please, may I be of help to Marie.*

At the hospital she stopped by the chapel and prayed, *Lord, may I heal and do no harm.*

Lilith received report on Marie and her other patient, Walt. After checking on Marie, she assessed, medicated, and charted on Walt. Lilith returned to Marie's room to assess her. Her ears buzzed.

She heard, *Lilith, please talk to me. What am I going to do? This is so hard. What if I go to prison? I'll be separated from my daughter, and husband. How will they handle it? How can I handle this myself?*

Lilith spoke silently, *Marie, did you see your daughter last night?*

Lilith heard, *Yes, I love her so much.*

Marie, you may have a long recovery ahead of you. And we do not know what will happen in regards to the accident. There may be some consequences. But wouldn't you rather fight through anything, and be able to see your daughter grow up? She needs her mom, Lilith said silently.

Lilith heard, *I love her so much. I don't want to be without her. I'm just scared.*

Lilith said silently, *Of course you are. But I bet you can be brave for that little girl. And it looks to me like you have a good man in David.*

Lilith heard, *I know. I'll try.*

Lilith spoke out loud to Marie. "Marie I'm turning off the paralyzing agent, and decreasing your sedation. I'll be checking your reflexes, and looking into your eyes to check your pupil response. You will still have the breathing tube until we know you can breathe on your own."

Over the next hour, Marie slowly had return of reflexes, and pupil response was equal but sluggish. She would withdraw her limbs when Lilith stimulated her, but did not follow any commands. Lilith decreased the sedation and pain medication a bit more.

Each time Lilith assessed Marie she spoke softly to her. "Marie, I'm Lilith the nurse taking care of you. You're no longer in a chemical coma. I'm decreasing your sedation and pain medication. Can you squeeze my hand? Can you open your eyes?"

There was still no response. Marie's monitoring devices read normal, and her ICP was normal. Lilith knew Marie would be showing signs of waking soon. Cindy was the oncoming nurse. This would be her first time taking care of Marie. Lilith gave her report, and they entered Marie's room. Lilith familiarized Cindy with Marie's monitoring equipment, and answered her questions. Lilith did a final neurological exam.

Lilith said, "Marie, can you open your eyes?"

Marie opened her eyes. She slowly blinked as if trying to focus.

Lilith took each of Marie's hands in hers, and said, "Marie, can you squeeze my hands?"

Marie squeezed both of Lilith's hands. Lilith was ready to withdraw her hands when Marie grabbed them. Lilith looked down at Marie's face.

Marie's eyes looked into Lilith's eyes and she mouthed, *"Thank you."*

Lilith said, "It was my pleasure working with you, Marie. You're going to be fine. Please be patient. We will let you rest on the respirator tonight, and try and wean you tomorrow. Weaning means that we decrease the settings on the ventilator, and allow you to try and take your own breaths with the support of the ventilator. You just keep thinking about your husband, and that beautiful little girl."

Marie mouthed, *"I will"*.

Lilith left the hospital with a spring in her step. Even though she would never know how Marie did in her long recovery since she would eventually transfer to another hospital for rehabilitation, she felt confident that Marie had a good attitude to start the process.

Lilith looked up into the beautiful blue sky scattered with white and pink fluffy clouds and gave her thanks. *Thank you, Lord, and thank you, my angels.* She smiled to herself as she unlocked her car to head home.

Lilith heard her angels' chatter. It was her female angel, Jade, whose voice was the loudest. Jade said, *We are so proud of you. You are growing with your gift and helping your patients.*

I'm thankful that you help me along the way. I have much to learn. Lilith responded as she drove toward home.

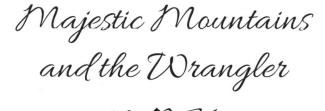

Majestic Mountains and the Wrangler

LILITH MARKED OFF THE DAYS ON her calendar in June until the 10th. She circled that date in rainbow colors. Brochures were tacked to her bulletin board. It was finally the day to pack. Samantha, Angie, and Rebecca, her suite-mates from college, were meeting her at the Always Summer Dude Ranch in southern Colorado. Lilith picked the ranch, because she remembered how beautiful it was when she had flown there in the helicopter to get a patient. It would be 7 days of relaxing fun. There would be games, food, drinks, hiking, swimming, and riding. And Lilith couldn't wait to see her friends. It had been a couple of years since they had all been together.

Samantha had married a Texan, and lived in Dallas with their three kids. She was an oil and gas lawyer, and her husband was one of the state's youngest judges. Samantha was blond, sweet, smart, and pretty. She fit in well with the Dallas crowd. It had been years since she had on a pair of jeans, and even longer since she had been on a horse.

Angie and her partner Sue lived in Santa Fe. They were both artists and owned a gallery. Angie painted landscapes in oils and pastels. She hiked and biked and was looking forward to learning to ride a horse.

Rebecca was a freelance journalist and writer of fiction. She had been touring and promoting her last book. She was anxious to see her friends and relax. The size and power of horses scared her, but she was up for the challenge.

The day was warm, and full of sunshine. The sky was crystal blue against the western mountains. Lilith drove south toward the ranch. Check in was at 1 p.m. That would give her time to unpack, and walk around a bit before her friends arrived near dinnertime. As she left the city, the landscape opened up to fields of green grass and scrub oak bushes. She spotted some antelope and deer grazing in the distance. There had been a lot of evening rain this June, adding to the vegetation. The sky was now blue with an array of purple, grey, and white clouds looming over the western mountains.

Perhaps rain tonight. Glad I brought rain gear, Lilith said to herself.

She spotted the large stone entrance with a wired sign hanging over the drive. It read WELCOME TO ALWAYS SUMMER RANCH. The long dirt drive wound past pastures with horses and stables. Up over a hill, Lilith spotted a large building with parking. She pulled in and parked and went in to register. Just past the desk she saw a large dining hall, and could smell barbeque smoking. A thin young man appeared and came to the front desk. He had sandy blond hair visible below his cowboy hat. He wore jeans, and a brightly blue-colored snap western shirt.

"Welcome to Always Summer Ranch, my name is Jason. Let's get you checked in," he smiled.

Lilith smiled, "Something smells delicious."

"That's Roy's famous barbeque. He likes to welcome the guests with his mouth-watering favorite." The young man laughed.

"I'm sure we'll love it." Lilith signed in, and Jason handed her a map and key.

She drove her car down the winding road and past many cabins, all named after trees. She pulled in the drive of Cottonwood. The cabin was rustic with knot holes and a porch with four rocking chairs.

Inside were four bedrooms and two bathrooms. There was a small kitchen, and a nice cozy living room with two over-stuffed couches, and a large stone fire place. The tiny refrigerator was tucked under the kitchen cabinet, and supplied with fruit, cheese, water bottles, sodas, and a bottle of white wine. The curtains, bedspreads, and towels had patterns of cowboys and cowgirls riding horses.

This will get us in the western spirit, Lilith said to herself as she smiled.

She unpacked and put on a pair of jeans, a western snap shirt in blue and purple, and one of her pairs of cowboy boots. She headed out for a walk. The grounds were beautiful with natural grasses and flowers. It was warm with a hint of moisture.

A storm must be approaching, Lilith said to herself.

Her wandering took her down to the stables. The horses were coming in closer for dinner. She watched as some of the crew hauled out bales of hay, cut them open, and threw the flakes into troughs. Lilith particularly noticed a tall man, probably in his forties. He was working alongside the younger wranglers. The wind teased his thick, black, grey-streaked hair under his cowboy hat. He had broad shoulders and fit his jeans well. Lilith saw him reach over and give one of the horses a soft rub. Just then he turned, and saw her watching him. He touched his hat, and nodded a hello. As his smile reached her, her checks flushed.

Lilith, what has gotten into you? she said to herself as she hurried back to the cabin; smiling at the memory of the cowboy, and embarrassed that she had been caught admiring him.

Lilith lay down on her bed and closed her eyes. She thought she would rest before her friends arrived. She knew they would be up late tonight catching up on each other's lives. But Lilith's mind drifted back to the cowboy. She took a deep breath in and could smell horse, and maybe a scent of man. She dozed off.

Lilith awoke with a start when her friends jumped on her bed squealing.

"Wake up, Sleeping Beauty. Time to party!" they yelled.

Lilith laughed. "I can't believe we're all here. Isn't this wonderful?"

The friends hugged and admired each other. They laughed and danced around.

"Good thing I brought some tunes. There's no TV or music in here. We have to have music!" Angie sang out as she danced around the room.

"Why don't you get unpacked? I'll open a bottle of wine." Lilith opened the refrigerator as the other women slipped into their rooms.

All four women gathered around the island in the kitchen. Lilith had poured four glasses of white wine. Each took a glass.

Lilith raised her glass and the others followed. "Here's to us. Wonderful friends together again, and embarking on a great adventure."

After they finished their wine, they headed for the dining hall. As they opened the door they were hit with the magnificent smell of smoked barbeque. The dining hall opened out onto a patio. There was already a line at the buffet table, so the friends filed in behind. Lilith grabbed a plate and moved down the line filling her plate with salad and vegetables. When she arrived at the meat table she was served a rib and a piece of chicken. She looked up to see the person serving her the meat, and was met with the familiar smile of the ranch-hand whose well-fitting jeans she had admired. Her face flushed.

He said, "Nice to see you again. My name is Roy. Hope you enjoy your stay."

"Thank you. My name is Lilith." Lilith extended her hand to shake his.

As she withdrew her hand he grasped it more strongly. "I know you. You're a nurse. You flew here a couple of summers ago in a helicopter to help one of my guests who had fallen from a horse."

Surprised, Lilith said, "I was here on a flight one summer. I remember that patient."

"I was impressed at how quickly you made her comfortable, and then lifted off for Denver." Roy smiled warmly and released her hand.

"I was glad to be able to help. Your barbeque looks delicious. I can't wait to try it." Lilith smiled, turned, and headed for a table. Her face was burning with a blush.

Angie caught up with her and leaned in close, "What was that all about? I think the cowboy has the hots for you. And judging from your face, you don't mind."

Lilith grinned, and took a swig of her cold dark beer. Her thoughts were swirling. The flirtation had felt good.

Dinnertime was full of chatter and laughter. The food was great, and filled the women up. After eating, they went for a walk. They took in the scents of evening as the cool night air hugged the warm earth. Once back at their cabin the friends went to their rooms to change into pajamas, and then returned to the den to visit.

As they gathered Angie danced around the room and sang. She sang out, "I have some news. Sue and I are going to have a baby."

Sam asked, "Which one of you?"

"Sue is pregnant. We picked a sperm donor, and Sue's due in January. We're so excited." Angie's smile filled her face.

The friends hugged Angie. Then Lilith noticed that Rebecca had excused herself to the bathroom. Her ears buzzed a warning.

She asked silently, *Is this about Rebecca?*

She heard, *Yes.*

Lilith quietly left and tapped on the bathroom door. "Rebecca, it's Lilith. Are you OK?"

There was silence, and then Rebecca said, "Yes, just a minute."

Lilith wasn't convinced. "Can I come in?"

Hesitantly Rebecca said, "Yes."

Lilith entered the bathroom and found Rebecca sitting on the closed toilet seat crying.

She knelt down next to her and said, "What's wrong, Rebecca? Are you all right?"

"Yes… No. I want to have a baby and Larry doesn't want to be a father." She let out a sob.

Lilith hugged her and said, "What do you want to do?"

"I want what Angie has. I want a baby, and a loving partner to be happy and excited to have a family with me." Rebecca rubbed her running nose.

Lilith asked, "Do you love Larry?"

Rebecca sighed and said, "Yes, but we want different things. I've been thinking and thinking about our situation. And, we even tried counseling. We're so good together in so many ways. But I know that I want to have a family. I thought he did too, but after we got established in our jobs, he shared that he really didn't. He feels he's too selfish to have a child. I have to talk to him. I don't know if I'll ever find someone to love, who wants a child. I might have to be a mom on my own. But this is what I want, and I'm sure of it. I'll have to tell Larry when I return." Rebecca took a deep breath, and let out a sigh. "Well, we better rejoin the group." She hugged Lilith. "Thanks."

Lilith hugged her, "Of course. I love you, dear friend."

When Lilith and Rebecca exited the bathroom they were met with the stares of Sam and Angie.

"What's going on?" they said in unison.

Rebecca approached Angie and pulled her into a hug. "I'm so happy for you, Angie. I hope to find that happiness someday," Rebecca said through tears.

"Thank you. I do hope you find it soon." Angie hugged Rebecca tight.

"Can you tell me how the sperm donor process works?" Rebecca said quietly.

Surprised, Angie said, "Sure, whatever I can do to help." She smiled at Rebecca as the two joined the others on the couch.

It was a long night of explaining and sharing. At midnight, Lilith reminded everyone that they had a long day tomorrow. They had breakfast at 8 a.m., and had to be at the stable at 9:30 a.m. to get placed with their horses for the week. Yawning, they all retired to their rooms. Lilith thought of the cowboy as she drifted off to sleep.

After eating a hearty breakfast of eggs, sausage, biscuits, potatoes, juice, and coffee, Sam, Angie, Rebecca, and Lilith walked down to the stables. They checked in, signed forms, and received horses appropriate to their levels of riding experience. Lilith was excited. She breathed in the smell of horse and leather. She couldn't wait to get started. Roy was the lead wrangler on his big bay, quarter horse gelding named Warrior. He had all the riders trot out and back down a short path to make sure they were comfortable, and the right fit with their horses. There were five women, three men, and two teenage boys. Roy gave some instructions, safety rules, and introduced Josh, the wrangler who would ride last and bring up the rear, assisting anyone who needed help.

Rebecca asked, "What's a wrangler?"

Roy smiled and said, "A wrangler is a handler of animals."

"Thanks." Rebecca responded, and gave her horse a pat.

The sun was warming as the end of the night-cool breeze kissed their skin and left. The sky was bright blue, and the warming air brought the smell of pine from the evergreens. Lilith rode a gray, half Arabian and half thoroughbred, named Josephine. She was impressive with how she held herself with a long flowing mane and tail. She reminded Lilith of her childhood red mare, Rosie. Rosie had been striking to look at. She would arch her neck with ears forward, and swish her tail.

The group rode through woods, meadows, along ravines, next to a waterfall, and spotted some elk in the distance. Everyone seemed to be enjoying the ride. After talking to each rider, Roy decided that all would pick up the pace and trot through the woods on a wide, nicely-cleared path. One of the boys tried to pass his brother by veering into the trees. He hit one hard with his shoulder, which knocked him off. His scream alerted the wranglers. Lilith was there in a flash, and off her horse. Roy climbed off his horse and retrieved the first aid kit from his saddle.

As Lilith knelt next to the boy lying on the ground she said, "My name is Lilith; I'm a nurse. I'm going to help you. Please lie still so that I can see if you're injured. What's your name?"

"Jimmy," he said as he grimaced.

Lilith could see that Jimmy was holding a misshapen right wrist. "Jimmy, I'm going to touch the back of your neck, and down your spine. Tell me if anything hurts."

As Lilith palpated Jimmy's neck and spine; Jimmy didn't respond that it was painful. She checked his pelvis, chest and abdomen.

"Do you have any numbness or tingling in your legs or arms?" Lilith asked.

"No, I landed on my right hand and rolled. Only my wrist hurts!" Jimmy cried out as he tried to move his wrist.

Lilith found that the wrist was Jimmy's only injury. Roy handed the first aid kit to Lilith. She found a splint in the box.

Lilith said, "I'm going to support your wrist with this splint and wrap it with the ace bandage."

After placing Jimmy's right lower arm in the splint, she wrapped it with the ace bandage.

Lilith instructed, "Hold it up against your chest so it won't throb, and hurt as much."

"It feels better. Thanks," Jimmy replied.

Jimmy' brother Tom rode up hesitantly. "You OK, Jimmy?" he asked.

Jimmy looked up at his brother and said, "Yah, I'm OK. No big deal."

Tom asked, "Do you want me to come back with you?"

Jimmy smiled at his brother, "Nay, you have fun. See you later."

Roy had phoned the main house to get the jeep to take Jimmy back down the trail. Josh arrived with the horse that Jimmy had been riding. The horse had wandered off to eat grass.

Lilith offered, "Roy, I'll ride back with Jimmy, and wait with him until his parents can take him to a clinic to get his arm set."

"Thanks, Lilith. I'll check in with you when we get back."

Lilith helped Jimmy get into the Jeep once it arrived. Mac got out of the Jeep, and tied both horses to the back. They slowly made their way back to the ranch. Back at the stable, Lilith put away the horses, as Mac drove Jimmy to meet up with his mom. Lilith ran to the main house, and stayed with Jimmy until his mother arrived. His mom had gone on a hike, and was being brought back by Jeep.

As the Jeep pulled up, Jimmy's mom rushed into the lobby. "Oh, Jimmy, are you all right?"

"Yah Mom, it's fine. Lilith put on the splint," Jimmy answered.

She turned to Lilith. "Thanks so much for taking care of him."

"You're very welcome. He was a brave young man." Lilith smiled and patted Jimmy on the back.

"I'll see you back here at supper," Lilith encouraged.

Jimmy turned toward Lilith. "No more riding for me, or swimming for that matter."

"There are other activities you'll enjoy." Lilith smiled.

"Bye." Jimmy waved as his mom's car pulled away, headed for Colorado Springs.

Lilith went into the library located off the main house sitting area. It was small with wall-to-ceiling built-in bookshelves packed with books. The chairs were large and overstuffed; there were table lamps in all corners. She perused the book selection as she waited for her friends to return. A loud bell sounded, notifying guests that lunch was ready. She found her friends in the dining hall.

Rebecca said, "Lilith, we missed you. The ride was great. We rode through some beautiful country. I am going to be sore, though. Probably start walking like a cowboy."

Samantha added, exaggerating her southern drawl, "Angie almost fell off when her horse jumped the creek."

Angie punched Sam in the arm. "I knew exactly what I was doing. I was just trying to show all of you how to jump." She smiled.

The friends grabbed some plates and helped themselves to salad and sandwiches. There were three kinds of salads; Caesar, chicken, and Cobb. The sandwiches were made from a variety of meats or vegetables. As they were enjoying their lunch, Roy entered the dining hall, and approached Lilith.

Roy leaned down next to Lilith and said, "Lilith, thanks for taking care of Jimmy. I heard from Mary, Jimmy's mom. The doctor said Jimmy has a hairline fracture of his ulnar bone at the wrist. He'll have a nice cast to show off. Sorry you missed your ride. Can I make it up to you, and take you for a ride this afternoon?"

Lilith looked from Sam to Angie to Rebecca; they all nodded. "We're probably going to rest our sore muscles and read, or maybe even nap," Rebecca laughed.

Lilith turned to Roy. "Sure, I'd love that."

"Meet me at the stable about 2?" Roy smiled.

"I'll be there." Lilith smiled back.

As Roy walked off, Angie, Rebecca, and Sam all kicked Lilith under the table.

Angie sang, "So, I guess we shouldn't say, Lilith has a boyfriend."

"No! I guess you shouldn't." Lilith couldn't help smiling to herself.

Lilith looked at each of her friends and said, "Seriously, are you sure you don't mind me going? This trip is for us to be together."

"Are you kidding? We want details when you get back." Sam laughed.

Lilith didn't bother to change her clothes, but she ran a brush through her long blond hair and clipped it back. She refreshed her makeup and put on some lip gloss. She thought of splashing on a bit of Jasmine cologne, then thought against it.

I would probably attract bees and get stung, she said to herself.

Lilith got to the stable at 2 on the dot. Roy was already there, and had both their horses saddled. Lilith noticed that Roy had a different horse.

"I am taking Ty since I rode Warrior this morning." He handed Lilith a rain slicker. "There are clouds coming over the mountains. We should be prepared, just in case."

"Good plan." Lilith strapped the slicker to the back of her saddle.

Once in the saddle, they headed down the path. Roy took them in a different direction from the trail they had followed in the morning. They went across a beautiful meadow with chicory flowers and a crystal-clear, blue-green lake. Lilith breathed in the grass smells, and let her body relax deep into the saddle.

Roy remembered that Lilith had experience riding so he asked, "Do you want to gallop?"

"Sure," Lilith replied as she urged Josephine forward. The two horses kept stride together.

The air was cooling, and they felt a few sprinkles as the grey clouds floated in from the mountains. Sprinkles turned to drops so they stopped, and put on their yellow slickers. The slicker raincoat covered their upper bodies, and split to cover the saddle and their legs.

Soon it was pouring, so they turned their horses to head back toward the ranch. There was a loud clap of thunder, and a bright flash of lightning, that caused the horses to bolt. As Lilith and Roy steadied their horses, they both realized that the hairs on their heads and bodies had reacted to the electricity of the lightning. Lilith, frightened, looked over at Roy, and he motioned for them to head toward a hunting blind that Lilith had not noticed before. The blind, Roy explained, was made of wood with a floor, walls, and roof. It would provide shelter from rain and lightning. Lilith and Roy dismounted, tied the horses to some roots coming out from the trees, and took off their saddles. They climbed into the blind. It was not high enough to stand so they had to crawl inside. Roy laid out the horse blankets, and they sat down to wait out the storm.

Lilith found she was shivering, not from the dampness, but the shock of how close they had been to the lightning strike. Roy instinctively put his arm around Lilith, and rubbed her arms and back to warm and calm her. Soon Lilith was shivering not from the storm but from the touch of this man who was sending a warmth through her that she had not felt in a long time.

There was another clap of thunder, and Lilith jumped toward Roy. He held her tight, and brushed her damp, blonde curls away from her fair, soft face.

Lilith looked up into Roy's eyes, and realized there was a charge of energy between them. Lilith felt light-headed as Roy gently tasted her lips, and they both found a hunger that had been buried too long. Soon, their limbs were tangled, and moving with a passion matching that of the branches in the storm.

Later, as the rain turned to drizzle, Lilith and Roy lay sated on the blankets, wrapped in each other's arms.

Lilith thought to herself, *I don't know anything about this man. But that was beautiful.* She snuggled up against his warm, lean frame.

Roy thought to himself, *Who is this amazing woman?*

They both smiled to themselves, and listened to the quieting of the rain.

When the rain stopped, they sat up, and pulled on their clothes and boots. They said not a word. Roy climbed out of the blind first, and helped Lilith out and to her feet. Their hands squeezed as they smiled at each other, and then turned to saddle their horses. Lilith turned to Roy just before mounting her horse. He kissed her forehead, and she smiled up into his face. They rode back toward the stable sneaking smiles at each other. At the stable, they put away the horses, and left for their separate cabins.

Lilith entered her cabin and was met with an inquisition.

Lilith put her hand up to quiet her friends, and with a smile she said, "I think I'll take a bath, and join you in a little while."

"What, no details?" Sam roared.

Lilith smiled as she closed the bathroom door. She wanted some moments alone with her thoughts and memories. As she soaked in the tub, her mind was swirling and floating. She felt amazing and dreamy.

What's gotten into me? She smiled to herself, and slipped down into the sudsy, warm water.

When Lilith came out of the bathroom her friends gathered her up, and cornered her on the couch.

"What kind of ride did you have? Why are you all smiles?" Rebecca asked.

"We were worried when you didn't come back during the storm. Where were you?" Sam demanded.

"What's he like? Did anything happen?" Angie shouted out.

Lilith pulled her legs up on the couch, and hugged her knees. "Well… The scenery was beautiful. We galloped along together, and then the rain started. We put on our slickers, but the rain came down harder. We were heading back when the lightning came close. We took shelter in the protection of an old hunting blind, and waited out the storm." She smiled and looked coyly down at her knees.

"That's not all you did!" Angie called out. "I can see it in your face."

Lilith hesitated, and then said, "Well, it was amazing. We enjoyed each other, and I'm just going to bask in the glow."

"Are you going to see him again?" Rebecca asked.

Sam piped in protectively, "Do you know anything about him?"

"No and no. I'm here to visit with you guys, not start up a romance. Now, what are we going to do tonight?" Lilith looked around warmly at her friends.

"There's a bridge game after dinner. That might be fun," Sam added.

"I haven't played in years," Angie said. "Let's do it."

Rebecca said, "I'm in. How about you, Lilith?"

"You know, I haven't ever played. I don't want to hold up the game.

I'll play if you don't have a fourth. If you do, I'm happy just to read in the library, and day-dream until you're done," Lilith said with a smile.

The women walked down to dinner, and filled their plates full of another good meal. Tonight was stew, and Roy wasn't around. Lilith found she was looking for him. After eating they wandered into the game room, and found that Lilith wasn't needed, much to her relief. She loved her friends, but didn't care for card games.

She said good luck to her friends, and headed for the library. She was looking through the books when she found one with a title that intrigued her. It read, *Beyond Faith, Grasping What You Cannot See* by Edgar R. Johnson, Ph.D. She pulled it out, and sat down to read.

After reading a while, Lilith could tell it was well written, and very open-minded. She decided to write down the title and author just in case she didn't finish it, and wanted to find the book at home. She looked at the back cover for information on the author, and there was a familiar face. He was dressed in slacks and a buttoned-down shirt. But it was Roy's face. Lilith was so stunned, and preoccupied that she didn't hear someone enter the library.

"So you've found me out," Roy said softly so as not to startle Lilith.

Surprised, Lilith asked, "Why did you use a different name?"

Roy offered, "Do you have time to come to my cabin? I'd like to show you why."

Lilith smiled. "Sure. My friends are playing bridge. It'll probably be a couple of hours before I need to be back."

Lilith got up and followed Roy out into the night air. Lilith took in a deep breath and breathed in the smells of the cool, damp air. The smells were fresh, delicious, and comforting. She looked up at Roy, and he smiled. They walked side by side, close but not touching. Lilith could feel the heat between them.

Roy's cabin was the largest on the property, and set apart from the others. He held the door open and stepped aside to allow Lilith to enter. As Lilith entered the cabin her ears began to buzz.

She heard, *Pay attention.*

She spoke silently, *I will.*

Lilith was surrounded by the warmth of the colors; deep reds, forest greens, sunlight yellows, and burnt orange. The furniture was in warm, two-tone browns that blended with the log walls and ceiling. Large suede couches and chairs looked comfy, and surrounded a tall natural stone fireplace. The wood floors were covered in beautiful Navajo rugs. Off to the left of the fireplace was an alcove library with floor to ceiling bookcases made of the same wood as the furniture. Most of the bookcases were filled with books except the fourth shelf, at eye level, which was filled with framed photographs. A desk sat in the center of the small room with a computer, printer, a few open books, and a stack of papers. Lilith moved in closer to view what looked like a picture of the main ranch house with two men and two boys in the foreground.

Roy followed Lilith into the study. "That's a picture of my grandfather, father, my brother and me. I'm the skinny one on the right."

Lilith looked closer and smiled. "Yes, it looks like you."

Roy said, "My grandfather bought this land, built the ranch and started the business. It was his dream to keep it in the family. My brother, Steve, one year older, and I grew up here and went to the local schools. My brother was interested in the family business, but I wanted to teach. After college my brother came back to the ranch, and I continued on to graduate school, and then got a job at an eastern university teaching philosophy and religion."

Lilith asked, "How did you end up here?"

Roy motioned Lilith over to the couch. "Why don't we sit? Can I get you a glass of wine, and finish the story?"

"That would be nice." Lilith sank into the cozy couch.

Her ears were buzzing. She said silently, *He has a lot to tell doesn't he?*

She heard, *Yes.*

Roy returned with two glasses of red wine. He handed one to

Lilith, and sat down next to her. He took a swallow of his wine and stared into the empty fireplace. Lilith waited patiently, sensing his pain.

Roy turned to Lilith and began, "Three years ago, my grandfather, dad, brother, and his wife were driving back from Colorado Springs after buying food and supplies. They were surprised by blizzard conditions, their car went out of control, and rolled down an embankment. All were killed instantly except my sister in-law, Caroline, who died days later in the hospital." Roy paused and took a quivering deep breath.

Lilith reached out and took his hand. The silence was filled with so much pain.

Roy continued, "When I heard, I took a leave of absence, and flew home. My brother and his wife had two sons ages sixteen and eighteen. Their names are Steven, named after my dad and my brother, and Clark, named after my grandfather. I was their only family. My grandmother had died before I was born, and my mom died of cancer when I was in college. I stayed to make arrangements and decide how to move forward. It was so sudden and so painful for all of us." Roy looked into Lilith's eyes. He rubbed his brow and took a deep breath.

Lilith waited patiently.

Roy continued again, "After a week or two or maybe three, I talked with the boys and we made a decision together that I would run the ranch. They would both go off to college when they graduated from high school. When Steven, who would graduate college first, came home, I would work with him until he was comfortable running the ranch, or until his brother was able to join him."

"That was a wonderful gift you gave your nephews, and a proper tribute to your father, grandfather, and brother. But it must have been hard leaving your life behind," Lilith said sympathetically.

"Yes, it was." Roy paused. "And there was a woman, Jane. She worked with me at the university. We had been together for five years, and planned to marry. We shared a house near the campus. But she didn't want to leave, and help run a ranch with me. So our relationship ended."

Lilith thought to herself, *I hope you know that I will be gentle with your pain.*

Roy got up and walked over to the fireplace, and sat on the stone hearth bench facing Lilith. "For the most part it's been great being with the boys; getting them off to college, having them back for holidays and summers. Having left the university, I decided to work on my writing. I never seemed to find the time when I was teaching. Now it fills the quiet time in the evening. I have been lucky enough to get one book published, and I'm working on a second one."

Lilith shone with appreciation. "It's amazing that you are able to write with the responsibility of running the ranch."

"I have good people who work with me. A few are permanent and live here, and then the seasonal young people come when there are guests. Summer is June through September for families and friends to experience the ranch, October and November there is elk and deer hunting, January and February is goose hunting, and April and May is turkey hunting. We are always closed Thanksgiving through New Year's. The boys and I prefer that. It has become our time."

Lilith's ears buzzed. She said to her angels, *Yes, I know he's special.*

Roy came back over to the couch, and joined Lilith. Lilith felt her pulse race as he reached for her hand, and held it in his.

Lilith said to herself, *I hope you want to kiss me.*

Just then, Roy looked deep into Lilith's eyes, and reached up and touched her cheek. He leaned in and softly kissed her lips, tasting their warmth.

Roy leaned back and said, "Lilith, I need to tell you something about myself."

Worried, Lilith responded, "OK."

Roy began, "I have a sense you have some insight, and will understand what I'm about to tell you. I'm telepathic. I can hear others' thoughts. Not all the thoughts, only the ones they address to me."

Lilith's ears buzzed, *See!*

Embarrassed, Lilith said, "So… you can hear my thoughts?"

Roy squeezed her hand, and pulled her to him. "Only the thoughts you address to me. For example when you said to yourself, "I will be gentle with your pain." It may not have been all you were thinking, but that thought you put out to me and I heard it."

Lilith, again embarrassed, said, "So, you heard other thoughts?"

Roy smiled, "Yes, you gave me permission to kiss you."

Now Lilith got up and paced. She said to herself, *Could I tell you about myself?*

Roy got up, and approached Lilith. He slowly took her into his arms. "You can tell me anything."

Lilith sighed loudly. "It hasn't always been safe for me to share my gifts. I've learned to keep them a secret."

Roy asked, "Do Sam, Angie, and Rebecca know?"

Lilith paused, "No, my friends don't know. They always say I'm intuitive, but they don't know much more. It was not in their belief system. I tried to talk to them in college. I told them my beliefs in a general way. I even tried to help Samantha when her mom died. But she felt it was too scary. She might have used the word *creepy*." Lilith looked up into Roy's face. "I have clairaudience. I can hear, and speak with spirits who have passed. I hear my own spirit angels, who are always with me, and I can talk with my patients when they are in altered states like a coma or in death."

Roy hugged Lilith, "That's an amazing gift. I've so many questions. How do you distinguish who is talking? It must be pretty loud, and confusing at times."

Lilith answered, "It was, at first. I had to learn to filter, and control the energy. Now, I feel very blessed. It has become part of my nursing care, and my life. And, I'm never alone. My angels are always with me talking, encouraging, and sometimes warning. You asked how I distinguish whose talking. Sometimes I know, and other times I have to ask them. It might take several questions."

Lilith relaxed into Roy. "It feels so good to be able to share with you."

"I was about to say the same thing," Roy laughed.

Lilith held tightly to Roy, breathing in the clean smell of soap and man. A clock chimed, and she startled. She looked up to see that it was 10 p.m.

She pulled herself away from Roy and said, "I must be getting back to my friends."

Roy held on to her and said, "Lilith, I like you, and would really like to get to know you better. I know you want to visit with your friends this week. But could you stay an extra day or at least the evening after check-out so that we could talk? I could make us dinner here, and if you wanted to stay overnight, I have a guest room."

"I would like that. Let me see what I can arrange." Lilith reached up, and gently stroked Roy's face. She said to herself as she looked up at Roy, *I like you too.*

Roy smiled, and lifted her up into his arms for a goodnight kiss.

"I'll walk you back to the main house." Roy opened the door for Lilith, and they walked hand in hand until reaching the building. "I'll say goodnight here. See you and your friends tomorrow." He squeezed her hand and released it.

Lilith walked up the steps and entered the main house. She saw that her friends were just finishing their bridge game. Entering the library, she checked out Roy's book. Then she joined her friends in the hallway.

Sam hugged Lilith. "Did you have a relaxing time reading?"

Lilith smiled slyly. "You bet."

"There's a story here. I can feel it." Angie giggled the same laugh that Lilith remembered from their college days.

"Tell us!" Rebecca tried to grab the book from Lilith, but she held it tight.

"Let's get in our pjs, and I'll entertain you." Lilith started out the door, feeling as if she were floating on air. Her friends followed.

After Lilith, Rebecca, Angie, and Samantha got ready for bed, they gathered in the den. They sat around together on the comfortable couch and chairs. Sam noticed Lilith still held tightly to her book.

Sam asked, "Is that the book you were reading while we played bridge?"

Lilith smiled, "Yes, it's very good." She held it up so they could read the title.

Rebecca said, "I see why you picked it. Didn't you minor in religion in school?"

"That's right. But take a look at the author." Lilith held out the book to Rebecca.

Sam and Angie leaned in to look at the back cover. "He looks like Roy. Is that Roy?" All three looked questioningly at Lilith.

Lilith told them of the meeting with Roy in the library, going to his house, talking about his books, job at the university and family. She was careful not to share personal information that she and Roy shared alone.

"He's a real gem," Sam said approvingly.

"What's going on between the two of you?" Angie asked.

"I really don't know." Lilith paused. "I like him, and want to get to know him better. But a long-distance relationship is hard."

"He's only three hours away. Long-distance relationships can be very romantic." Rebecca hugged herself as if remembering.

Lilith said softly, "He invited me to stay an extra day after our week here so we can talk."

"Talk!" Angie laughed out loud. "Are you going to stay?"

"I think I will. It's so easy to be around him. And he *is* hot!" Lilith laughed.

"Well… this has been a busy first day. I think we should get some sleep. We have another ride in the morning," Lilith said and turned to her friends. "I'm so glad to be here with all of you."

Lilith grabbed her book, and hugged it to herself. The women slipped into their rooms and closed the doors. Sam called her husband to say goodnight, and check on the kids. Angie called Sue to see how she was feeling. Rebecca chose not to call Larry. And Lilith touched the picture of Roy on the back of his book, gave thanks for her blessings, and slipped off to sleep.

The next four days were full of great food, morning rides through beautiful country, swimming, tennis, volley ball, hikes, fishing, music, a play put on by the staff, and a guest rodeo. On the last day there was a hay-ride up into the mountains with a lunch cookout. Lilith, Sam, Rebecca, and Angie enjoyed the fun, exercise, the outdoors, and just being together. And it never went unnoticed how Roy and Lilith would nod at each other from across the room.

The last night Roy stopped by their table at dinner. "Hello, ladies. Have you enjoyed yourselves?"

All said, "Yes."

Lilith said to herself as she looked up at Roy, *I will stay an extra night.*

Roy smiled at Lilith and nodded. He then turned and joined another table.

Angie said, "Lilith, it looks like you two have a secret communication."

"Perhaps we do." Lilith smiled and looked dreamily out at nothing and everything.

Lilith looked over at Roy, who was sitting and talking with a female guest. Envy and jealousy flashed through her. She didn't remember ever feeling like that, not even in high school. It was not a feeling she was proud of, or would share with her friends. She realized that she really did like this man.

The last day after breakfast, everyone was given a sack lunch to take to their various activities. Lilith, Angie, Rebecca, and Sam headed for the stable for their last ride together. The ride took them through brush, and along a river to a gorgeous waterfall. They tied their horses to the trees along the water and gathered with the group for lunch. After lunch they rode back to the ranch to pack and check out.

After checking out, Lilith hugged her friends. "I'm going to miss you all so much. This was such fun."

Rebecca hugged Lilith, and whispered in her ear, "You deserve some fun and romance."

"Thanks. And you take care of yourself. Honor your dream. And call me if you ever want to talk. I love you." Lilith hugged her back.

"Angie, blessings to you, Sue, and your baby. Can't wait to hear." Lilith hugged her friend.

"And you, Sam, mother, wife, and professional, I'm so glad you could get away for this trip." Lilith hugged Sam.

"Me too." Sam hugged Lilith back.

Lilith stood on the main house porch, and waved as her friends drove down the long drive. She could see Roy approaching with a smile just for her. She picked up her bag, and shortened the distance between them. Roy grabbed for her bag, gently brushing his hand down her arm to her hand. Their eyes danced together.

Possibilities

ROY AND LILITH WALKED HAND IN hand up to his cabin. As they approached the porch Roy turned to Lilith.

Roy asked, "Would you like to go for a ride?"

"I'd love to," Lilith said as Roy grabbed her bag, and placed it just inside the door.

At the stables they found their horses, brushed them, and saddled up. It was a beautiful afternoon. Lilith noticed there were no storm clouds, and she smiled to herself remembering. They traveled together up a trail, and then into the piney woods. There was a smell of dampness. The trail opened up to a clearing, and the sound of rushing water. As they neared the water, Lilith saw a crystal blue lake that was fed by a waterfall crashing down the rocks. They allowed their horses to get a drink before continuing up the trail at a gallop. At the top they pulled their horses to a stop as they approached the ridge. The ridge overlooked the ranch and valley with its rolling hills. Some of the horses had been turned out and were grazing in the distance. As the sun was slipping behind the mountains, the valley showed rich hues of purple, deep green, sienna, and blues.

"It's so beautiful and peaceful here. What a great place to grow up," Lilith said as she turned to Roy, and saw the colors reflected in his eyes.

Roy nodded, and said softly, "It is a wonderful home, and so full of memories."

Lilith could hear the pain in Roy's voice. She sat quietly as they both took in the beauty and so much more. Lilith could feel his sadness as if a dark rain cloud had shadowed them. Coyotes howling a warning in the distance caused her to shiver. Roy turned his horse to face Lilith.

He said, "Shall we head back?"

"Sure, I'm getting hungry for the meal you promised. I have been fed so well here that my stomach is anticipating the next feast with your fresh vegetables." Her eyes smiled.

They trotted back to the road and then slowed to a walk to cool down the horses as they turned toward the ranch. Unsaddling and brushing the horses, Lilith and Roy chatted about their horse experiences. There was no one else around. The staff had gone into town to party before coming back in the morning to get ready for the next group. Lilith gave the horses some grain and water before Roy opened the gate to allow them to join the others.

"Race you back to the cabin?" Lilith took off at a run.

Roy held back. Lilith knew he was watching her. He then took off, easily catching up with her with his long legs. They both laughed as they breathlessly entered the cabin. Lilith was hit with the most delicious smell.

"What smells so good?" Lilith asked.

"I'm cooking beef bourguignon and vegetables in the slow cooker. I just need to make some rice, and toss the salad. Do you want to get cleaned up? The guest room is on the right at the top of the stairs. Clean towels are on the bed."

Lilith bounded up the stairs. "I'll be right back to help with dinner."

Roy called after Lilith, "No rush. Take your time. I think I'll shower as well. If I'm not out yet, just make yourself at home."

Lilith was downstairs, and in the kitchen before Roy. He had set out an open bottle of red wine to breathe. Lilith poured herself a glass. She took a sip and the red warmed her tongue and throat as she swallowed. She slowly walked around the living room just off the open kitchen. She could feel the loving energy in the room.

Her ears buzzed an unfamiliar voice. She asked silently, *Are you familiar to me?*

She heard, *No.*

She asked silently, *Are you familiar to Roy?*

She heard, *Yes.*

She asked silently, *Are you his family?*

She heard, *I'm Steve, Roy's brother.*

Your brother is a good man, Lilith said silently to Steve.

Lilith heard, *I know. I'm so proud of him and grateful for what he is doing for my boys. I hope you can tell him.*

I will try, Lilith promised silently.

Lilith turned, and saw Roy approaching. She placed her wine glass on the beautifully carved chopping block. She moved easily into Roy's arms, and gave him a warm kiss.

"Thanks for inviting me. This is such fun." Lilith smiled.

Roy returned her smile, and gave her a hug. "We are just getting started with the fun." He laughed.

Lilith helped put a salad together with Roy's fresh-smelling ingredients.

Lilith thought to herself, *These vegetables are so fragrant.*

She could smell the tomatoes, peppers, carrots, zucchini, and greens. She closed her eyes, and breathed them in.

She heard, *Those are from my green house.*

Lilith spoke silently, *Is that you, Steve?*

Lilith heard, *Yes.*

Lilith turned to Roy, "Do you grow your own vegetables? They're so fresh and fragrant."

"Yes, they come from our greenhouse. It was my brother's passion to live off the land. We raise cattle, grow vegetables, herbs, and some fruit. Just haven't been able to do the dairy cow thing." Roy laughed.

I love your laugh, Lilith thought to herself.

"Thanks." Roy smiled again, surprising Lilith with the depth of his gift.

Lilith heard Steve say, *I use to hate that I had to be careful what thoughts I put out there.*

"Your answering my thoughts will take some getting used to." She smacked Roy's arm.

Roy asked, "Would you like to see the greenhouse after dinner? It would be good for me to check the sprinkler system since my staff is away."

"Sure." Lilith's thoughts were drifting to Steve, and what he had said to her.

Lilith and Roy chatted about the week as they finished dinner. They both got up and cleared the table. They laughed as they did the dishes together. Once the dishes were put away, they walked out the door hand in hand up the hill toward the greenhouse. It was set away from the main house and cabins, and faced south. The warm evening light reflected off the solar panels, and specially tinted glass windows. Roy opened the latched door and Lilith was overwhelmed by the colors, and smells of vegetables and flowers.

Her ears buzzed, and she spoke silently to Steve. *Steve, this is a beautiful place. You put a lot of work, and love into it.*

Lilith turned to Roy. "I've only been in a few greenhouses, but nothing as grand and intricate as this one. The flower and vegetable beds lined in railroad ties are amazing."

Roy paused, "It was Steve's pride and joy. I have tried to keep it just as he did."

Lilith heard, *Lilith, tell him he has done a great job with everything.*

Lilith said silently, *I will tell him.*

Then silently to herself she said, *Roy, how do I tell you that your brother has a message for you.*

Roy turned quickly to Lilith. "Steve is here?" Tears welled up in his eyes.

Lilith took Roy's hand. "Yes, he's here, and wants you to understand some things."

Roy looked intently at Lilith. "Please tell me."

Lilith shared with Roy all that Steve had said. She told him how grateful Steve was that the boys were with him. Lilith paused as tears rolled down Roy's face, and he turned away embarrassed.

Roy turned back to face Lilith. "I've always been afraid I would disappoint Steve. I wanted to raise the boys as I thought he and Caroline would have done."

Lilith heard, *He is and so much more.*

Lilith smiled warmly. "Roy, Steve is very pleased and grateful."

Roy hugged her tight. "Thank you," he said as fresh tears welled in his eyes.

Lilith's hands reached up to gently brush away the tears from Roy's face. He caught her hands, and brought them to his mouth, giving each a tender kiss.

Roy whispered in Lilith's ear, "Is Steve still here?"

Lilith asked silently, *Are you still here, Steve?*

Lilith listened, and heard nothing but the beating of her heart.

"No, he's gone," Lilith replied.

Roy pulled her to him, and they embraced and explored the warmth of each other as their passion ignited into the night air. Clothes were tossed, and Roy gently lowered Lilith down. He explored Lilith's curves as she softly moaned and leaned into him. After, they lay tangled and sated on the soft, damp earth. As the air cooled, Roy covered Lilith's smooth, naked body with his shirt.

Roy laughed. "You know, I do have a bed that might be more comfortable."

Lilith snuggled against his warm, tanned skin and smiled. "This is perfect."

As the night grew darker, the evening temperature dropped. Roy and Lilith shivered as they gathered their clothes and dressed.

"Do you want some dessert?" Roy asked.

Lilith laughed. "I thought we already did." She grabbed at Roy.

Roy laughed as he pulled her close. "Yes, indeed. But I do have some homemade ice cream and strawberries. It might taste good after we get inside and warmed up. Are you interested?"

"You don't have to ask me twice," Lilith answered.

Leaning together, they walked to Roy's house. With heaping bowls of ice cream and fruit in hand, they sat next to each other on the couch, their legs intertwined.

Between bites of the creamy dessert Roy said, "Lilith, I would love to hear more about your gift. I have so many questions."

Lilith grew quiet and said to herself, *This causes me such anxiety. It has not been safe for me to talk about my gift. Can I tell you?*

Roy set his bowl down on the side table and put his arms around Lilith. "I want you to learn to trust me, and know I will keep your confidence. You can tell me anything. May I ask what has happened to you to make you so afraid?"

Lilith paused and then spoke. "Except for three people, no one I shared with believed me. The only ones that did were my mom, who is now passed, my mentor, Paula, and one of my friends, Michele, who has gifts herself. I tried to share with my priest and he sent me to be exorcised. I tried to share with some men that I dated and they tried to fix me."

Roy asked, "What about at work? You said you use your gift at work."

Lilith sighed and said, "My work is my livelihood. Some of my coworkers feel I'm intuitive, but I have kept the rest a secret. My work is important, and I don't want to jeopardize it. I just don't feel it necessary for anyone to know. I don't want distractions to keep me from being available to the patients that I want to help."

Roy hugged Lilith and said, "Our world is made up of all kinds of people. Some are frightened of things they can't see or don't understand. And others are just plain closed-minded." Roy paused and then began again, "I don't tell people about my gift. My brother knew, and my fiancée. But I was afraid that people would think I was intruding on them if they knew I could read some of their thoughts. I always keep it confidential. Their thoughts are not mine to tell."

Lilith said, "Has it been hard not to be able to share?"

Roy answered, "Not really. Most of the time, I ignore what I hear. Sometimes it is something that someone wants to say out loud to me, but they are hesitant. I can usually coax it out of them without revealing that I heard their thoughts."

Roy looked into Lilith's eyes, noticing they became a deeper blue with her change in mood. "Can I ask about your angels to whom you talk?"

Lilith's ears buzzed and she heard, *You can trust him.*

Lilith silently said in response, *I know.*

Lilith reached across Roy, brushing against him playfully, and set her now-empty bowl down on the table next to his. She settled back into the couch, brought a pillow to her chest, and hugged it tight. Roy, seeing this, reached over, pulled Lilith up into his lap, and surrounded her with his arms. She stared up into his face.

She began slowly, "I have three angels with me at all times, and I have others who are familiar from my past they come and go. Of the three, one is a dove, and two are angels, one male and one female. The dove reminds me that she is there by touching my left check, head, or left shoulder. She sends doves in my path when I need to pay attention or need encouragement. The female angel, Jade I call her, is the talker and the male, Ralph, gives comfort and reassurance silently with his powerful presence. Ralph does not speak much, but visually has come to me throughout my life. I call on them to assist in speaking with the angels of others, and to answer my questions or concerns. They also offer unsolicited encouragement, praise, excitement, and suggestions."

Roy asked, "Remind me how you know who is speaking?"

Lilith replied, "I don't always know. If I don't, I ask and they tell me."

Roy asked, "Are they telling you things right now?"

Lilith replied with a smile, "Yes."

Roy hugged Lilith tightly, breathing in the sweet scent of her blond curls. "So, Lilith, where do we go from here? I like you very much, and would like to see you again. I'm not very available except the weekend between groups here at the ranch. Can we keep in touch by phone and email, and see what we can work out?"

Lilith smiled up into the face of this man who had shared her inner secrets. "I would like that," she replied, and sealed it with a kiss.

Dog Sense

Lilith's heart was warmed by the memories of her vacation. But it was the man she saw in her rearview mirror waving goodbye to her that burned her to her toes. As she drove back to her life, job, and friends in Denver she wondered how this new kindred spirit would fit. Her mind replayed the week, and the lovely last night. But she could only think of Roy for half the drive home; she needed to plan for work tomorrow.

Lilith thought to herself, *Let's see, I need to stop at the store; there is nothing in the refrig. Gas, pick up my mail, laundry. Oh and check to see if there are any bills I need to pay. I will also send an email to Roy. Oh there's that warm feeling. He's going to be hard to shake. Maybe I won't have to.*

Lilith's ears buzzed and she heard, *We are happy for you.*

Thanks, Lilith said silently to her angels.

5 a.m. came early. Lilith felt as if she had just laid down her head. She slid out of bed, drank some coffee, and watched the news as she ate her oatmeal. Lilith smiled to herself remembering her jeans and cowboy boots as she put on her navy scrubs, and headed to the hospital.

On arrival to the hospital, Lilith was surprised to see Ruth, her boss, with a large black Labrador dog. Her expression was perplexing. She approached Lilith, and handed her the dog's leash.

"This is your project. I hope you'll agree," Ruth said to Lilith.

Lilith laughed in surprise. "What do you mean?"

Lilith's ears buzzed. She heard, *This is good.*

Ruth pointed to the dog at Lilith's feet and said, "This is Jack. He's a service dog for the blind. A blind female teacher, and her seeing-eye dog came to Colorado from Texas with her students to hike. She had a heart attack up in Summit County, and was flown here to the hospital with her dog. She's in the cath lab now. There is no one to care for the dog. Jack's owner will be your only patient."

"How long until the patient comes out of the cath lab, and what's her name?" Lilith asked.

"About an hour, and she's a forty-one-year-old female, Nancy Wilson," Ruth replied.

"I'll get her room ready, and then take Jack out for a walk." Lilith headed for ICU room 12.

Once in room 12 Lilith talked softly to Jack. "Jack, my name is Lilith. I am going to take care of Nancy. You're a good dog. I know you're worried, but everything is going to be all right. Let's get some supplies so we're ready for Nancy." She took off Jack's service harness, and placed it in the window. Jack's collar displayed in broad letters that he was a service dog, but he didn't need the harness until Nancy was up and walking.

Lilith tied the leash to her belt, and Jack followed slowly along behind her as she went to the stock room and gathered supplies. They then went into Nancy's room and restocked the nurse server with syringes, blood pressure cuffs, alcohol wipes, tape, monitoring cables, and extra linen. She checked the oxygen and suction equipment. The heart monitor was on and ready. Lilith looked down at Jack. He was looking around with quick movements of his head and sniffing the air.

Lilith said to herself, *This is going to be tricky. I'm going to have to bond with Jack so he'll trust me when I work with Nancy.*

Lilith's ears buzzed. She heard, *Talk to Michele.*

Lilith said silently to her angels, *Great idea. My friend Michele is the expert with animal communication. I'll call her now, and have her talk with Jack.*

Lilith took Jack outside, and he seemed relieved to be out on the grass, sniffing around. She called Michele, told her that she had a patient with a seeing-eye dog, and needed help assuring him that she was helping his owner. She also asked Michele to explain to Jack that she was in charge, and if she asked him to sit and stay, he needed to listen.

Lilith sat on a bench outside with Jack curled up next to her on the grass. Michele was going to communicate with Jack remotely from her own house. Lilith sat and watched Jack to see his reaction. He lay quietly at first with his eyes closed, and then they opened. He blinked, squinted, and his ears twitched. He appeared to be listening or paying attention. After about fifteen minutes Jack turned and looked at Lilith. She smiled and reached out her hand. Jack got up and put his face in Lilith's hand.

"It's going to be all right, boy. You sweet, good boy," Lilith said as she patted his head.

Lilith rose, and they both headed back into the hospital, and down to the ICU. Jack's stride stayed even with Lilith's. Some of her colleagues nodded as they saw her go by with Jack sporting his brown service dog collar. Once in the ICU, Lilith sat down to review Nancy's records on the computer. Jack lay down, curled around Lilith's feet.

The phone rang in the unit. "Lilith, your patient is on her way out," Marie, the unit secretary, called out.

After a few minutes Lilith's patient arrived, wheeled in on her bed by the cardiac catheterization team. They all entered the room with monitors beeping and intravenous fluid hanging from poles. Nancy had long, coal-black hair with graying around her temples. Her eyes were an ice blue. Her color was pale; her brow was furrowed as if tired and worried.

Lilith touched Nancy's hand. "Nancy, my name is Lilith. I'm your nurse, and I have Jack here to see you. I will put down your side rail, and lower your bed so you and Jack have easy access to each other."

Nancy hung out her hand, and Jack put his head in the crook of her arm. Lilith got report from Jane, the nurse who had taken care of Nancy during the procedure.

Jane began, "Nancy has 100% to 90% blockages in all three of her main coronary arteries, the LAD, RCA, and Circ. She does have good collateral circulation, so she has some blood flow to her arteries from these small vessels. Her chest pain is gone after a Nitroglycerine drip at 20mcg/min and 10mg of IV morphine sulfate. She will need bypass surgery tomorrow morning. It is scheduled for 8:00a.m. Her sheath has been removed. So with her catheter removed from her groin, a percutaneous closure was used to seal her artery. Her groin site is without oozing or ecchymosis. It looks good. But Nancy still has to lie flat for four hours. Do you have any questions?"

"No. Thanks so much," Lilith replied.

After Lilith got report her ears were buzzing and her mind whirling. She thought to herself, *Open heart surgery, the dog, the recovery, the blindness. How do I teach her and help her with her dog?*

Lilith knew how serious it was to have three vessels blocked, LAD, left anterior descending, RCA, right coronary artery, and the Circ, circumflex. Her sighted patients watched a video about the procedure. Lilith remembered that there was an audio CD. Her thoughts were interrupted.

"What about Jack? How can I take care of him? My sister can't get here for two days," Nancy cried out loud.

Lilith moved close to Nancy, and took her hand. "Nancy, we'll help you. I'm going to step out of the room, and talk with my boss. I'll be right back."

Lilith saw Ruth standing near her office. She approached her and asked, "Ruth, my patient will have open heart surgery tomorrow.

Could I stay in the hospital during the night with her dog, and be her primary nurse during the day?"

Ruth smiled, "That's a great idea. You can stay in one of the call rooms just outside the unit. Thanks for taking this assignment, Lilith."

"You're welcome. I'll go tell Nancy." Lilith headed to Nancy's room.

Lilith knocked on Nancy's door and said, "Nancy, it's Lilith. I'll take care of Jack until your sister arrives. We have made arrangements for him to stay with you during the day. I'm going to sleep nights in our call room, and he can stay with me. I'll make sure he eats, drinks, and gets out for his bathroom walks. Don't worry. You rest and let me take care of you. You will have to stay in bed flat and not bend your right leg or raise your head for four hours. The artery in your leg had a big catheter called a sheath in it that gave the doctor access up into your heart to see if you had any blockage in your heart arteries. After the procedure the sheath was removed, and a closure device was used to help seal the opening. If you move your right leg or lift your head you could open up the artery, and it would bleed under the skin, causing you to have pain and bruising. If you need to cough or sneeze hold pressure on your right groin site. Take your right hand, and feel the site where I'm touching."

Nancy felt her right leg at the groin, and said as she touched, "It's tender."

"Yes, that's to be expected. But it is soft and has no bruise," Lilith added. "I'll be checking your heart, breathing, blood pressure, groin site, and pulses frequently. Please, you need to tell me if you are having any pain of any kind. I have to ask you some medical history questions." Lilith squeezed Nancy's hand. As she was about to release it, Nancy grabbed Lilith's hand.

"But surgery? What's involved? How am I going to do this?" Nancy pleaded. Nancy cried into her hands. "I'm sorry. I don't mean to sound so desperate. This is just so much to take in. I'm usually so independent, and now I feel helpless and alone. This isn't a comfortable feeling for me."

"Would you like me to call anyone for you?" Lilith inquired.

"I called my friend Jessie. I left a message so she should be calling later today. I know my students will be all right. We have some great parents who came along on the trip." Nancy clasped Lilith's hand in both of hers. "Thank you for being so kind."

"It's my pleasure, Nancy. And please let me know how I can be helpful and do what is most comfortable for you. Would it help if I describe your room, the doorway, and how the nursing unit is set up?" Lilith asked.

"Yes, that would help. I hear voices, but I don't know if they are just walking by or in the room," Nancy replied.

Lilith explained the size of Nancy's room, what was in it, what monitors made noises, and what the noises meant. She explained the circular nursing unit with the circular desk in the middle of the unit where the nurses, doctors, secretary, and ancillary staff sat, reviewed records, and did computer charting. She told Nancy that the unit had fourteen ICU beds, and was staffed with 7 to 8 nurses. Lilith told Nancy that there was always someone to help her even if she wasn't available.

Lilith calmly said, "I'll explain your surgery, and your cardiac surgeon will be in later to talk to you as well. We will make sure all your questions are answered. Right now I need to ask you a few questions. Nancy, when did your pain start?"

"When we were hiking up in the mountains on our first day, I was out of breath, and had tightness in my chest and neck," Nancy replied.

"Had you ever had this pain before?" Lilith asked.

"No, but my parents both did. My dad died of a heart attack at age fifty-eight, and mom died last year after her second heart attack. Mom had two stents placed, but her heart was too weak. I had regular checkups, normal cholesterol and blood pressure. I had no pain or difficulty breathing, so my doctor felt I was fine." Nancy paused and appeared saddened.

"I'm so sorry about your parents," Lilith replied softly.

"I miss them a lot." Nancy was quiet as Jack stood next to her bed with his head in her arms. Nancy combed through his fur with her fingers.

"Nancy, I've reviewed your history. Do you have anything to add?" Lilith asked.

"Do I have to have the surgery here? What about going home and having it there?" Nancy asked.

Lilith sighed. She was expecting this conversation. "It is of course your decision, but you have coronary heart disease with three vessels blocked. Could you go back home for surgery? You could, but it's not without risks. You could have another heart attack, and destroy more heart muscle, or you could have a lethal heart rhythm and die. When the surgeon comes in this afternoon you can talk with him, and make your decision."

Lilith paused to see if Nancy wanted to respond. Nancy continued rubbing Jack's head. Lilith began again. "Would you like some lunch? You could take a break, and then either listen to a CD about the procedure, or I could explain the procedure and answer questions when you are ready."

"Yes, I could eat, and maybe rest a while." Nancy spoke in a monotone voice.

"Nancy, I'm going to order a sandwich for you. And I'm going to have Marie, our secretary, get Jack some dog food. Is there anything special he needs to eat?" Lilith paused for a response. She thought about where to get some bowls. She remembered two large bowls in the nurses' lounge.

Nancy interrupted her thoughts. "Jack likes just about anything. His digestive system does best with the most natural ingredients. But we'll not be too picky in this situation. I'm just so grateful that you are taking care of my boy."

"I'll let Marie know. Here's your call light. It has a raised knob where you push it if you need me for anything. Try it to see how it feels." Lilith placed the call light in Nancy's hand so she could practice.

Lilith stepped out of the room, and called the kitchen to order Nancy a box lunch of turkey, lettuce, and tomato on wheat bread, an orange, and a bottle of water. She gave Marie some money and instructions on Jack's dietary needs, and thanked her for running the errand.

Nancy was resting with her eyes closed when Lilith entered her room with the sandwich, and dog food. "Nancy, it's Lilith. I have your sandwich. I'll place it on your tray, and move it close to you so you can reach it. I'll lay a towel across your chest. It's hard to eat lying down. I also brought a bowl of water, and some dog food for Jack."

Lilith opened the box, and told Nancy what she had brought for her. She then placed the two bowls on the floor near Nancy's bed. In one she put water, and in the other dog food. She motioned for Jack to take a look. Lilith leaned down, and stroked his head while her mind was making lists. Nancy's reply interrupted her thoughts.

"Thanks," Nancy replied in a low tone, shaking her head from side to side as if having a conversation silently.

"Nancy, I'm here to help in any way I can. Call me if you need anything. I will be right outside the door." Lilith said, and left the room.

Lilith's mind was racing as she tried to think how to describe the surgery to a blind woman. She knew Nancy could listen to the CD. She then remembered that the education department had a heart model. She could let Nancy feel it as she explained her heart disease, and the surgery she would be facing. The light lit up above Nancy's door.

Lilith entered the room. "Hi, Nancy, it's Lilith. Can I get you anything?"

"I'd like to listen to the CD about my surgery." Nancy looked resolved as she rubbed Jack's head.

"I have it right here. After you listen to it, I'll go through the procedure, and answer any of your questions," Lilith said.

Lilith put the CD in the player, and showed Nancy the buttons to stop, rewind, pause, and play. The buttons were imprinted with symbols that would assist her touch. Nancy practiced in front of Lilith to make sure she understood the buttons.

"Nancy, do you have any questions?" Lilith asked.

Nancy sighed. "No, I just need some time to listen, and think about my questions."

"How about I take Jack for a walk? When we return, I'll let him back in the room and give you some time alone. Just push your call light if you need anything. If I'm not back in the unit when you call, one of the other nurses will help you." Lilith paused for a response.

"Sure, Jack probably needs to go out. Thanks," Nancy responded.

Lilith left the room with Jack on his leash, and headed down the hall to the exit door. Lilith walked Jack around on the grassy area outside the hospital. She took out her phone, and called her friend Michele.

Lilith had to leave a message. "Michele, could you do a communication with Jack tonight? His owner has to have open heart surgery tomorrow at 8:00 a.m. She won't be back into her room until mid-afternoon. Can you tell him she'll be asleep or sleepy and smell different, and the room will be busy with people for a while? He'll have to listen to me. Assure him that I'll take care of his owner, and keep her safe. 8:00 p.m. would be a good time to talk with him. Let me know if that doesn't work? Thanks."

Back in the ICU Lilith took Jack off the leash, and he joined Nancy in her room. Lilith sat at the nurses' desk to catch up on her computer charting. She remembered the heart model, and headed to the education department to get it. When she returned to the ICU, Nancy's call light went on.

Lilith went to Nancy's room, and asked, "Nancy, can I help you with anything?"

"I've listened to the CD. I think it would help me if you explained the procedure, if you have time now." Nancy was fidgety. She was picking at the covers on her bed.

"I'd be happy to. Just a minute while a get a model of the heart." Lilith retrieved the heart model from the desk. She handed the model to Nancy. "This model is about the size of a human heart. It pumps nourishing blood throughout the body. The heart needs nourishment as well. It gets its blood supply from the arteries on the outside of the heart." Lilith took Nancy's fingers and showed her the arteries on the outside of the heart model. "This is where you have blockage in your arteries. An artery in your chest and a vein from your leg will be used to bypass, or go around, the blockage and give blood to your heart." Nancy held the model, and touched the arteries.

Lilith asked, "Had you been feeling tired, or having any trouble catching your breath when you were at home in Texas?"

Nancy replied, "At home I've been tired, but I thought it was just working too much, and getting ready for this trip. Since I've been here in Colorado, and especially once we were up in the mountains it's been hard to catch my breath."

Lilith patted Jack, and touched Nancy's hand. "Your heart was not getting enough blood to pump properly. In Colorado, with the higher altitude, the air is thinner, and it takes weeks to raise your oxygen-carrying hemoglobin so you feel normal breathing and exercising. If you have blockage in your heart arteries, it makes the heart struggle, causing pain, and difficulty breathing. That can lead to a heart attack or even death."

"I guess I was lucky. I could have died." Nancy grabbed at the fur around Jack's neck.

Lilith knelt down next to Jack and Nancy's bed and gently took Nancy by the shoulders, "Nancy, you survived. And we're going to help make your heart well." Lilith gave Nancy a reassuring hug as she felt Nancy's tears fall onto her shoulder. "This is a lot," Lilith added sympathetically, placing a tissue in Nancy's hand.

"It's hard to believe. Some vacation." Nancy tried to chuckle.

"Do you want to hear about the surgery now, or do you want to rest?" Lilith offered.

"I think I'm ready," Nancy replied.

Lilith pulled up a chair next to Nancy and Jack. Jack was sitting patiently next to Nancy's hospital bed as if he, too, wanted to understand the surgery. "The surgery will take four to five hours. In the operating room you will be given some medication to relax you, and then some anesthesia to put you to sleep. The anesthesia doctor will place a breathing tube in your mouth, and into your trachea, and you will breathe with the help of a respirator. You will have special IVs placed at your right chest, and in your wrist to help monitor your heart and blood pressure. Your chest and legs will be cleaned. You will have an incision down the middle of your chest, and an incision through your sternum to give access to your heart. You will have a surgeon working on your heart, and one working on one of your legs to retrieve a vein to use for one or two of your grafts."

"Will it hurt?" Nancy asked anxiously.

"No, you'll be asleep with machines breathing for you and an anesthesia doctor monitoring you to make sure you are comfortable," Lilith said. She paused to see if Nancy had any more questions. Lilith continued, "Once your heart is exposed, you will be placed on a pump that will circulate your blood, bypassing the heart so that the grafts can be placed on a quiet heart. You will be on this pump for thirty to ninety minutes. Once the grafts are placed, you will be taken off the pump, and your heart will be allowed to restart on its own."

"How are you doing so far? Do you need a break?" Lilith waited for a response.

"OK, let's continue," Nancy responded, biting her lip.

Lilith began again. "Your sternal breastbone will have special sternal wires, and internal and external sutures. Initially you will have a lot of tubes monitoring your heart, and your fluids in and out. You may have some chest tubes to remove fluid that builds up in the space between your lungs and the chest wall. In a matter of a day or two these tubes will be removed. Your heart will not hurt. You will feel pain at the chest incision site, and your leg incision. You will be given pain medicine to make you comfortable. Most likely the breathing tube in your throat will be taken out in the operating room. But if not, you will probably only have it for a day. It will be removed when you are awake enough to breathe on your own. If you come to your room with a breathing tube, you will have soft wrist restraints to remind you not to pull out the tube. It has a balloon that holds it in place, and if you accidentally pull it out it can hurt your vocal cords."

Lilith paused and then said, "Nancy, this is a lot of information. You probably won't remember all of it so we can repeat anything you need. Would you like to take a break, and think about what I've said, or do you have any questions so far?" Lilith inquired.

"Please tell me what to expect after surgery. When can I go home?" Nancy tightened her jaw.

Lilith said, "That depends how well you get up and around, manage your pain, and start eating. We'll also have to teach Jack how to walk slowly with you as you recover." Lilith reached for a heart-shaped pillow she had brought into Nancy's room. She placed it next to Nancy's hand. "Nancy, this is called a heart pillow. You will hug it tight to your chest when you take a deep breath, and cough to clear your lungs after surgery. It will help support your sternum."

Lilith watched as Nancy felt the fabric, and held the pillow to her chest. Lilith couldn't imagine how overwhelmed Nancy must be now with a heart attack, surgery, a different town, and no friends or family. Just then as if he heard her thoughts, Jack looked over at Lilith.

Lilith thought to herself and to the dog looking on, *Well of course she has family, she has you, Jack. You're a good boy.* To Lilith's surprise, Jack wagged his tail as he continued looking at Lilith.

Lilith's ears buzzed and she heard, *He understands you.*

I see that, Lilith answered silently.

Lilith continued, "When you come out of surgery you will be

pretty sleepy. You'll hear the voices of the surgery staff giving me report when you get into your room. The first few hours I will be busy monitoring your heart, blood pressure, and fluids. I'll be watching you closely to see how your heart and lungs react to the new blood flow. You'll have a lot of monitoring devices attached to you that help me monitor you, give you medicine, and assist your heart and lungs. We both will need to reassure Jack. You will smell different due to the medicine and antiseptics. Once you are stabilized, I mean your heart and lungs are recovering, and you are awake, we'll sit you up, and dangle your feet at the side of the bed. This will progress to sitting in a chair, getting tubes taken out, walking around the nursing unit, and then finally down the hall. When we walk together, Jack will be at your side so he can learn from you how fast or slow you can go. You'll start eating clear liquids, and progress to soft, and then a regular cardiac diet. A nutritionist will be in to talk with you about grocery shopping, and choosing heart-healthy food. Do you have any questions?"

"Yes, but I don't know what they are yet. When does the surgeon come?" Nancy asked.

Just as Lilith was about to respond, the surgeon knocked on the door to Nancy's room. "Nancy, my name is Dr. James Waken. I'm one of the cardiovascular surgeons. I'd like to talk with you about your heart, and what surgery could do for you."

"Nice to meet you, Dr. Waken," Nancy put out her hand to shake his. "I'm blind and these are my eyes." Nancy patted Jack's head as Dr. Waken took her hand.

"May I sit down, Nancy?" Dr. Waken asked.

"Yes, of course," Nancy replied.

Lilith rose from her chair. "You can sit here. I'll step out and give you a chance to talk." Lilith turned to Nancy before she left. "Nancy, call if you need anything."

"I will. Thanks," Nancy responded.

Lilith left the room, and sat at the nurses' desk to chart. After about thirty minutes, Dr. Waken came out of Nancy's room. He approached Lilith, and handed her some papers.

"Nice lady," he said. "She signed the consents for surgery. I'm afraid it made her cry when I went through the risks of surgery. Do you have her chart? I want to write some orders for her. We'll come and get her about 6:30 in the morning."

"She'll be ready. Here's the chart. I'll go check on her." Lilith handed him the blue plastic chart which held Nancy's hospital papers.

Lilith got up to check on Nancy. When she got near Nancy's room, she could hear crying. Lilith could see that Nancy was talking on the phone to someone as she wiped at her eyes. Jack sat with his head on Nancy's lap. Lilith quietly closed the curtains to Nancy's room, and returned to the desk. Ten minutes passed, and the light above Nancy's door went on.

Lilith pushed back the curtain. "Nancy, it's Lilith. Do you need anything?"

"Jack needs to go out," Nancy responded, crying.

Lilith approached Nancy's bed. "May I sit on the side of your bed?"

"Yes, I could use some comfort." Nancy sobbed into her hands.

Lilith hugged Nancy. "How can I help you?"

"You're doing it." Nancy hugged her back.

After a few moments Lilith said, "Nancy, you can move your leg now. Why don't I get a wheelchair with oxygen and an IV pole, and you and I both take Jack outside?"

"Can we really?" Nancy asked with a smile.

"I'll go get the chair. You'll still be connected to the heart monitor. It can come off the wall and be portable. I'll be right back." Lilith left the room.

Lilith returned with the wheelchair and some blankets. She transferred the IV fluid and pumps to the pole on the chair, and hooked Nancy's oxygen tubing to the portable oxygen tank. The portable heart monitor fit on the back of the chair. Lilith helped Nancy sit up, and waited a few minutes to see if she was dizzy.

"How do you feel?" Lilith asked Nancy.

"Ready to escape this place," Nancy tried a laugh.

"Well, let's go." Lilith helped Nancy into the chair. Lilith, Nancy, and Jack went out of the ICU, down the hall, and into the sunlight. Nancy put her head back, closed her eyes, and smiled. Jack sniffed around at the bushes. Lilith kept a close watch of Nancy's heart rhythm on the monitoring device.

After basking in the sun, they returned to the ICU. Lilith helped Nancy get settled in her room, sitting in a comfortable chair for dinner. She gave Jack some fresh water, and another cup of dog food. The night shift was arriving, so Lilith excused herself to give a report on Nancy to the night nurse, Tom.

Lilith greeted Tom, "Hey, Tom, nice to see you."

"How was your shift?" Tom asked.

"One of your patients is a very interesting case." Lilith smiled.

Lilith gave Tom report, including information about Jack. She explained that she'd be sleeping in the call room with Jack and might come in to check on Nancy through the night. After report, Lilith and Tom entered Nancy's room.

"Nancy, it's Lilith and Tom, your night nurse," Lilith announced.

"Hi Nancy, it's nice to meet you," Tom added.

"Hi Tom," Nancy responded slowly and very softly. She rubbed Jack's head. "This is Jack."

In a softer voice, Tom said, "Hi Jack, I'll be taking good care of Nancy tonight. You can come and check on her anytime you like."

Lilith noticed that Nancy smiled. "Nancy, would you like me to take Jack out for a long walk? I want to show him where we will be staying tonight."

"Sure. Jack would like that," Nancy replied.

"Nancy, I'm going to get report on my other patient. I'll be back in to check on you in a few minutes. At that time I'll listen to your heart, lungs, and belly and then check your vital signs and pulses. Do you need anything before I go?" Tom inquired.

"No, thank you," Nancy replied.

"I'll see you in a little while." Tom left the room.

Lilith said, "Nancy, I'll bring Jack back to see you after our walk, and then help him get settled to sleep in our room. I'll give you my phone number if you need me or Jack for anything."

Lilith placed the leash on Jack and patted her leg, "Come, Jack."

Nancy reached out for Lilith's hand. "Thanks, Lilith," she said as tears spilled from her eyes.

Lilith sat next to Nancy's chair and took her in her arms. "You're going to be fine! Think of the hikes you'll be able to do with Jack!"

Nancy hugged Lilith tight and laughed. As she released Lilith she said, "Jack, you be good for Lilith." She hugged Jack, and gave him a kiss on the top of his head.

Lilith walked with Jack to her locker to get her purse. She stopped by the call room, and saw her name taped to the door by her boss, Ruth. The note said thanks on the bottom. Lilith smiled as she let herself and Jack into the room. Lilith plopped down on the single bed in the room. She looked around as Jack went about sniffing every inch of the place. There was a bathroom with towels, washcloths, soap, toothpaste, and a new toothbrush. In a small closet she saw extra scrubs. Lilith sighed. She could feel how tired she was. The day hadn't been particularly physically demanding, but she was emotionally exhausted.

Lilith looked over at Jack and said, "Come on, boy; let's go for a walk. There's a beautiful lake across the street. And we can stop at the sandwich shop, and get me some dinner. Oh, I almost forgot. You have a session with my friend Michele the animal communicator at 8 p.m. She's going to talk to you about tomorrow. Maybe I can eat while you talk with Michele."

Jack cocked his head as he listened to Lilith. She smiled, patted him on his head, and rubbed his ears. Jack leaned into her hand as she rubbed.

"You've had a long tiring day too, haven't you, boy?" Lilith rose and motioned for Jack to follow as they headed down the hall.

Lilith and Jack took a long walk around the lake. She knew that Jack might play since he was not in his harness. She kept him close on the leash on her left side. The water was inviting, but Jack had been trained well, and stayed at her side. After two laps they stopped for a sandwich; pastrami on rye with mustard and tomatoes sounded good to Lilith. They then found a picnic table for Lilith to eat, and Jack to have his session with Michele. Michele had not called Lilith back so she knew the 8 p.m. appointment was on her schedule.

Lilith settled onto the bench, and quietly munched her sandwich with eyes watching Jack to see if he reacted to the session. Jack was looking out toward the lake as a small boy skipped a stone across the dark blue-green water. Then his ears twitched. He looked around, and then became very still. Jack's eyes moved and ears twitched, and then his tail wagged back and forth. After a while he looked at Lilith.

She smiled and motioned for Jack to come close. "You're such a good boy. Let's go say goodnight to Nancy."

After Lilith dropped her trash in a bin next to the trail, she and Jack headed back to the hospital. Their stride was slow, and they leaned into each other. The fatigue of the day shadowed them.

Once near Nancy's room in the ICU, Lilith took Jack off the leash, and he darted into the room. At the sound of his paws on the floor Nancy squealed in delight. Lilith gave them a moment, and then entered Nancy's room.

"Hi Nancy, it's Lilith. We stopped by to say goodnight. Is there anything you need?" Lilith asked.

"No. I appreciate you coming, and bringing Jack," Nancy replied.

Lilith noticed tears welling in Nancy's eyes. She moved closer, sat down next to Nancy, and took her hand.

With a firm grasp of Nancy's hand, Lilith said, "You're going to be fine. You're young, and this surgery will make your heart strong so you can get up, and do all the things you want to do."

Nancy wiped her tears and gave out a weak laugh. "Like run right out of this place?"

"That's right. You and Jack run like the wind!" Lilith laughed with Nancy, and gave her a hug.

Lilith and Jack left the ICU, and got settled in their room. Jack fell asleep next to the bed. Lilith slipped into the bathroom for a shower. The warm water felt good on her tired muscles. She breathed in the steam slowly, and then exhaled out, letting the water wash her worries and fears down the drain. Once in bed she softly patted Jack's fur as he slept. Then, she fell fast asleep herself.

Lilith was awakened by an unfamiliar sound. She opened her eyes in the darkness, and was disoriented until she remembered where she was sleeping. Then there was that sound again. It was a whimper or whine.

She called to Jack, who rose and came over to her bed. "What's wrong, boy? Do you need to go out? Are you worried about Nancy?"

Lilith turned on the light, and looked at her watch. It was 4 a.m. She stretched, and climbed out of bed. After dressing, she motioned to Jack.

Jack rose and came to her side. "Let's go outside for your walk, and then check on Nancy. Then we'll have some breakfast, finish getting ready for the day, and go see Nancy off to surgery."

The two walked down the hall and outside. A security guard nodded a greeting as they passed through the doors. Jack took care of his needs quickly, and was ready to go back into the hospital. They walked side by side down the quiet vacant halls. Once in the ICU, Lilith and Jack entered Nancy's room. It was just a little after 4 a.m. and Nancy was still sleeping. As if sensing her slumber, Jack approached Nancy's bed slowly, and breathed her in. He then turned, and walked back to Lilith. They both quietly exited the room, and went to get some breakfast.

After breakfast, Lilith and Jack came back to Nancy's room. Tom, Nancy's night nurse, had just come out of her room. He was finishing up paperwork and making sure Nancy was ready for the surgery team. He saw Lilith, and gave her an update on Nancy.

Lilith and Jack entered Nancy's room. "Nancy, it's Lilith and Jack." Nancy said, "I'm so glad you're here. Jack, come here, boy."

Jack trotted over to Nancy, and they snuggled together. Nancy leaned over, and whispered into Jack's soft fur. She sighed deeply, and reached out her hand to Lilith.

Lilith came over, and took Nancy's hand. "How did you sleep last night?"

"Tom gave me a sleeping pill. I did sleep, but had strange dreams. I'm still sleepy and I'm scared," Nancy replied.

Lilith took Nancy in her arms. "Of course you are, but you're going to be fine. Jack and I will be waiting to greet you when you come out of surgery."

The surgery team came in to take Nancy into the operating room. Lilith and Jack followed her to the doors of the OR, and said their goodbyes as she was rolled through the doorway.

Lilith patted Jack's head, and motioned for him to follow her back to Nancy's room so Lilith could prepare it for her return. Lilith got out extra monitoring cables to monitor arterial blood pressure, swan ganz cables to give number values to determine if Nancy's heart is pumping adequately, and adjusting to the new vessels that are nourishing it with blood. The swan ganz measures cardiac output, pulmonary artery pressure, cardiac index, and central venous pressure. Lilith knew all of these numbers were vital to monitor how Nancy's heart and lungs were reacting to the surgery, and new blood flow to the heart. She got a level stick so that she could measure the transducer of the heart catheters to Nancy's left atrium of her heart, or her midauxillary line. This would give the most accurate readings. Lilith also collected towels, washcloths, a new gown, and mouth swabs.

Now it was a long wait for Nancy to return from surgery. It could take 4 to 6 hours with the preparation time. Lilith checked in with her charge nurse to see if she was needed anywhere while she waited for

Nancy. The procedure unit needed help getting patients ready for their procedures. She could help there, and then take an early lunch before Nancy came out of surgery. Lilith gave her cell phone number to the unit secretary so she could get updates about Nancy, and be alerted if she was coming out of surgery early.

Jack followed along with Lilith which delighted, and distracted the patients from the anxiety of their procedures. Jack was exceptionally well behaved. He stood back and waited while Lilith worked. She'd always introduce him, and after the work was done, most patients asked if they could pet him. Jack would look up at Lilith for instructions, she would smile, and give him the go ahead.

Lilith got a call at 11:00 a.m. that Nancy was off the heart and lung pump. Lilith knew they had about thirty to sixty minutes before Nancy would be out. Lilith and Jack went outside for a short walk, then to the cafeteria for Lilith's food. Then they went to the call room for Jack to have some food. Lilith sat on her bed and ate. She was tired, but adrenaline pumped through her in preparation for Nancy's return to the ICU. Open heart patients were so exciting for nurses. They were stimulating to the nurse's brain. A nurse could use her critical thinking skills at an intense rapid pace. Lilith was in job mode just as Jack would be when Nancy needed him. Lilith's phone rang alerting her that Nancy was coming out of surgery in thirty minutes. She finished lunch, and took Jack out for another walk.

When Lilith and Jack returned to Nancy's room, Lilith motioned Jack over to the corner under the window. She scanned the room to make sure everything was ready.

"Jack, you stay here. It's going to be busy for a while with a lot of people. You're a good boy." Lilith patted his head. Jack lay down, waiting.

The team arrived pushing Nancy's bed. Lilith noticed that the anesthesiologist had extubated Nancy, so she no longer had a breathing tube, but oxygen by mask. Lilith got report from the team; how long Nancy had been on the heart lung pump that circulated oxygen rich blood to her body while her lungs and heart rested during surgery; how her heart responded; the vital signs of heart, blood pressure, respirations, and temperature. There was information about blood loss, fluids received, IV drips hanging, heart function numbers of cardiac output, cardiac index, pulmonary artery wedge pressure, and central venous pressure. After receiving report and getting the necessary documents, Lilith thanked the team, and they left. Lilith worked quickly and confidently setting up her drips and IV lines, making sure the equipment was on and working. She reached for her level stick, and found it not on the hook where she had put it.

Lilith leaned her head outside Nancy's room. "Does anyone have the level stick?"

"Oh, sorry Lilith, I borrowed it." Pat, one of the nurses, went into her room, and then came out with the stick. Lilith met her halfway, and headed back to Nancy's room with the stick.

With the stick out in front of her, Lilith quickly moved toward Nancy. Jack rose, stood between Lilith and Nancy and growled. Lilith stopped dead in her tracks. She had briefly forgotten about Jack.

Lilith took a deep breath, and let it out slowly. In a soft voice she said, "Jack, it's OK, boy. This is to help Nancy. Come here, and you can sniff it." Lilith knelt down, and put the stick close to the floor. Jack gave it a sniff. "Now let's go see Nancy."

Lilith approached the bed with Jack. "Nancy, it's Lilith and Jack. Your surgery is over. You're doing great. Can you open your eyes?"

Nancy tried to open her eyes, but she was too groggy. She extended her right hand, and Jack put his face in her hand. Lilith used the level stick to balance the transducer with Nancy's heart, so that there would be accurate numbers. The numbers looked good. Lilith listened to Nancy's lungs, and her strong beating heart. She checked the surgical dressing down her chest, and two chest tubes that were emptying fluid from her chest cavity. Nancy had a catheter in her bladder so Lilith could measure the fluid that went in and out. Her left wrist had a catheter that measured her arterial blood pressure.

She had a catheter in the right side of her neck measuring her heart and lung functions.

Lilith coached, "Nancy, I need you to take a deep breath. Good. Now another one. Good. I'm going to put a pillow over your incision on your chest. I'll take your right hand, and you hold the pillow firmly to your chest. Now take a deep breath, and give out a cough."

Nancy attempted a weak cough. "Ouch."

"I'll give you some pain medicine. It will make you more comfortable. I'll keep asking you to breathe deeply and cough. You need to blow off the anesthesia and keep your lungs clear. I'm going to put a clean gown on you."

Lilith injected Nancy's IV with some morphine sulfate for pain. She placed a clean gown on Nancy and inspected her right leg incision. She had strong pulses to her foot. Over the next few hours Lilith monitored Nancy's heart, respirations, blood pressure, lung function, chest tube drainage, urine output, and pain. She encouraged Nancy to take deep breaths and cough. Lilith turned Nancy, alternating left and right side every hour.

Toward the end of Lilith's shift, Nancy was more awake. "My mouth is soo… dry," Nancy called out.

"I can swab out your mouth to moisten it. We'll start with that, and when you are awake enough to swallow, you can start with ice chips," Lilith told her as she swabbed out Nancy's mouth.

Nancy responded to the swab wash, and lifted her hand to assist. Lilith handed her the swab, and moved Nancy's side table closer to the bed. It held a cup of ice and a spoon.

"Nancy, I'm going to raise the head of your bed to see how you feel in a sitting position. If you feel all right, I'll give you some ice chips."

Nancy was thrilled to be sitting up. She called to Jack. He came to her side, and put his head in her hand. Lilith had adjusted the monitoring equipment to read Nancy's arterial blood pressure while she was in a sitting position.

"How are you feeling?" Lilith asked Nancy.

"Pretty good," Nancy replied slowly.

Lilith noticed that Nancy was losing the color in her face. She looked up at the monitor, and saw that Nancy's heart rate had elevated from 78 to 101, and her arterial blood pressure had changed from 112/58 to 90/49.

Lilith put her hand on the bed control and said, "Nancy, I'm going to lower the head of your bed now."

"Why?" Nancy asked. "Oh, I feel dizzy." Nancy's eyes rolled back in her head as she began to lose consciousness. Jack whined in alarm.

Lilith took a quick deep breath, and let it out slowly as she lowered Nancy's bed to a flat position. In a calm voice she said slowly, "Jack, Nancy is OK. She was just not ready to sit up. It's OK, boy."

Lilith patted Jack's head as she adjusted the monitoring equipment to Nancy's changed position. Nancy's heart rate, and blood pressure returned to normal. Nancy's eyes opened.

"What happened?" Nancy asked.

Lilith touched Nancy's arm. "Nancy, you're fine. Your heart is adjusting to the change in blood flow. Your blood pressure dropped when you sat up, and that's why you lost consciousness. We'll try again later. Why don't you rest now? Here's your call light. I'll be just outside the door if you need anything."

It was the end of her shift, and Tom had just come into the ICU. Lilith exited Nancy's room, and settled at the nurses' desk to give him report. After reporting on Nancy's surgery, progress, and blood pressure dropping, Lilith re-entered Nancy's room.

"Nancy, it's Lilith. Tom is here now so I will take Jack out for a walk, and get him some dinner. We'll be back before you go to sleep for the night. Is there anything I can do for you before I go?" Lilith waited for a response.

Nancy paused and then spoke, "Lilith, am I doing all right?"

Lilith came over to the bed and took Nancy's hand. "Yes, Nancy, you're doing great. It's not uncommon to have a drop in your blood pressure when you first sit up after this surgery. You'll do better tomorrow."

"Thanks," Nancy replied.

"I'll see you in a little while, OK?" Lilith asked.

"OK, see you later. Be a good boy, Jack," Nancy said as she rubbed the scruff of Jack's neck.

Lilith and Jack left the ICU for a walk around the lake, dinner, and then went back to see Nancy. Lilith could feel the tight, sore muscles in the back of her neck and shoulders. She let out a slow breath.

Once back in the ICU, Lilith knocked on Nancy's door frame. She said, "Hi, Nancy, it's Lilith and Jack."

Jack trotted in to see Nancy as she put out her hand. Lilith was pleased to see she was sitting up in bed. Lilith held back to give Nancy and Jack a moment.

"Lilith, are you still there?" Nancy called out.

"Yes, I'm here. I was just letting Jack have some time with you." Lilith approached Nancy's bed. "How are you feeling?"

"I'm sore, but feeling more like myself," Nancy replied with a smile.

Lilith touched Nancy's hand. "I'm so glad. It will get better. As you heal and feel stronger on day 2 or 3 it's common to feel like you've been run over by a truck. This feeling doesn't mean you are going backwards or getting worse; it's common in the healing process."

"Wow, I'll look forward to that!" Nancy replied with a laugh. Then, she said, "Ouch! It hurts when I laugh."

Lilith handed her the heart pillow and said, "Hold this pillow to your chest. It will support your chest incision when you cough or laugh."

Nancy took the pillow and hugged it. "My sister comes tomorrow. She's going to be staying in the Sister House near the hospital. And she can take care of Jack. Lilith, thank you for all you're doing for Jack and me." Nancy reached out to Lilith.

Lilith took Nancy's hand. "You're so welcome. And I'll be nearby if you need anything. Jack and I will go, and see you in the morning. Sleep well. You are doing beautifully."

"Thanks," Nancy replied as she squeezed, then released Lilith's hand, tipped her head toward Jack, and blew him a kiss.

Lilith and Jack headed down the hall to their room. Lilith couldn't wait to get into the shower. As she stood and let the warm water wash over her, she thought of sweet, handsome Roy in his snug jeans.

Lilith said to herself, *I was going to email him days ago. I'll give him a quick call when I get out of the shower.* The thought of Roy made her smile.

Once she saw that Jack was settled and asleep, she climbed into bed and reached for her phone to dial Roy. It was about 9 p.m.

Roy picked up on the second ring. "Hello?"

"Hi, Roy, it's Lilith."

"I was beginning to think I dreamt you," he said with a laugh.

"Well, it was dreamy." Lilith laughed as well. "I've had a very intense couple of days at work. I'll tell you about it later. I'm so tired."

"You sound exhausted. Call me when you've gotten some rest and can talk. I'll be here," Roy said cheerfully.

"Oh, and how are you?" Lilith asked sleepily, feeling Roy's smile.

"I'm fine. Let's talk another time. You get some rest. I look forward to hearing from you," Roy added.

"OK. Bye for now." Lilith shut off her phone with a smile.

Her ears buzzed and she heard, *Nice man!*

She answered out loud, "I know!" She rolled over and was soon fast asleep.

Lilith was awakened by the now familiar sound of Jack's whine. "OK, boy, I'm up."

Lilith put on a pair of fresh scrubs, and the two went out and down the quiet hall. It was 4 a.m. They stepped into the darkness. The smell of the cool earth on the early morning breeze drifted to Lilith. There was the music of bird songs in the air.

"We aren't the only ones up, boy." Lilith leaned down, and gave Jack a hug. "Your auntie arrives today, and she'll be looking after you. I'm going to miss our time together."

Lilith hugged Jack with emotion that surprised her. Jack leaned into her, and seemed to feel the same. Lilith straightened, stretched, and with Jack headed back into the hospital.

Once back inside Lilith, and Jack headed for Nancy's room. They both peeked inside, and found Nancy sleeping. Jack looked up at Lilith.

Lilith leaned down and whispered, "You can go check on Nancy."

Jack walked in the room quietly, and set his head down on Nancy's bed. Lilith could see that his big dark eyes were scanning Nancy. After a few moments he returned to Lilith's side. The two left to get breakfast, and prepare for the day.

Lilith and Jack returned to the ICU at 6 a.m. Nancy was awake, so Jack went in to see her. Lilith found Tom, Nancy's nurse, and got an update. Nancy no longer required a one-to-one nurse so Lilith got report on Tom's other patient as well.

After report, Lilith entered Nancy's room. "Nancy, it's Lilith. How are you doing today?"

"Sore, but doing pretty well I think," Nancy responded.

"Well, today we will get you up to the chair for breakfast, get you cleaned up while in the chair, then back to bed for a nap. Of course your doctors will be coming in to see you. Your heart rate, respirations, blood pressure, cardiac output, and pulmonary artery pressure all look good. After your nap we'll take a short walk. Getting up will help the chest tubes drain," Lilith explained.

"Walk, with all of this stuff hooked to me!" Nancy responded with her hands moving around her.

Lilith encouraged, "Yes, we have ways to make it work. Don't worry. It'll make you feel better to get your circulation going. I'll give you pain medication, and the exercise will help your medicine work more effectively. I'm going to see my other patient, and then I'll get you up in a chair for breakfast. I'll be back in about ten to fifteen minutes." Lilith left the room.

After assessing, and medicating her other patient, Lilith returned to Nancy's room. Dr. Waken was talking with Nancy.

As Lilith approached Nancy, Dr. Waken turned and addressed her. "Hi, Lilith. Nancy is progressing well. Let's remove her arterial line and her left chest tube. The right chest tube is still draining so we may remove it tomorrow." Dr. Waken answered Nancy's questions and left the room.

Lilith helped Nancy sit on the side of the bed, dangling her legs for a few minutes to check to see if she was dizzy. Since she was not light-headed, Lilith helped her walk to the chair, maneuvering with her chest tubes, urinary catheter, and intravenous lines.

"Once you feel the chair with the back of your legs, bend your knees to sit yourself down," Lilith explained.

Nancy held the heart pillow to her chest as she slowly sat in the chair. Her face showed a mixture of uneasiness and accomplishment. Lilith's thoughts were overwhelming. She couldn't imagine what it was like for someone like Nancy to be blind, away from home, family, and friends, and then to have major surgery and be facing the recovery. But here she was, blessed to be a part of this brave, extraordinary woman's life. Lost in the wonder, she shook herself back to the present, got Nancy's breakfast, and set it before her. She told her what was on the tray and the position of the food, gave her the nurse call light, and excused herself to take care of her other patient.

Lilith returned to check on Nancy. She was just hanging up the phone and looked troubled.

"Nancy, are you all right?" Lilith asked.

"Oh Lilith, that was my sister, Fran. Her car broke down, and she can't get here until sometime tomorrow." Nancy sobbed. "I don't know why I am so emotional." Nancy sobbed harder.

Lilith got Nancy a box of tissues, and sat with her. "Nancy, it's normal to have waves of emotion after major surgery. And you have had extra stresses with your blindness, with being from out of town, and now with your sister being delayed. Your emotions will be up and down as you recover. Now, try not to worry. I'm relieved to have another evening with Jack. We've become good friends. And if you need a shoulder to cry on, I'm here," Lilith said.

Nancy took Lilith's hand. "How can I ever thank you?"

"No need. It's my pleasure. I'm going to take your breakfast tray, and give you a warm basin of water, a toothbrush, and paste. You can get cleaned up and then back to bed." Lilith removed the tray and set up the bath water.

After Lilith worked with her other patient she came back and helped Nancy finish her bath. She got more warm water and bathed the areas that Nancy could not reach; her back and legs. She helped her put on a fresh gown, brushed her long black hair, and helped her back into bed. Nancy was medicated for pain with two Percocet. Lilith removed the arterial line from her left wrist and the left chest tube. Nancy was visibly fatigued. She had trouble holding a conversation, and her eye lids were heavy over her eyes.

"You rest now. Your call light is next to your right hand. I'll be back in an hour, unless you need me sooner. Sleep well. You're doing great," Lilith whispered into Nancy's ear.

Nancy rested until lunch. Lilith got her up in the chair to eat, and placed her tray in front of her. She informed Nancy about where and what was on her tray.

There was a knock on Nancy's door. "Nancy, it's Sadie and my mom, Trudy. Can we come in?"

With excitement Nancy responded, "Yes, come in. I am so glad you came. This is my wonderful nurse, Lilith."

Lilith greeted the freckled, red-headed young Sadie and her red-headed mother. Sadie's exaggerated hand shake demonstrated her excitement at seeing her teacher well. Sadie's mom, Trudy, was one of the parent drivers for the trip. The kids had recorded a CD with songs and stories of their adventures hiking and camping. After Nancy had a visit with Sadie and Trudy, they left to rejoin the group in the mountains. Lilith put the CD in the player for Nancy to listen to while she finished lunch. There were funny jokes and words of encouragement that made Nancy laugh.

After lunch, Lilith rolled a wheelchair into Nancy's room. Nancy heard the squeak of the wheels and asked, "What's that, Lilith?"

"It's a wheelchair that will carry your monitor, chest tube, and urinary catheter. It has an oxygen tank to attach your oxygen tubing. We're going for a walk. And if you get tired, you can sit in the chair. I'll push the wheelchair on your right side, Jack will be on your left, and we will walk. You'll have a belt around your waist so I can assist you if you get wobbly. And we'll take your heart pillow to hold up against your chest in case you need to cough. Any questions?" Lilith waited.

"No. Let's do it," Nancy responded.

Lilith placed a robe around Nancy's shoulders, and put the belt around her waist. She went to get Jack's harness from the corner of the room.

Just then Nancy said, "Wait, I'm not sure I'm ready to walk by myself. Do you think I can hold onto the wheelchair?"

Lilith saw the anxiety in the frown lines around Nancy's eyes and mouth. "Of course, I'll just have Jack walk along the side of you without the harness, and you can hold the chair. I'll be behind you with my hand on your waist belt just in case you need me."

Lilith helped Nancy up and out of the chair. Nancy felt for the wheelchair, and stood behind it. The three walked out of Nancy's room, and around the nursing unit. Some of the nurses sitting at the desk saw Nancy as she walked around the circular unit. They called out encouragements: "Good job!" Nancy straightened her back and nodded.

"Nancy, we have done one loop around the nursing unit. Would you like to do another loop?" Lilith asked.

"I'm tired, but would like to try another loop," Nancy replied.

The three walked another loop around the nursing unit. They stopped at Nancy's room and went inside. Lilith helped Nancy back to bed, and re-positioned her equipment. Jack lay down in the corner.

"I think I'll take a nap now. I'm really tired," Nancy said with a yawn.

"Your sweet dog is already asleep in the corner. You get some rest. Here's your call light. Call if you need anything." Lilith left to check on her other patient.

Lilith took care of her other patient, and then checked on a sleeping Nancy. When the dinner trays came, she got Nancy up to the chair for dinner. It was about time for the night shift to arrive, so Lilith finished her charting. She gave report to Sara, one of the night nurses, and went in to tell Nancy goodnight.

"Nancy, it's Lilith. Sara is here to care for you tonight. I'll take Jack out. I'd like to go for a run. I'll bring him back while I run, and then come and get him for the night."

Nancy responded, "Lilith, Jack loves to run. At home when he's out of his harness, I can hear him running around the back yard. He makes a loud noise when he jumps against the fence, probably chasing something. You can take him with you if you like."

"OK. Then we'll both be back a bit later," Lilith said. Then she called to Jack.

Lilith had a pair of running shoes in her car. She thought they could go down to the cafeteria and get some dinner, put the food in their room, and then go for a run. The cafeteria was only open another half hour so they had to hurry. Lilith and Jack took the back elevator next to the ICU down to the lower floor. They started down the long hall that led to the cafeteria.

Lilith looked down at Jack. "Do you want to run?" Jack looked up at her with a jump of his head and a yip.

Lilith took off the leash and the two took off at a run. They slowed just before the turn for the cafeteria. Lilith smiled and Jack wagged his tail, and licked her as she fastened the leash at his collar.

The night routine was pretty much the same except for a run around the lake. After saying goodnight to Nancy, it didn't take long for Lilith and Jack to fall fast asleep. Jack didn't wake until 5a.m. He awoke Lilith with his whine.

"Boy, you slept in." Lilith laughed as she rose, and dressed.

Lilith took Jack outside, then back into the ICU to check on Nancy. Jack sniffed the sleeping Nancy, and returned to Lilith. They went down the elevator, ran down the hall, and walked into the cafeteria to get some breakfast. After breakfast Lilith and Jack walked back into the ICU. Jack joined Nancy in her room, and Lilith got report on Nancy and her other patient.

Dr. Waken came in to see Nancy, and ordered removal of her right chest tube, urinary catheter, and swan ganz catheter. He said that she would probably be in the ICU until tomorrow, and then could move to the telemetry unit.

"What is a telemetry unit?" Nancy asked.

"It's a medical floor that has the ability to monitor your heart from a box in your pocket attached to wires like you have now, but it is portable," Lilith explained.

"Oh," Nancy responded.

"You'll be graduating out of the ICU! This is wonderful!" Lilith said excitedly.

"Are you sure I'm ready?" Nancy frowned, and tears welled up in her eyes.

Lilith moved next to Nancy, and took her hand. "We'll not move you unless you are ready. But you're doing great."

"I don't know. I'm so sore. I ache all over. I don't think I feel like getting out of bed or eating." Nancy sighed deeply.

"Nancy, do you remember I told you that you would have a day where you would---" Nancy interrupted, "Yes, I feel like I've been run over by a truck." She gave out a meek laugh.

"Let me get you your pain medication. Would you like to have breakfast in bed?" Lilith offered.

"Yes, that sounds better." Nancy let out a slow sigh.

Lilith brought in Nancy's pain medication, and gave it to her. "After breakfast, I'll take out your chest tube, urinary catheter, and swan ganz catheter. I'll let you nap. After a nap we'll get you up for a walk. How does that sound?" Lilith waited for a response.

"You're the boss," Nancy responded and then added, "I don't mean that in a derogatory way. I just feel so helpless and scared. I have been independent for so much of my life; this is hard."

"I'm sure it is. Nancy, we'll take small steps forward so you can gain your confidence." Lilith gave Nancy a hug, and Nancy clung to her for a while. Lilith didn't let go until Nancy relaxed, and released her.

Lilith brought in Nancy's breakfast, and set it in front of her. She explained what was on the tray, and where it was positioned. After working with her other patient, she returned, removed the breakfast tray, and placed Nancy's bed flat. She removed the chest tube, urinary catheter and swan ganz catheter. Nancy was visibly sleepy, so Lilith raised the head of the bed slightly, and left her to nap.

While Nancy was sleeping, Lilith noticed her oxygen saturation was 100% on the 2 liters of oxygen through the cannula in her nose. She quietly entered Nancy's room, and turned off the oxygen to see what her saturation would be on room air. She was delighted to see it was 97%.

Nancy slept until lunch. Lilith entered her room to check on her.

"Hi sleepy head, are you hungry?" Lilith inquired.

"I must have been tired. And yes, I could eat something," Nancy responded.

Lilith helped Nancy get up to the chair after using the bathroom. Lilith knew it was important for Nancy to try and empty her bladder after having the catheter removed. Nancy had no problem. Lilith brought in her lunch tray, set it in front of her, and told her the position of the food.

"I'll take Jack out for a walk, and be right back," Lilith said.

"I think he needs to go out. Thanks," Nancy added.

Lilith and Jack left the ICU, and went out for a stroll. Jack sniffed all kinds of interesting things, and left his mark. Lilith smiled to herself as she watched him.

Jack looked up at Lilith. She leaned down, and gave Jack a hug. "I'm going to miss you, sweet boy."

Jack and Lilith paused, and breathed each other in. Lilith straightened, and the two walked back into the hospital. It was time for Nancy's walk; she would be freer without all of the tubes.

Jack walked in, and sat next to Nancy. "How about a walk?" Lilith asked.

"I think I'm ready," Nancy responded.

"I'll put the belt around your waist. I'll carry your heart monitor and travel on your right side. Jack will be in harness on your left. You don't need a chair, because you don't have any other equipment," Lilith said cheerfully.

"OK. I'm a bit nervous," Nancy said slowly.

"You and Jack set the pace. I'll be right here," Lilith said.

Lilith stood by as Nancy rose from the chair. Jack already in harness was at her side ready for work. Nancy started out slowly and then became more confident. They did one loop around the nurses' station and headed down the hall leading to a second ICU. It was a long hall with windows. The sun was streaming in, bathing them in warmth. Nancy turned her head as if taking in the rays. As they turned to head back to Nancy's room, Lilith saw a familiar woman. The woman had black hair with gray, and looked very much like Nancy, but older. She had a big smile on her face, and appeared to be wiping tears from her eyes.

"Nancy, I think your sister might be here now. There is a woman who looks a lot like you at the end of the hall," Lilith said.

Nancy called out, "Fran, is that you?"

Fran approached. "Yes, dear sister, it is." The two sisters hugged.

"You're looking great," Fran added.

"Sisters lie." Nancy laughed. "Oh, this is my wonderful nurse, Lilith."

"It's so nice to meet you, Fran." Lilith put out her hand, and shook Fran's.

"Nancy, let's get you back to your room. Do you want to sit in the chair or get in bed?" Lilith asked.

"I think I'll sit up for a while," Nancy responded.

Lilith helped Nancy to the chair, and got a chair for Fran. She removed Jack's harness, and he went to greet Fran with licks and a wagging tail. Lilith gave Nancy her call light, and left the room. She turned and saw Nancy happily talking with her sister. She knew Nancy was on the way to recovery. She'd probably move to the telemetry unit tomorrow. Lilith would visit her there and see Jack. And soon those three would head back to Texas. Lilith sighed. She'd miss them. But she felt humbled to have been a part of this amazing woman's illness and recovery. Lilith made a mental note to herself to call Michele, and thank her for helping with Jack.

The Weekend

LILITH LEFT WORK EXHILARATED, BUT EXHAUSTED. She had a three-day weekend to relax, sleep, and have some fun. Maybe she would have a chance to talk with Roy, and see how he was doing. She had an urge to share her week with him. Lilith realized it felt good to have a man with whom she could share. She then smiled as she remembered Nancy and Jack.

When Lilith got home, she gathered her mail, leafed through it, and set it on the kitchen counter. After putting on her running shoes, shorts, and a top she headed out the door. It was still hot out so the shade of her neighbors' trees that lined the path provided welcome relief. The run felt good. But she couldn't ignore her tired, sore neck and shoulder muscles. After a mile she cooled down to a walk.

Once home, Lilith took a cool shower, put on a pair of light lavender pajamas, and had a dinner of beans, rice, and a salad. After she cleaned up the dishes she settled on the couch to call Roy. He didn't answer, so she left a message. Sipping a glass of ice water she gazed out her window at the creek that ran behind her house. Through the open patio door she took in the scents of mint, Russian olive tree blossoms, and fresh cut grass. The smell of freshly cut grass made her think of watermelon. The sound of running water from the creek was relaxing and she had her quiet time with her angels. Her angels were softly chatting with her about the days and nights with Jack and Nancy. They were always her champions. She smiled as she felt surrounded by her constant companions.

As she closed her eyes to doze, the phone rang and Roy answered her hello with, "Nice to hear your voice."

Lilith could hear him smiling. He asked about her week, and listened quietly as she excitedly told him of the blind patient and her dog. Lilith was always careful not to disclose personal identifying information about her patients. Roy asked questions and was impressed with the diversity of her job.

Lilith asked about Roy's week and heard funny stories about the guests. Lilith could almost smell the barbeque as he talked. His week was winding down, and the guests were heading home tomorrow. The staff would clean and get ready for the next group of dudes. Roy laughed and Lilith realized she was missing him.

"What are you doing this weekend?" Roy asked.

"I haven't really made any plans," Lilith responded.

"Would you like to get together? I could come there, or you could come to the ranch. I have Saturday afternoon until Sunday afternoon before the next groups of guests arrive at the ranch." Roy sounded excited; there was a change in the pitch of his voice.

"I'd be happy for you to come here, but you know, I could use a ride in the country," Lilith added.

"Then it's a date. Can you come tomorrow afternoon? I'll be available after 2 p.m." Roy waited for a response.

"I'll be there about 2 p.m. And this time I'll bring dinner to cook. Do you like curry?" Lilith asked.

"I like just about anything, especially if you're doing the cooking," Roy answered.

"Well then, see you soon." After Roy's goodbye, Lilith smiled as she hung up the phone.

The once-tired Lilith now had renewed energy as she made her list of things to take, and food to buy. She was warmed all over at the thought of Roy. Her ears were a buzz of chatter from her angels.

She heard, *Your energy is electric. We love to float in it.*

Lilith answered out loud with a smile, "I know. That man does something nice to me."

Lilith thought a curried chicken, rice, and a vegetable dish would be a nice change from the ranch barbeque. And she would get fresh fruit for dessert.

Taking her overnight suitcase out of the closet she packed jeans, tops, swim suit, shorts, pretty sundresses, cowboy boots, and her toiletries.

Lilith talked to herself. *Too many clothes for one day, but it's hard to know what to bring. And what to wear when I arrive, riding clothes or a sundress? It would probably be too hot to ride just when I get there. So a sexy little dress would be fun. Oh, that's hot.* Lilith laughed out loud. *And this nightgown, sexy, whether I wear it or not.*

Lilith lay on her bed dreamily thinking of Roy. The voices in her ears were all chattering. She put her finger to her lips to quiet them, pulled the covers over her head, and fell fast asleep.

As Roy hung up the phone he caught his reflection in the wall mirror. He was beaming from ear to ear. He slapped his leg, and did a hop. He then scanned the room, noticing the mess. He rushed to the main bedroom, and stripped the sheets. He grabbed the towels from the bathroom and hand towels from the kitchen. He headed down the hall to the washer and dryer. Placing the dirty items in the machine, he added soap and closed the lid.

"Got to clean," he said out loud.

He gathered up papers and clothes. He dusted every surface, every book on the shelves, then pulled out the vacuum, and roared around the house. As he was putting away the vacuum he thought about flowers.

"I'll get some flowers from the greenhouse. She'll like that," he said out loud.

He sprinted to the greenhouse. He knew if people saw him, they would wonder about his urgency. As Roy opened the greenhouse door, his nostrils were hit with the fragrances of the flowers, the smells of greens, onions, and tomatoes. He wandered down the cool dirt aisles, and smiled at the memory of showing Lilith the greenhouse. His body flushed warm as he remembered their embrace, the dirt and leaves in Lilith's hair, her laughter, and her touch.

He shook his head with a smile. "Need to focus. Have a lot to do," he said out loud.

Roy gathered bunches of daisies, pansies, irises, and three dark red fragrant roses. Back at his house he checked on the laundry and found he hadn't started the machine. Laughing to himself he turned the setting knob, and pushed the start button.

Guess it's a good thing I'm not doing anything serious tonight. My mind is elsewhere, he said to himself.

Roy finished cleaning, and then placed the flowers around the house with the three roses on the bedside table. The roses were reflected in the mirror that hung behind them. He checked the refrigerator to make sure he had breakfast and lunch supplies, wine, cheese, crackers, coffee, fruit, and juice. He could get vegetables from the greenhouse once he knew what Lilith was bringing for dinner.

Roy returned to the laundry room, and put the sheets and towels in the dryer. He went into the kitchen, took a beer out of the refrigerator, and sat in his favorite brown suede chair. Roy rubbed the back of his neck, sighed, and closed his eyes.

Smiling and stretching his arms behind his head, he said to himself, *I should be tired. It was a busy day with the end-of-the-week party, and dance. But I'm finding that woman gets to me more than anyone I have ever known.*

The next morning Lilith got up early, went for a run, showered, dressed, and drove to the store. She filled her cart with wild rice, yogurt, garlic, curry, strawberries, whipping cream, and angel food cake. Stopping at the butcher she picked out a fresh chicken. She bought a bag of ice for her cooler and stopped at the liquor store for some champagne. She was so excited, and a little nervous. She wanted this dinner to be special. She thought she could make a salad from Roy's fresh vegetables. Lilith smiled at the memory of the greenhouse.

Once home she packed her car, and headed for Always Summer Ranch. Her radio played Martina McBride singing "Anyway". She sang along as she narrowed the distance between herself and Roy.

Roy spotted Lilith's car. He went out onto the porch and waved. He met her as she pulled in, and popped the trunk after she parked. Recognizing her suitcase, he pulled it out and reached for the cooler. As he straightened and turned, Lilith stood in front of him smiling warmly. Roy set down the suitcase and cooler, and pulled her into his arms. He breathed in the scent of her skin and hair.

He whispered, "I missed you."

Lilith wrapped her arms around his neck and said, "I missed you, too." Their lips touched.

Grabbing Lilith's hand, Roy picked up the suitcase. Lilith carried the cooler as they walked toward the house. Roy set Lilith's suitcase in the bedroom. Lilith put the groceries in the refrigerator.

Roy approached, "What would you like to do? We could saddle up the horses and take a ride into the mountains. No storm in the forecast." Roy grinned.

Lilith smiled remembering their time in the storm. She moved into his arms. "Why don't you help me change, and we can go for a ride."

Roy leaned down, and kissed her hot eager lips. He lifted her up off her feet and carried her into the bedroom. He set her gently on the bed, and lay next to her.

Lilith said, "I smell roses." She turned to see the three red roses. "Oh, Roy, they're beautiful! From your greenhouse?"

"Yes." Roy smiled as he removed his shirt.

Lilith sighed as she caught sight of his tanned chest. She took a slow breath in, and enjoyed the fragrance of the roses. "Why three of them?"

Roy smiled broadly. "Because this is the third time we're together."

Lilith reached up, and pulled him to her. They rolled, losing their clothes, and finding the tenderness and heat of each other. Fingers of sunlight moved across the floor keeping time with the lovers.

Lilith and Roy lay together in each other's arms, sated and dozing. The chiming of the grandfather clock in the den startled Lilith awake. She smiled at the sleeping Roy, and snuggled into him. He stirred and kissed her forehead.

In a sleepy whisper, he asked, "Do you feel like getting up and going for a ride before dinner? Or shall we rest, then ride, and have dinner?"

Lilith, tired from her week, and happy in Roy's arms, said, "Rest, ride, and dinner would be my vote."

Roy let out a slow sigh, and then said, "OK, rest it is."

Lilith awoke to find Roy had slipped out of bed. She called out to him, and got no answer. She thought maybe he needed to attend to something on the ranch.

"I must have been tired to not notice Roy getting up," Lilith said aloud.

She dressed in jeans and a tank top and put her cowboy boots by the front door. Just as she set them down the door opened. Roy entered holding a basket of fresh vegetables, tomatoes, lettuce greens, parsley, cucumbers, and green bell peppers.

"Those look beautiful," Lilith said as she admired the basket.

"I thought we could use them for a salad tonight," Roy said.

"I was going to suggest that myself." Lilith smiled.

"I see you're ready to ride. I'll put these away, and we can go." Roy headed to the refrigerator. He put the basket inside and took out two cold bottles of water. He handed one to Lilith.

"Good idea; thanks," Lilith said as they headed out the door and down to the stables.

Roy brought Warrior over to be brushed, and saddled. Lilith found Josephine grazing near the stables. She breathed in the smell of her horse. It brought back so many memories of her childhood, riding her favorite horse Rosie. After brushing, applying fly spray, and saddling her horse, Lilith climbed up, ready to ride.

As they left the stables Roy said, "I want to take you on a different trail that winds through the woods."

The air was hot, but a breeze and the shade of the pine trees helped as they climbed. Even the horses seemed more energetic. The horses tossed their heads, and twitched their tails as they pranced. Lilith took off at a gallop, and Roy joined her. They had galloped for a while when Roy raised his hand, pulling in his horse. Lilith did the same.

Now at a walk, Roy said in a quiet voice, "This is a crossing. Watch carefully; you might see deer or elk."

Just as they came to a stop, up ahead a few yards, a nose peered out of the woods. Then a beautiful deer walked out and stood in the path facing them. Behind her moved two spotted fawns, slowly at first, then scampering off. The doe seemed to nod before turning and bounding off behind her family.

"Wow, that was amazing," Lilith said.

"They have gotten used to me traveling up here. We respect each other's space," Roy added. "These woods are alive with movement, so it's best to walk. We don't want to disturb the wildlife, or cause the horses to spook."

Lilith nodded. Her ears were filled with a buzz of excitement and appreciation.

They came to a clearing, and climbed to an overlook of the valley below. It was a different vantage point than Lilith had seen before. She could see the ranch below. It was quiet without activity except for a few of the employees moving around delivering fresh linen and supplies to the cabins. Lilith spotted the main house, and saw some smoke coming from the roof. Alarmed, she turned to Roy.

He smiled, knowing what she had seen. "That's the barbeque smoker."

"Oh, you're making your mouth-watering barbeque for the group arriving tomorrow." Lilith smiled at the memory of her first day here at the ranch.

"It's the hook to get you attached to the place." Roy grinned at Lilith.

"Worked on me," she said. Lilith reached for his hand, and gave it a squeeze.

"Are you ready to head back for some dinner? Can't wait to see what you're going to cook up," Roy said.

"Sure. This ride was just what I needed." Lilith took one last look at the valley that held the ranch where she had met this amazing man.

Lilith took the water bottle out of her saddle bag, and drank thirstily. They turned their horses, and headed back to the stables. Lilith realized she was relaxed, and her sore neck and back muscles were no longer noticeable. The weekend was doing her good. Her stomach growled as she thought of the dinner she was going to make.

Back in the ranch house, Lilith headed for the kitchen. She turned on the oven. "I'm going to put the chicken in to bake. Then I'll go shower and change, and be back to fix the rest."

"I'll set the table. Do you want me to make a salad?" Roy asked.

"That would be great." Lilith mixed the curry sauce, poured it over the chicken, and slid the dish into the oven. She set the timer, and hurried to the shower.

Roy made a salad of vegetables from the greenhouse. He placed the bowl in the refrigerator to keep cool. He was setting the table when he saw Lilith appear in a dress that fit her form perfectly. Her hair was still wet from the shower, and she smelled of soap and shampoo.

Lilith caught Roy looking at her and said to herself, *Do you like how I look?*

Roy laughed and said, "You bet I do. And you smell wonderful."

Lilith looked coyly away. "I better tend to dinner." She was smiling to herself.

Roy excused himself and left to shower and change. Exiting the bedroom, Roy could smell the curry. He happily joined Lilith. He kissed her cheek, took the champagne out of the refrigerator, and popped the cork. He filled two flutes and handed one to Lilith. They clinked their glasses together.

Lilith smiled and said to herself, *To the weekend.*

Roy chimed in, aloud, "Yes, to the weekend."

Roy and Lilith chatted while they ate the curried chicken, wild rice, and salad. There were strawberries, cake, and whipped cream for dessert. After cleaning the dishes, they settled on the couch with a second glass of champagne and more strawberries.

Lilith asked, "Would you be willing to read me some of your book? I would love to hear it in your voice."

A little startled, Roy modestly asked, "Really?"

Lilith nodded.

"OK. I just finished a chapter. I'd be interested in your opinion." Roy went into the den and picked up a folder.

Lilith's ears buzzed with excitement. She heard, *This is amazing.* She answered back silently, *I have a feeling I'm going to like it.*

Roy sat on the couch with Lilith and she swung her legs onto his lap. He began to read. Lilith was surprised, and pleased by his words. His writing was sharp, articulate, spiritual, and full of insight. She heard about his views on enlightenment, awareness, purpose, and being present. He gave examples of non-judgemental awareness. He had a beautiful reading voice. She was mesmerized. She appreciated the unusual combination of education, spirit, and cowboy. Roy was warming her heart.

Roy stopped reading and saw that she was smiling. "What's so funny?" he inquired, smiling.

She laughed. "Not bad, cowboy." Lilith tickled him.

Roy grabbed her up into his arms. "There's more to this cowboy than what meets the eye."

Lilith took Roy's face in her hands and kissed him gently. She whispered in his ear, "I love your writing."

Roy looked into her blue eyes and was pleased. He reached over and turned out the light. As he rose from the couch he pulled Lilith up and led her to his bed.

Hours later, the phone interrupted the happily sleeping pair. Roy answered, "Hello?"

Lilith was groggy as her ears buzzed, alerting her.

"I'll be right there." Roy hung up the phone, and turned to Lilith. "Get dressed; there's a situation in the bunk house. One of the crew woke up screaming, and hallucinating. I could use your medical help. I hope he hasn't been doing drugs." Roy's furrowed brow showed his concern.

They dressed quickly and headed toward the bunk house. A few of the boys were standing outside, and one approached Roy. "It's Ryan.

I don't know what's wrong with him. He woke us up screaming, and saying something about seeing someone who wasn't there."

Lilith's ears buzzed, and she heard, *There was someone there.*

I will check it out, Lilith answered back silently.

Lilith and Roy entered the cabin and asked that the boys give them some privacy with Ryan. As the boys left, Lilith could see Ryan huddled in the corner of the room on the floor. She approached him slowly, noticed that his bed clothes were wet, and his hair was matted wet against his brow. His head was down, and he was crying.

"Ryan, my name is Lilith. I'm a nurse. Roy and I want to help you." She moved slowly closer, and leaned down on her knees. "I'm going to touch your wrist, and feel your skin and pulse." Lilith slowly reached for Ryan's wrist.

His skin was cool and clammy. His pulse was strong and rapid. He looked up at Lilith with sad, frightened eyes. Lilith noticed that his pupils were normal in size and equal, so she wasn't concerned about drug use.

"I saw him!" Ryan called out.

"Who did you see?" Lilith asked.

"My brother, David," Ryan answered quietly.

"Does he work here as well?" Lilith asked, and looked back at Roy, who shook his head.

"Noooo," Ryan cried out.

Lilith's ears buzzed.

She asked silently, *Are you familiar to me?*

She heard, *No.*

She asked silently, *Are you familiar to Ryan?*

She heard, *Yes, I'm David.*

Lilith got up, and walked over to Roy. "Do you mind if I speak to Ryan alone? His brother is here."

"Oh." Roy was surprised, and not sure quite what to do. He said, "Sure. I'll be right outside if you need me." Roy left the cabin.

Lilith sat down next to Ryan and asked, "Ryan, can you tell me what happened?"

Between sobs, Ryan straightened up and began, "My brother David died 6 months ago in a car accident. It has been awful for my family and me. Now I'm the only child. I was supposed to go to college next year, but Mom and Dad don't want me to go. The last 6 months of my senior year of high school were rough. I didn't think I could do it. Then I started feeling as if David was with me. I know that sounds crazy." Ryan paused, and wiped away a tear.

"No, that doesn't sound crazy," Lilith said softly, looking at Ryan.

Ryan began again. "Well, when I felt that David was with me it was as if he wasn't gone, and I had my brother back. I was able to study, and finish the year. I'd always wanted to work at a dude ranch, and I talked my parents into it even though they didn't want me to leave home." Ryan started to cry, and Lilith put her arm around his shoulder. He leaned in to her. "When I got to the ranch it was exciting, but as the sun went down, and I was away from home I missed David so much. It was as if I had lost him all over again. When I finally went to sleep, I dreamt of being with David. We were playing in our old fort in the backyard. I was so happy. Then something woke me up, and I realized it was a dream. I opened my eyes and ..." Ryan started sobbing.

Lilith hugged Ryan. "You love your brother very much. I know your brother loves you too."

"You're going to think I'm crazy." Ryan sniffed.

"No, I'm not going to think that about you." Lilith continued to hug Ryan.

"I saw David sitting on my bed. He was smiling at me. I just screamed. I was happy, and scared all at once," Ryan said.

"You did see David. He's here, and has some things to tell you," Lilith said softly.

"What do you mean? You can see him?" Ryan looked at Lilith with a surprised expression.

"I have a gift of hearing spirits, but I don't usually see them. I can hear David," Lilith added.

"Really, so I'm not crazy? What's he saying?" Ryan said excitedly.

"He wants you to know that he is so proud of you, and loves you very much. He is fine, and with you right now to make sure you're all right. He wants you to go to college, and live your life. He said that your mom and dad will be all right," Lilith explained.

"He's OK? Tell him I love him. He's the best brother ever," Ryan said between sobs.

"He is OK, and he heard you. He loves you, too," Lilith said.

"Thanks, Lilith. I can't tell you how good it feels for you to believe me. What should I tell the guys?" Ryan said hesitantly.

"You can tell them whatever you like. It could have just been a bad nightmare." Lilith winked.

"I like that." Ryan smiled.

"Now try to get some sleep. I'll tell the guys for you if you like." Lilith rose to leave.

"Yes, please. And thanks again." Ryan got up, and gave Lilith a hug.

Lilith hugged Ryan back, and didn't let go until he released her. She opened the door, and headed toward the boys. When she saw Roy, she told him to tell the other boys that it was just a bad dream. He went over and talked with the guys, and they all filed back into the cabin for bed. Lilith and Roy walked hand in hand back to his house as Lilith shared what happened with Ryan and David.

Roy listened intently. When Lilith had finished he held her tight and said, "I'm sure lucky you decided to come to my dude ranch this summer."

Lilith hugged him right back, and said, "I'm lucky, too."

The moon cast a warm light on the two, tenderly kissing.

Halloween

LILITH KNEW THAT THERE WERE MANY different kinds of relationships: one could be related by blood or marriage, or one could have a romantic or sexual involvement. Attraction, common interests, and mutual respect were important, but what about like-mindedness?

Lilith had only had a handful of relationships. There was sweet Jeremy, her neighbor, best friend, and first lover. She smiled, and teared up as she remembered Jeremy. He was such an ardent lover. It had been the perfect first love experience. Yet as close as they were, Lilith held back from telling Jeremy all her secrets. It was only in death that he became aware of her gifts.

In college she became close with Jesse. He was in the nursing program with her. They were often lab partners, and studied after class together. They were drawn together by their love of medicine. And Jesse could not take his eyes off Lilith. He called her Lithe. He said she was graceful, with a fragile quality about her. Lilith wasn't sure she appreciated that description, but she kept her feelings to herself.

In their third year of school, Jesse's mom died suddenly. Lilith accompanied him to the funeral, and found Jesse's mom was excited that Lilith could communicate with her. She had things that she wanted Jesse to know. Lilith gently told Jesse of her gift, and that his mom was with them and had messages for him. Jesse, in his anguish, was thrilled to know that his mom could talk through Lilith. His mom stayed around for a few months, and then said goodbye.

Lilith and Jesse moved into campus housing together, and continued with their relationship, and studies. Near the end of their last year before graduation Lilith came home from class, and found some literature on the kitchen table. She sat down, and started to read. It was a new surgical procedure to stop tinnitus or ringing/buzzing in the ears. Lilith's stomach flipped, and she found she was nauseated and sweaty.

Her ears buzzed, and she heard, *He doesn't understand.*

How could that be after I helped him with his mom? Lilith answered back silently.

When Jesse returned that evening she heatedly asked, "What is this article?"

Confused by Lilith's reaction he said, "I just wanted to help you to get rid of your tinnitus."

"I don't have tinnitus. I have the gift of clairaudience. I helped you speak to your mom after she died," Lilith shouted.

"I believe you think you did, and believe me I wanted to believe it too. But Lilith, it just isn't possible," Jesse said as he shook his head, and paced around the house.

In tears, Lilith said, "You don't believe me!"

Jesse pleaded, "Lilith, I love you. We can work it out."

Lilith answered, "I would love to work it out. Do you think that you can learn to believe my gift?"

Jesse said, "Lilith, honey. It's a lovely dream to think you can talk with the dead. But, honey, when you die, you're gone. We deal with so much life and death in nursing. It is understandable that you feel close to your patients at their death, and grieve them. And in grief the mind can play tricks on you."

No amount of talking changed his mind, or eased Lilith's discomfort with continuing their relationship. He didn't believe her. It was plain and simple, but painful. Both Lilith and Jesse were heartbroken.

After college Lilith dated Craig for a while. They had some mutual friends and interests. But he was infuriating. He was desultory about everything. He had no plans or goals. He had a hard time making a decision about where to go for dinner. He said he was just too much of a free spirit. He was too flighty, and unorganized for Lilith. She couldn't imagine sharing her world with him.

Lilith closed her eyes, and dreamily thought back to the time when she knew Russ. He was drop-dead gorgeous. His kisses were so sweet, and tender that they took her by surprise. She always melted into him, and burned in the fire. Russ was passionate in all he did. He was audacious. He skied, and drove his car, and motorcycle at high speeds. He was fueled by speed, and the risk of danger. Lilith's job showed her too often the result of such reckless behavior. She had backed away from Russ. She couldn't tolerate the worry or the risk.

And then there was Ken, the pharmacist. They were progressing in their relationship when Lilith shared her gift. Ken, like Jesse, felt he needed to fix her brokenness.

Now Lilith wondered how she would define her relationship with Roy. He was the first man who was like-minded. Would that be enough?

She said to herself. *We're fond of each other, enjoy being together, and the sex is incredible. He understands me like no one has before, and we can easily talk with each other. But where's this relationship going? He's committed to helping his nephews with the ranch for an undetermined amount of time. What will he do after that? What about my job? We've been seeing each other for five months. Why am I feeling restless?*

Lilith plopped a big pumpkin onto the newspapers covering her kitchen table. She got out a carving knife and a marker. As she studied the pumpkin, and tried to decide what to carve on the face, an image popped into her head.

She laughed as her ears buzzed, and she heard, *You worry too much. Your future will unfold before you.*

She said silently in answer, *I know I worry too much. But what does that mean, my future will unfold? Are you telling me to be patient?*

She heard, *Yes, and we are with you.*

She answered silently, *I know.*

Picking up the marker, Lilith drew a face on the pumpkin. She cut out the top, and scooped out the strings and seeds. Carefully she carved the face. When she was finished she laughed. She had carved a defiant face with the tongue sticking out of the mouth.

"That's how I feel about life sometimes!" she said, smiling as she admired her work.

Halloween had been a growing challenge for Lilith. As a child she could feel the energy, but could not quite understand it. She tended to stay away from parties and neighborhood "trick-or-treat" events. Not only did her ears buzz but her whole body hummed. Her like-minded friends, Michele and Paula, helped her understand that Halloween was a spiritual time when spirits that had passed from this place came back to visit. So now Lilith prepared the spiritual celebration, and she hoped to have a visit from Jeremy, her mom, and hopefully her dad. She set her lit pumpkin on the doorstep with a basket of candy. Lilith didn't want to answer the door tonight. She was expecting visitors who wouldn't use the door. She placed a single candle and a bowl of water on a low table in her living room. Lilith knew that the candle welcomed, and the water was a conduit for energy. Lilith relaxed on the couch to meditate with her angels, and asked that her visitors come forward.

Lilith's ears buzzed and she heard, *They're coming.*

Lilith waited patiently and then felt a dizzying swirl of wind. The couch shifted as if someone sat down. She looked over, and saw a dent appearing on the couch cushion. She said, "Jeremy, you always have the same entrance."

She heard, *That's right. I wouldn't want to disappoint you. I'm so glad you call to me every year. How are you, Lil?*

"Always good when I get to talk to you. What's it like where you are?" Lilith asked.

She heard, *It's amazing. I'm so busy, and learning so much. You'll love it, someday. But now you still have to go through all the human stuff. How's that working out for you?*

Lilith hesitated.

Jeremy yelled and Lilith heard, *You've met someone haven't you? Tell me all about it. Does he know about me, that I was your first love? Does he know what you can do?*

Lilith took a deep breath in and sighed. "Yes, yes, and yes." She smiled.

She heard, *What's the story? What are your plans?*

Lilith said out loud, "Jer, calm down. You act like we're kids. Aren't you grown up yet?

She heard, *Here I can be whatever age I want. Lil, you are my best friend, and the sister I never had.*

Lilith said, "I feel the same. And yes, I've met someone. His name is Roy, and I like him very much. It's complicated. We are good together, but I don't know if we can work it out."

Lilith heard, *You'll figure it out. He can't be as good as me! Ha, ha! Well it's time for me to go. Someone else wants to talk to you. Love you Lil.*

Lilith called out, "Love you too, Jer!"

As Jeremy left, the room filled with the smell of cinnamon. Lilith clapped her hands together with joy and anticipation. She knew it was her mom's smell.

Lilith heard, *Honey, it's me.*

"Oh, Mom. I miss you so much. I'm so grateful I can talk to you." Lilith wiped tears from her eyes. "There are so many things I want to tell you."

She heard, *Much has happened to you.*

Lilith sighed and responded, "Yes!" Then with surprise she asked, "You know about Roy?"

Lilith heard, *Honey, I know you care about him.*

"Did you know Dad was the one?" Lilith asked.

Lilith heard, *I just listened to my heart. If you do that, you'll know too.*

Lilith sighed and asked, "Is Dad with you?"

Lilith heard, *Your dad is never far away from you. He sends his love, and admiration through me. He never had the vastness of your gift. He had a sense, a sensitivity, and heard things but wasn't able to respond back to the messages he received. We're both so proud of how you use your gift to help others.*

"Mom, I have so much more to learn," Lilith said with both hope and frustration.

We all do, even after you leave this place, Julia explained. *Tell me what troubles you now?* Julia asked.

"Oh Mom, I've had such difficulty with men. It's so hard to feel safe sharing my gift. It's really hard to find like-minded men," Lilith said.

Lilith heard, *And now?*

Lilith began, "I've found a like-minded man in Roy. But I don't know if our worlds can come together."

The cinnamon smell grew stronger, and there was a warmth in the air. Lilith felt as if she was being hugged. She closed her eyes, and leaned into it.

Lilith explained, "Roy is a good man. I like him very much, but there are complications."

Julia added, *There always are, but if a relationship is worth it both of you will figure a way to make it work.* Julia paused and then said, *You're scared.*

Lilith started to cry, "More like terrified. What if I give him my heart and it doesn't work out? What if he doesn't want children? I know I want to have a baby."

Honey, Julia said softly, *you could protect yourself forever, and never take a chance. But is that the life you want to live? You have so much love that you give to everyone around you. You give to your patients, their families, the spirits that you help pass on, your friends, and coworkers. Isn't it time for you to love and be loved? I know it's scary and you might, probably will, get hurt at some point. But that is the beautiful way of living. If you just keep yourself safe you'll never feel the pain, and joy of love. I want you to feel the ups and downs and the amazing in-between. Even though I only had a short time with your father, it was one of the best parts of living, especially because that love brought me you. I hope you won't deprive yourself of this wonderful journey. You have the strength to handle whatever comes your way.*

Tears filled Lilith's eyes as she took in her Mom's wisdom. "Mom, I love you so much. I'm so grateful that I can talk with you."

I'm grateful too. I have to go now. I love you, Lilith. The smell of cinnamon swirled around Lilith, and she felt her mom's love.

Lilith breathed in the savoring scent as it dissipated. She closed her eyes, and leaned back into her soft, comfy, red couch. Thinking about what her mom had said, she wondered if she could meet Roy half-way. It was hard to image how they could make it work. What she did know was that she liked him, a lot. The phone rang, interrupting Lilith's thoughts.

She cleared her throat before answering. "Hello?"

"Lilith, it's Roy. Glad I caught you at home."

"Hi, Roy," Lilith said with surprise.

Roy remembered it was Halloween and said, "Did you get a lot of trick or treaters?"

Lilith paused, thinking of her visitors. "No, I celebrate Halloween in a different way." Lilith thought to herself, *Do I tell you?*

Roy said, "Lilith, I hope you can feel safe to tell me anything."

Startled, Lilith said, "I forget your gift can work over the phone."

Roy sighed, "Sorry, sometimes I forget to think whether something is spoken to me out loud or silently. I tend to do that mostly with you."

Lilith smiled pensively, and said to herself, *Here goes.* She began, "Some people believe…"

Roy interrupted, "You mean, you believe?"

Lilith stopped, smiled to herself, and said, "Yes, I believe there is a thin veil at Halloween that allows spirit energies to travel between this world, and the next. They can communicate with sensitives from this world."

Roy asked, "Did you have spirit visitors tonight?"

Lilith smiled at the memory. "Yes, I did. Mom always comes to visit, and check in with me. So does my friend Jeremy. I told you about him. He was my next door neighbor, and best friend when I was young."

"And your first love!" Roy added.

Lilith laughed, "Jealous?"

"Well, maybe a little. He knows you better than I do." Roy laughed.

"Perhaps we should do something about that," Lilith teased.

"What do you have in mind?" Roy asked.

"Well, I work Thanksgiving Day, but I have the weekend off, Friday through Sunday. Can you come for the Thanksgiving weekend?" Lilith paused aware of Roy's commitments to the ranch, and his nephews who come home for the holidays. She was wondering if their worlds could blend. There was a silence, and Lilith thought to herself, *Are you still there?*

Hearing her, Roy answered, "Yes, I'm here. I was just thinking. I heard from the boys that they're not coming home. They are going to Hawaii with friends for Thanksgiving. The ranch will be closed for the holiday. I'd love to come and see you. Maybe you could show me what you like to do on weekends?"

"Great. I'll make Thanksgiving dinner on Friday since I work Thursday," Lilith said.

"Actually, if you don't mind, how about I come Thursday and

make you Thanksgiving dinner for when you get off work?" Roy asked excitedly.

"Really? You wouldn't mind?" Lilith asked, as she smiled to herself.

"It'll be fun," Roy added.

"I'll get the food, and make some of the trimmings. What are some of your favorites?" Lilith asked excitedly.

"I like just about anything. Well, I do like sweet potatoes with marshmallows. Oh, and pie," Roy laughed.

"I can handle that. I usually make pecan and pumpkin. How's that?"

"With whipped cream?" Roy asked.

"Of course!" Lilith laughed.

Roy and Lilith shared turkey stories and talked until they were both yawning. Lilith needed to get some sleep, since she had to work the next day. Roy had busy weeks ahead with his hunting groups.

"I'll try, and call again soon to firm up our plans," Roy said with a yawn.

"We have a few weeks yet." Lilith laughed.

"Well, I need an excuse to call you," Roy added.

"No you don't. Call anytime. Goodnight," Lilith said.

"Goodnight to you, too," Roy answered, and the phone connection ended.

Thanksgiving

LILITH, NOW 33 YEARS OLD, THOUGHT back to Thanksgivings of the past. Her mom's cinnamon yeast rolls, the golden turkey and gravy, cornbread stuffing, green beans, chilled cranberries, creamy potatoes, and lots and lots of pies. Jeremy and his family usually came over. Friends from her mom's work who didn't have family around were also invited. There was so much food that there were plates of leftovers. And everyone ate too much. Lilith smiled at the memory. Then a tear slipped from her eye. She took in a quivering breath. Her mom had been gone ten years. Thanksgiving, as of late, had been only with friends from work. She breathed in, and smiled. This would be a first with Roy.

Roy was thinking back to his childhood Thanksgivings on the ranch with his family, and the ranch guest families. Those were happy busy times. His last Thanksgiving with Jane, his fiancée, was filled with planning their future: one or two kids, and teaching together into their later years. Then the tragic loss of his family ended his relationship with Jane, and placed him in the parent role to his nephews. Thanksgivings at the ranch with the boys had become comfortable. There was still sadness, but they managed to have fun, and enjoy themselves. This year was a change since the boys planned a holiday with friends in Hawaii. Roy was glad he was closing the ranch early for the holidays. He wanted some time to work on his second book. And he was looking forward to being with Lilith.

Lilith and Roy talked often on the phone. They were becoming more involved in each other's lives. Lilith returned home from work on Wednesday, the day before Thanksgiving. After showering and changing into some comfy jeans and a top, she turned on the country music, and danced into the kitchen. She had put the frozen turkey to thaw in the refrigerator, and now checked to see that it was ready. She smiled to herself as she touched the tender bird. She thought of Roy slicing the turkey at her table.

Singing out loud to Clint Black's "Like the Rain", Lilith made pie crusts, and pecan and pumpkin fillings. She stirred the spices into the mixture as she sang out the lyrics to Faith Hill's "Like We Never Loved Before". After carefully placing the pies in the warmed oven, she set the timer for the pumpkin. Lilith knew she would have to take it out, and allow the pecan to cook longer. She twirled around her kitchen singing with her arms dancing in the air.

The phone rang, and Lilith grabbed it and said, "Hello?"

Roy heard the music blaring in the background and asked, "What're doing?"

Lilith laughed and turned down the music. "I'm baking to my country favorites."

"Smells good!" Roy said with a smile.

"So you have another gift you forgot to mention?" Lilith said laughing.

"Oh, I'm full of surprises." Roy was enjoying the banter. He smiled as he imagined Lilith dancing. He laughed out loud.

Lilith asked, "Are you making fun of me?"

Laughing, Roy said, "I'd never do that!"

Lilith felt his smile, and found it contagious. They talked about the meal. Then the oven buzzer went off.

"Hold on a minute," Lilith said as she set the phone down.

She took the pumpkin pie out of the oven. She placed it on a hot pad rack that was lying on the counter. Opening the oven again, she moved the pecan pie to the center of the rack, and reset the timer to allow for the extra cooking time.

Leaning over the pumpkin pie she took a whiff, and smiled as she said to herself, *You'll like this with whipped cream.*

She picked up the phone and said, "I'm back."

Roy said, "Did you make pumpkin pie to have with whipped cream?"

Surprised Lilith said, "I'm going to have to watch what I think around you."

Roy softly said, "I'm sorry, I hope my intrusion in thoughts doesn't make you uncomfortable, or upset you. Remember it is only the thoughts you put out to me."

Lilith said silently, *I'm not upset with you. It will just take some getting used to. It feels good to have a comrade-in-arms.*

Roy said out loud, "It sure does. I look forward to seeing you tomorrow night," Roy added.

"Me too," Lilith responded. "The key is under the angel to the right of the door. The rolls will be rising in the refrigerator. I left instructions for the turkey, stuffing, and rolls on the counter."

"Thanks. This will be fun. I'll do my best to have it all ready," Roy said.

"It's so sweet of you to cook for me. See you tomorrow night. Bye now," Lilith said.

"Bye to you." Roy hung up the phone.

The pie timer buzzed. Lilith took the pie out, and switched off the oven. She set the pecan pie next to the pumpkin pie on the cooling rack. In a bowl she mixed the ingredients for her mom's famous cinnamon yeast rolls. She mixed up her favorite recipe of corn bread stuffing. After covering the stuffing, and placing it in the refrigerator, she kneaded the rolls, and then placed them next to the stuffing to rise. Lilith knew that her mom's yeast rolls needed to rise a couple of times in the refrigerator.

Lilith scanned her house, and found things in order. She had cleaned a few days ago. She made notes with instructions for Roy, and sleepily went into her bedroom. Slipping into her pjs, and brushing her teeth, she caught a glimpse of herself in the mirror. Even though she was tired, she had a happy glow.

She said out loud, "That man does something to me." Once in bed she was quickly asleep.

After hanging up the phone with Lilith, Roy made some lists of things to take: sweet potatoes, marshmallows, green beans from the greenhouse, and flowers. He packed his bag and smiled as he thought of his conversation with Lilith. His body warmed.

He said to himself, "That woman sure has an effect on me."

Lilith's alarm sounded at 5 a.m. She got up, dressed, ate breakfast, and drove her car toward the hospital. After parking the car, she walked down the hospital hall toward the chapel. She dipped her fingers in the holy water, and made the sign of the cross.

Lilith said silently, *May I heal, and do no harm.*

She continued on into the ICU, and got report on her two patients. During the course of the shift, one of her patients was well enough to transfer to the step-down unit. Lilith was then next in line to get a new admission.

Around 2 p.m. Lilith was notified by the charge nurse that she was getting a 72 year-old female in septic shock who would be transferred from the emergency room. Within 30 minutes Natalie, a nurse from the emergency room, called Lilith to give her a report on the patient.

"Hi Lilith, this is Natalie. Happy Thanksgiving! Are you getting Marie Sanchez?" Natalie asked.

"Hi Natalie. Yes, I am, and Happy Thanksgiving to you, too," Lilith answered.

Natalie began, "This is a sad one. Marie's husband, who had end stage liver cancer, ate Thanksgiving dinner with the family today. While the women were cleaning the dishes he went out on the back porch, and shot himself in the head. The family called 911, and the husband was pronounced dead at the scene. Marie collapsed, and the paramedics found that she had a weak pulse of 50 beats per minute, and low blood pressure of 70/49. She was in and out of consciousness, and was brought to the emergency room."

"That poor family," Lilith said.

"You're right," Natalie added and began again, "Her diagnosis is urosepsis. She apparently had bladder infection symptoms, but they went untreated due to caring for her husband. We did blood work and cultures, and have given her three liters of fluid. Because of her unconscious state, she was intubated, and placed on a ventilator to protect her airway. She was started on antibiotics, according to the sepsis protocol. The fluid did not help her blood pressure so she was placed on Levophed at 15 mcg per minute. There is a slow response to the medication. Her temperature is 103 degrees, heart rate 112, respirations with vent 16 breaths per minute, and her blood pressure is 90/58. No urine output at this time, so haven't been able to send any urine for culture. Her white count is elevated, as well as her Bun and Creatinine. She has two daughters with her, and two granddaughters. The patient and family are bilingual. There is no communication barrier. As you can imagine, they're traumatized. The chaplain is with them. Do you have any questions?"

"Could you show them the waiting room just outside the ICU, and tell them I will come get them as soon as I get Marie settled?" Lilith asked.

"Sure," Natalie responded.

"Thanks, Natalie. See you soon," Lilith said.

Lilith received her patient, Marie. The nurses carefully transferred her from the stretcher to the ICU bed. Jan, the respiratory therapist, connected her to the ICU ventilator, and checked the settings. She then listened to Marie's chest to check lung sounds. Lilith attached all the monitoring cables, and assessed Marie.

Lilith's ears buzzed an unfamiliar voice. She silently said, *Are you familiar to me?*

She heard, *No.*

She silently asked, *Are you familiar to Marie?*

She heard words in Spanish, and she did not understand the language. Silently Lilith said, *I don't speak Spanish. I don't understand you.*

Then, she heard, *I'm John. What happened to Marie? Where are we? Why can't she talk to me?*

Lilith said silently, *John, Marie is in the hospital, and is very sick. I'm her nurse. I need to attend to her right now, and then I will answer your questions.*

Lilith assessed Marie's neurological status, and found her still unresponsive with sluggish, equal pupils. She continued the intravenous fluid, and increased the Levophed to 20 mcg per minute to support Marie's blood pressure. She drew some labs from the arterial line that had been placed in the emergency room, and saw that Marie was still not producing urine. Lilith knew she might need dialysis support if her kidneys failed. She briefly left the room, and had one of her coworkers watch Marie. She went to the waiting room to update the family, and request that only two visitors come in at a time due to the small space to care for Marie, and her need of rest.

Lilith found the family weeping loudly in the waiting room. Chaplain Susan was with them. After Lilith explained about their mother's condition, and how she would look with the equipment attached to her, they wept more loudly. She put her arm around one of the daughters who was holding the hand of her grown daughter, and led them to the ICU room. On entering the room the daughter stood back. Lilith helped her go close to the bed, and hold her mom's hand.

The daughter threw her body across her mom's, and wailed loudly, "Mama, don't leave us! We can't lose you, too!"

Lilith's eyes filled with tears as she watched the sudden outpouring of emotion. She could feel the grief of this family. She noticed Marie's eyes flicker open, and then shut again.

Lilith's ears buzzed and she heard, *I don't want to live without him.*

Lilith silently said, *Marie, is that you talking?*

Lilith heard, *Yes. What happened? How can you hear me?*

Marie, my name is Lilith. I'm the nurse taking care of you. You came to the hospital very sick. I have a gift of hearing people even if they are unconscious, Lilith said silently.

Lilith heard Marie cry, *Where's my husband?*

Lilith silently explained, *Marie, he died at your house.*

Lilith heard, *What? Oh, that's right. It was awful. He'd been so sick. But I never thought he would end his life like that. What's wrong with me?* Marie sounded worried.

Lilith silently explained, *Marie, you had a bladder infection that became very serious. You are very sick, and we are working hard to help you get better.*

Lilith heard John's voice in her ears. *What? I'm dead?*

Lilith had been busily monitoring Marie. She had adjusted her medications as she talked with her. She'd forgotten that John had spoken to her earlier.

Lilith said silently, *John, yes, you died. You shot yourself on the porch after the Thanksgiving meal. Marie is very sick, and missing you. But she can't talk with you. I can try to give her a message from you.*

Lilith heard John reply, *Please tell her I'm sorry. I wasn't leaving her, my love. I just couldn't take the pain. She needs to get well for the children. She still has a whole life. Tell her I'll love her always.*

As tears rolled down Lilith's cheeks she heard Marie say, *John, I hear you. I love you too. I will miss you. Wait for me.*

Then Lilith heard, *I will my love. Please get better. I love you.*

I love you too, Lilith heard Marie respond. And then Lilith heard some beautiful words in Spanish, but she did not understand them.

Lilith looked at the monitor in Marie's room. Her blood pressure was stabilizing, so Lilith could decrease the medication. Two more members of Marie's family were now at her bedside.

Lilith leaned down, and whispered in Marie's ear, "You're doing well, Marie. John is looking out for you."

Lilith left Marie's room. She took a deep breath in, and let it out slowly. After she was composed she entered her other patient's room.

At 6:30 p.m. the night shift started to arrive. After giving the night nurse report, Lilith left the ICU, put on her coat, and headed out into the Thanksgiving night. The chill in the air surprised her. The wind whipped around her, pulling at her coat. She closed her eyes, and breathed in the cool air. Tears frosted on her face. She thought of the love and loss of Marie and John. She was thankful to have gotten a glimpse of their feelings for each other. After climbing into her car, she called Roy to let him know she was on her way.

Lilith opened the door of her house, and entered. Roy looked up, and smiled from the kitchen. The house was filled with wonderful smells of spices, turkey, and her mom's cinnamon yeast rolls.

As Lilith approached, Roy took her into his arms, and gave her a warm kiss on her lips, and the tip of her nose.

"It must be cold out. Your nose is freezing," Roy said with a smile.

"Not bad. It was actually refreshing after working indoors all day. It smells wonderful in here." Lilith hugged Roy tight.

Roy released Lilith suddenly and said, "I forgot to set the timer for the rolls."

Lilith got a pot holder, and opened the oven. She took out the hard dark rolls and burst into tears. She leaned over the counter with her head in her hands, and wept for her mom, the rolls, Marie and John.

Roy slowly came to her side. "I'm so sorry about the rolls. Is there anything I can do?"

You didn't do anything. It's Mom, and my patient and her husband. The loss! Lilith said to herself.

Hearing her thoughts, Roy took Lilith into his arms and said, "Let me absorb your loss." He hugged her tight.

Lilith let Roy hug her, and she melted into him. She sobbed until she was limp. He continued to hold her.

Embarrassed, Lilith straightened up as Roy released her. "Thanks. It was a rough day at work, and the burnt rolls reminded me that Mom isn't here anymore."

Roy reached out, and took Lilith's chin in his hand. He raised her eyes to meet his own. "No apology needed. I'm here for you. Now, are you hungry?" Roy asked with a smile.

Lilith threw her arms around his neck, and gave him a hungry kiss as her body pressed against him. "Yes, I'm hungry." She winked at him as she released him.

Roy sliced the turkey as Lilith placed the bowls of stuffing, green beans, sweet potatoes, cranberry sauce, and gravy out in a line on the counter. They both filled their plates, and went to take a seat at the table.

Lilith took hold of Roy's hand and said, "I'm thankful for this day, its challenges of joy, loss, and love. I'm thankful for this beautiful meal that was prepared by this wonderful man who I'm so very thankful for. Amen."

Roy squeezed Lilith's hand and said, "I'm thankful for life, memories old and new, and my darling, Lilith. Amen."

With eyes smiling at each other, they ate heartily.

Between mouthfuls of food, Lilith said, "My mom and I would sing just before eating. Would you like to hear the song?" Lilith asked Roy.

Roy put down his fork and answered, "Sure."

Lilith sang, "The turkey sat on the backyard fence, and he sang this sad, sad song.

Gobble, gobble, gobble, gobble, gobble, gobble, gobble. I don't like Thanksgiving Day. Gobble, gobble, gobble, gobble, gobble, gobble, gobble. I would like to run away..aaaah." Lilith started laughing, and Roy joined in.

After they finished eating, Lilith asked, "Pie?"

"I'm pretty full. Can we take a breather, and have it later?" Roy suggested.

"Why doesn't the cook relax, and I'll do the dishes," Lilith said. She rose and took their plates into the kitchen.

"Not a chance, fair lady. You worked all day. You change while I do the dishes, and put the food away?"

Roy strategically placed himself at the sink with legs spread wide so Lilith couldn't move him. With a laugh, Lilith conceded, and went off to shower and change. Roy was finishing up putting the food away when Lilith re-entered the room. A delicious surprised smile crossed Roy's face as he saw her naked except for a whipped cream bikini and whipped cream lipstick. She smiled as she seductively licked her lips. Roy's body flamed. He dropped his clothes to the floor as he approached Lilith with eyes locked on her. He lifted her into his arms and carried her into the bedroom.

After the night passed, the sun peeked through the curtains, and beams of light touched the sleeping pair. Lilith opened her eyes, and stared at the man lying close to her. She watched his quiet breathing as he slept. She knew she was falling hard for this man.

Roy blinked, and looked over at Lilith smiling. She looked beautiful with her blond curls all about her face. And her smile, it held him like a warm hug. He felt he could bathe in her glow forever.

Roy stretched, and said, "Good morning."

Lilith smiled. "Good morning to you. I think I will shower. I seem to be a bit sticky." Lilith laughed as she climbed out of bed. As she started walking to the bathroom she turned, and said with a grin, "Do you want to join me?"

Roy was out of bed in a flash. After showering, they dressed. Lilith stripped the sheets from the bed. She carried them to the laundry room, and put them in a basket. Gathering some clean linen from the closet she started making the bed. Roy joined in to help.

They walked arm and arm into the kitchen. Roy poured orange juice as Lilith started some coffee to brew. Lilith looked in the refrigerator, and took out some eggs. She also gathered the vegetables and herbs Roy had brought from his garden. There were also tomatoes, basil, spinach, and some mushrooms Lilith had bought. She took out a block of cheese to grate.

"Would you like an omelet?" Lilith asked.

"That sounds great. I'll set the table." Roy smiled.

While eating breakfast they scanned the paper, and talked. The sun was warming the day outside. Lilith looked out the window, and had a yearning for a run.

"Do you want to go for a walk or run?" she asked Roy, not knowing whether he liked to run.

"Sure, but I feel stuffed from breakfast. How about we start out at a walk, and then do a run?" Roy said as he remembered that he had packed a pair of Nikes.

Lilith did the dishes and then joined Roy in the bedroom to change. They both put on workout pants, shirts and windbreakers. Lilith put on her running shoes, and looked over at Roy.

She said to herself, *This is fun being together.*

Roy looked over at her, smiled and said, "It sure is!"

As they stepped outside, the cool crisp morning air caused them to zip up their jackets and put up their hoods. With their outside hands in their pockets, they walked hand in hand a mile to a nearby park. The park had a path that wound through the trees around a small lake. Lilith stopped to stretch, and Roy did the same. She then took off at a run and Roy, with his long legs, easily caught up with her. They did two laps around the park, and slowed to a walk. The sun was warming, and the rise in temperature was bringing people to the park. All of a sudden there were bikers, runners, dog walkers, and families. Lilith stopped to watch a toddler making her way down the hill, falling and getting up laughing. The sight made Lilith laugh.

Lilith remembered the conversation she had with her mom on Halloween. She was ready to put herself out there with Roy. "I want to have a baby someday," Lilith burst out. "What about you?" She looked over at Roy as she held his hand.

"Oh, I thought I did at one time. But since having the boys I pushed it out of my mind," Roy said looking out as if deep in thought.

Lilith's stomach dropped. She found it hard to breathe. She wondered why they hadn't talked about this before. She felt light-headed, and panicked. Her ears buzzed, but she didn't want to listen. She was careful not to put out thoughts to Roy. She didn't want him to hear her until she knew what she wanted to say.

"I'm not feeling very well. I think I should head back," Lilith said to Roy.

"OK. Is there anything I can do?" Roy asked with concern.

"I think I'll take a shower when I get back, and lie down for a while," Lilith said as she held her churning stomach.

They walked back in silence. Roy wondered if it was what he had said about children that had made Lilith sick. He didn't want to ask. He could tell she was not putting any thoughts out to him. He was glad. He wasn't sure he wanted to know. This was new territory for him. He needed to understand how he felt.

Lilith entered the house without speaking, and headed to the bathroom. She closed the door quietly behind her. After turning on the shower, she sat on the lid of the commode, and cried body-racking sobs. Once the room filled with steam, she took off her running clothes, and placed them in the hamper. She eased under the warm water and let her tears flow as the water washed over her. She had opened her heart, and hoped. She wondered why she'd jumped so fast only to fall on her face. Lilith lathered her hair and body. She trembled as she rubbed her skin trying to ease the pain. The suds washed off her skin and down the drain, but she felt no better. She slid down the wall and sat. The water ran down on her and puddled.

She cried to herself, *I like him. I think I love him. Why? Why?* After a quivering breath in and out, she thought to herself, *I will have to say goodbye. I want a baby and a family. It's been great, but I want more.* She sobbed harder.

Roy had watched Lilith quickly enter the bathroom, and close the door. He wasn't convinced she was just feeling sick. He got himself a glass of water, though he was thinking a scotch would be better, and went to sit by the window. Looking out as the dark clouds shaded the sun, his energy drained. He hadn't dealt with so much emotion in a long time. Something inside him made him want to run. Run back to the ranch, and his quiet life. He thought of his life over the past few years. It was a comfortable routine. Oh, he had had problems that came up with his nephews and of course the ranch, but it was a quiet life. He appreciated the calm after his family loss and grief. Then he thought of Lilith. He had never felt so energized. He was even writing more than he had in years.

Roy looked over at the closed bathroom door. Lilith had been in there a long time. He could still hear the water running. He wondered if she was all right.

Lilith cried to herself, *I have to let you go.*

Roy heard Lilith, and his heart dropped in his chest. He rushed to the bathroom, and opened the door. He saw Lilith through the glass shower door. She was sitting with her knees bent, holding them close to her chest. Her head was down, and he could see she was crying. He opened the shower door, and sat beside her as she looked up.

Touching her arm he said, "Lilith, please don't let me go. We are so good together. This is just a lot for me to take in. Please give me some time. Give us time to talk, think, and work it out together."

Lilith looked up at Roy. Words escaped her. Tears continued to flow.

Roy wasn't sure what to do or say, so he just pulled Lilith into his lap and rocked her against his body as the water showered around them.

Lilith leaned into him and realized that she had stopped crying. She felt exhausted, yet she felt herself starting to relax. She looked up at Roy, and said with a smile, "Sir, you are soaking wet in your clothes."

"Well, madame, in my defense, I didn't have time to dress, or undress accordingly." He laughed. "How about we dry off, and take a nap?"

Lilith leaned into this man, and let herself fall. At this moment she didn't care about the "what-ifs". She just wanted to be.

Christmas

THE THANKSGIVING HOLIDAY WEEKEND HAD BEEN a mixed bag of romance, misunderstandings, making up, and getting to know each other better. On the last day, Roy worked on his book while Lilith read as the sun beamed through the windows. It was nice just being together. Roy looked over at Lilith, and smiled. She felt his eyes on her, and looked up and smiled back at him.

Roy's new book was about mindfulness. Lilith loved that he would share with her his points of view on the topic. He sometimes wrote a paragraph, and read it to her to get her impression. She would comment, and ask questions. It was a nice way to share their thoughts and beliefs. Lilith realized she was more traditional than Roy, but their belief systems meshed well together.

After lunch on Sunday, Lilith and Roy lay on the couch together, and listened to a medley of classics: Bach, Beethoven, and Tchaikovsky. They relaxed, and breathed in rhythm with each other and the music.

Before Roy left to return home, he invited Lilith to spend the Christmas holiday with his nephews and himself. He wanted to start to share his life with her, and it started by meeting his nephews. She was thrilled to have a family gathering to attend for the holidays.

Lilith had worked at her hospital for more than thirteen years, and had her pick of holiday vacations. She received vacation time for Christmas Eve through January 2nd. It had been a long time since she'd taken this holiday off. Since her mom had died, she'd chosen to work most holidays so that her coworkers could have the holiday with their families. It was too painful to be off, and spend the holiday alone missing her mom. She was excited to have a holiday with Roy and his family. She could bring the memories of her mom with her.

Lilith's ears buzzed. She heard, *There is excitement ahead!*

Lilith answered silently, *I hope so.*

Roy and Lilith had phoned each other often since Thanksgiving. They made plans, talked about holiday foods, hunting for a Christmas tree on the ranch, and decorating it. Roy shared parts of his book, and Lilith talked about her work. Lilith had asked many questions about the boys so she could buy them meaningful presents. Roy gave her some ideas, and she went shopping. After purchasing a couple of flannel western shirts, she wrapped, and stored them away next to the present she had gotten for Roy. She smiled to herself as she gazed at Roy's present.

Lilith said out loud, "I sure hope you'll like what I got for you. Actually, I know you will."

The week before Christmas, Lilith's coworkers teased her about her vacation. Lilith blushed broadly and showed how pleased she was to go. She could hardly wait to see Roy, meet his nephews, and enjoy the celebration of the birth of Jesus.

Roy was at his desk. He had just finished working, and was thinking of Lilith. The clock chimed noon as the door opened. His nephews, Steven and Clark, clambered through the doorway. With the ranch closed since Thanksgiving, it had been pretty quiet. Their noise was a welcome sound. He'd gotten a lot of work done on his book, and was ready to see the boys.

"Hi, guys. How're you doing?" Roy called out.

"Great, Uncle Roy," yelled Steven. "Anything to eat around here?"

"Yeah, we're starved. Something smells good," added Clark.

Roy got up and hugged his nephews. They were getting so big. Nice young men. Clark was unshaven, and looked tired. Steven had cut his hair, and was looking more like his dad every day.

"I made an elk stew. It's in the slow cooker. Wash up, and I'll put the biscuits in the oven, and make a salad." Roy smiled to himself as he headed toward the kitchen.

After hanging their coats in the closet, the boys bolted up the stairs with their luggage. They disappeared in their rooms, and washed their hands in the adjoining bathroom.

Clark flung himself on his bed. He felt rested after sleeping during the drive. "Are you going to miss your gal?" he asked Steven.

Steven dipped his head and said, "Yes/No. We broke up."

Clark sat up and said, "Sorry, man. I thought she was nice."

Steven looked at this brother. "Well, nice isn't always good enough."

Clark tried to sound chipper. "Guess there'll be no more vacations to Hawaii?"

Steven playfully lunged at his brother, and punched him in the arm. "No, at least not with that family. Now, let's go eat."

The boys went downstairs, and sat at the table. Roy had placed a bowl of salad on the table, and they helped themselves and started eating. The buzzer went off. Roy dropped the biscuits into a basket, and spooned out elk stew into bowls.

The table was silent as the boys filled their bellies, and got second helpings. As they slowed their eating, Roy asked them about school, and their Thanksgiving holiday in Hawaii.

Steven ran up to his room, and got some pictures to share. After gazing at the beautiful pictures of the ocean, forest, waterfalls, and volcanoes, Roy saw some of the funny candid shots of his nephews. He laughed at their stories, and realized how good it felt to see them again.

The boys, who had heard about Lilith, asked about Roy's Thanksgiving. Roy talked about their weekend of cooking, running, reading, and working a bit on his book.

Roy said cheerfully, "Boys, I invited Lilith to have Christmas with us."

There was silence. Then Clark said strongly, "No way. We don't know her. This is supposed to be our family tradition, and celebration. We're all that is left of the family. It's only been three years."

Roy was stunned. "But I've already asked her, and she's planning on coming."

"No. It's hard enough not to have Mom and Dad here, but to share the holiday with a stranger!" Steven shouted angrily, near tears.

"Boys, Lilith is very important to me!" Roy said louder than he meant to.

"We don't know her. We want it just to be us," Clark yelled. Steven nodded.

Roy gathered up the dishes with a heavy heart. He understood the loss the boys were experiencing. He felt their loss, too. And he loved them. He didn't want to cause them any pain. They were his priority. His mind was whirling. But Lilith, she'd be so disappointed. How could he tell her? What would he say? She had had her losses too. He'd handled this badly. He should have talked with the boys first. He'd just assumed. But he shouldn't have.

That night Roy tossed and turned. He needed to think about what to say. He decided he would call Lilith early the next morning before she started packing.

Lilith arrived home from work excited about her trip. She showered, and changed into her pjs. She decided to make some cinnamon sticky buns to take with her, and a pumpkin pie as well. While the rolls and pie were baking, she packed her bag, and made lists so she wouldn't forget anything. As the timer went off, first for the rolls and then for the pie, she put them in the garage on a shelf to cool, and keep chilled. The drop in temperature made the garage the same temperature as her refrigerator. She smiled to herself as she thought of Roy. She slipped under the covers, and fell fast asleep.

At 7 a.m. the phone rang. Lilith sleepily reached for it and said, "Hello?"

"Hi, Lilith, it's Roy. I hope I didn't wake you," Roy replied.

"It's OK. Your voice is much nicer than my alarm clock. How are you doing? Did the boys get home OK?" Lilith yawned.

"Yes, they're here." Roy paused. "Lilith, I have some, I need to…I don't know how to say this…"

Lilith's ears buzzed. But she didn't have time to listen. She sat up in bed with alarm. "Roy, what's wrong. Are you OK?"

Roy started again, "Lilith, I'm so sorry, but I need to change our plans for Christmas. The boys were looking forward to having Christmas with just the three of us, and sharing our love and memories. I just can't disappoint them. They've been through so much, and I'm their only family. I'm so sorry."

Lilith felt as if the wind had been knocked out of her. Tears streamed down her face. Somewhere deep inside she understood Roy's commitment to the boys, his nephews, but her ache and disappointment pushed those thoughts from her mind.

Lilith was brought out of her thoughts with Roy's pleading voice, "Lilith, are you still there? I'm so sorry."

Lilith took a deep breath and replied, "Yes, Roy, I'm still here. I'm sorry it didn't work out. You have a nice holiday. I need to hang up now. Goodbye."

The connection was ended before Roy could reply. He said to himself, *Wow, she took that well. No drama. She must understand. I'll find a nice way to make it up to her. I'm sure she's disappointed. But I'm relieved that she understands.* Now relaxed, Roy dressed, and headed out to the kitchen to make blueberry pancakes with Vermont maple syrup, the boys' favorite breakfast.

After hanging up the phone Lilith wanted to throw or punch something. She took the present that she had picked out specially for Roy, and she threw it across the room. Of course it didn't break. There was nothing breakable about a cashmere sweater and cashmere bikini. But the gesture made her feel better. She got up out of bed and paced. She cried and was angry, but mostly she was disappointed and sad. Her immediate reaction was that the relationship was over.

Lilith said to herself, *We're at such different places. We want different things. He has commitments to his family, and the ranch. He lives so far away from my life. What could I have been thinking? And now I have the holiday, with two weeks and no work, no plans. This just won't do.* Lilith's thoughts rambled as she paced.

Lilith felt a swoosh and paid attention. She heard, *Love is not easy.*

She answered, *I'm learning that over and over.* She felt the hugs of her angels and said, *Thanks.*

Lilith grabbed her phone, and called the ICU unit. After the second ring she was connected. "ICU, this is Tania."

Lilith cringed. Tania was the biggest gossip. "Hi, Tania, this is Lilith," Lilith replied.

"Hi, Lilith. What are you doing calling us? Don't you need to be packing for your holiday at the dude ranch with the hot cowboy?" Tania asked.

Lilith took a deep breath. "Well, my plans changed, and I thought I could work if you need me."

"We've gotten very busy. You can take your pick of days," Tania added.

"Please put me down for tomorrow, and then I'll fill in the rest when I come into work. Thanks. See you tomorrow." Lilith said trying to sound cheerful.

She got up, and poured herself some coffee. She carried the steaming cup back to bed, and tried to read. Tears leaked out of her eyes. She was so disappointed and hurt. The tears spilled onto her book. She felt so lonely. In truth, she didn't feel Roy was rejecting her. She just wondered if their lives were too different to work out between them. She believed the best thing to do was to stay busy, and see how she felt after the holidays. The coffee tasted good. She breathed in the aroma, and it relaxed her.

After reading for a while, and taking a nap, Lilith went for a run. When she returned, she cleaned her house with a vengeance. When she was done, she started on her closets. She made a pile of clothes she knew she wouldn't wear anymore, organized her shoes, and cleaned out her drawers. Distracted, she forgot about the clothes in a pile on the floor, and tripped over them, twisting her ankle. She sat on the floor and sobbed.

After a good cry, she said out loud, "Shit, this is pathetic. I need to get back to work, and stop feeling sorry for myself."

Lilith knew from experience that taking care of the critically ill put her life into perspective. She carried the discarded clothes from the floor to her car, and placed them in the trunk. She'd take them somewhere to donate. Going back inside her house, she made a sandwich, and settled on the couch to watch mindless TV. At 9:30 p.m., she showered, and went to bed.

The alarm startled her awake, and she rose to get ready for work. The ICU was busy and the day flew by. Lilith had a few friends who asked about her change in plans, but she shrugged it off gently, and kept busy. She checked the schedule. She planned to work up until Christmas, and take Christmas Day off, since she wanted to go to midnight mass on Christmas Eve.

The days were so busy that Lilith only worked, ate, and slept. The busyness kept her mind off Roy, and her disappointment. Working in the hospital grounded Lilith, and prevented her from feeling sorry for herself.

On Christmas Eve, Lilith received report on her two patients. One of her patients was a fifty-year-old female with scleroderma that had advanced, and tightened the connective tissue of her lungs. Her name was Sue. This autoimmune disease that causes tightening of the connective tissues of the body, tightened around Sue's lungs. She had been unable to expand her lungs, and breathe by herself. She was intubated and placed on a ventilator. She had increasing air hunger, and rapid breathing, tachypnea. She had been given high doses of steroids with no effect. It had become difficult for her lungs to expand even with the peep pressure on the vent. Lilith knew that the high levels of peep, positive end-expiratory pressure, helped the lungs remain open to receive oxygen, but it didn't help with Sue's deteriorating condition. Sue had been hoping to live through the holidays, but her condition deteriorated after Thanksgiving. The high settings that were required on the ventilator, Sue's advanced disease, and her painful struggle to breathe indicated that she had only days or hours left to live.

Sue was surrounded by her husband, David, and children, Sean and Linda. Sue wrote a note to Lilith telling her that she was ready to go, and be with Jesus. Lilith looked from the note to the family. Tears welled in Lilith's eyes as she looked at the note, and then at the tearful family. They nodded their acceptance.

Lilith explained, "I'll notify the doctor of your wishes, Sue. When you're ready, I'll give you some morphine to relax you. Once you're relaxed, I'll turn off the respirator, and pull out your breathing tube. I can give you oxygen by mask, or a small cannula in your nose." Sue motioned for the cannula. "OK. I'll place a cannula of oxygen in your nose. Your family can be with you as long as you like. Would you like me to call the chaplain?"

"Yes, please do," David replied between sobs.

Lilith called the doctor, and got the order to withdraw ventilator support. She had Lisa, one of the nurses she was working with, listen to the telephone order with her. Two nurses had to hear a telephone order from a physician to withdraw lifesaving support like a respirator.

She went into the medication room to get some morphine. Holding the morphine in her hand she leaned into the counter and cried. She felt the pain of Sue, David, Sean, and Linda. Lilith felt honored to be a part of this brave family's decision to honor their mom's wishes, and let her go.

When Lilith approached Sue's ICU room, she knocked on the door. David invited her to enter. Lilith found David sitting at the head of Sue's bed. Sue was resting against his chest, and he had his arms around her. Sean and Linda were on either side of their mom, holding her hands.

Lilith said softly, "Sue, are you ready?"

Sue nodded. Lilith said, "Sue, I'm going to give you some morphine to help you relax, and feel comfortable. It will make you sleepy."

Sue looked around the room at her family, and mouthed the words, "I love you."

Lilith gave her the morphine, turned off the ventilator, and disconnected it from Sue's breathing tube. She let the air out of the balloon that held the tube in place, removed the breathing tube, and wiped Sue's mouth. She placed a cannula of oxygen in Sue's nose. Chaplain Jan appeared in the doorway. Lilith stepped back to give the family their time.

David put his lips to Sue's ear and said, "Go to Jesus, my love. I love you always."

Both Sean and Linda said together, "Mom, go to Jesus. We love you."

Within minutes, Sue slipped away peacefully. Lilith cried for the love and loss of this beautiful family. And she cried for her love and loss of her mother. It had been ten years since her mom had died. She missed her still. And then there was Roy. She squeezed her eyes together, releasing more tears.

When Lilith got home she showered slowly. She wanted to wash the pain down the drain and just hold the wonderful memories. Lilith knew that was what Christmas was all about: celebration, memories, family, and the birth of Jesus. She put on a long dress and boots over her wool socks. It was Christmas Eve, and she wanted to go to midnight mass. She made herself some spaghetti, and ate as she thought of her blessings, and the blessings of the birth of Jesus.

It was a beautiful candlelight mass with ritual, songs, and celebration. Lilith looked around at all the families celebrating together. She realized she didn't envy them, but was pleased for them. She watched the sweet children: some sleeping in their parent's arms, some sleeping on the pew, and some mesmerized by the candles and the beautiful music. She knew she would have a family someday soon. Lilith lit a candle for the blessings of her mom, dad, Jeremy, and Sue.

Lilith said to herself, *Merry Christmas, Mom: Merry Christmas, Dad: Merry Christmas, Jer: and Merry Christmas, Sue.*

Lilith's ears buzzed and she heard, *They are sending you love and wishes too.*

Lilith arrived home after mass. She realized she wanted to have a family even if it meant raising a child on her own. The idea of a baby warmed her. She had plenty of room at her house. She knew of some lovely women from her church that cared for infants of new moms. She changed into her pjs, and opened her computer. She searched sperm banks, gathering information as she started her quest for a family. She reviewed adoption sites. After an hour, she turned off her computer, slipped her tired body into bed, and fell fast asleep. Lilith was dreaming of babies, birthdays, Christmas, and blessings.

Roy awoke realizing he had been dreaming of Lilith. He sat up, and put his feet on the floor. He ached for her. The holiday had not gone as he'd planned. He tried to shake the feelings as he dressed, and wandered out to the kitchen. The house was quiet. The boys were sleeping. It was Christmas Eve, and they had a lot to do. He put on a pot of coffee, and put out some oatmeal to cook when the boys awoke.

He'd give them another hour to sleep. With his cup of coffee Roy settled into his chair by the window. It was a beautiful sunny day, and he could see clouds hiding the distant mountains.

He said to himself, *Looks like we're going to have a white Christmas.*

Roy was lost in his thoughts of past family Christmases, and now of Lilith when he heard footsteps on the stairs. He looked up and saw Steven.

Roy said, "Yah, how'd you sleep?"

Steven tried to shake the sleep, or lack of it from his head and answered, "All right, but I tossed and turned a bit."

Roy straightened in surprise. "I thought you boys would sleep like logs after all that riding we did yesterday. Were you sore?"

Steven sat on the ottoman across from his uncle. "No, my body isn't sore, but my heart is."

Roy leaned in and asked, "What do you mean?"

Steven began, "Heather and I broke up. I don't know what happened. We seemed to have a great time in Hawaii, but when we got back to school she was distant. Said she needed some time to think, and then she said we needed time apart." Steven hung his head. "Girls can be so confusing."

"Yes, that's true. But they're worth the risk of getting hurt," Roy added, thinking of Lilith.

"Did you feel confused about the woman you were going to marry before you came here?" Steven asked.

"Well, not exactly confused, but more disappointed. We were able to talk, and found out that our future plans, once the same, were now different. A life together was not possible," Roy explained. "Do you think you and Heather could try and talk things out?"

"Perhaps, but what if she just didn't have the courage to tell me she didn't feel the same about me anymore?" Steven asked.

"Wouldn't it be better to know?" Roy added.

"Probably." Steven's blue eyes looked sadly at Roy. "Uncle Roy, I'm sorry I reacted so strongly about having Lilith here. I think it wasn't just about Mom and Dad. I couldn't stand seeing you with someone when my heart was breaking."

"Thanks for saying that. I'll arrange another time for you to meet Lilith." Roy smiled with pride at how Steven was growing into such a nice young man.

When Clark got up the three had oatmeal, juice, and coffee. After the boys dressed they all went down to the stables. They hitched up two of the horses to a wagon and headed into the forest to select a tree. Roy had brought along some hot chocolate and cookies, a childhood favorite of the boys. They enjoyed the food and drink after selecting, cutting, and hauling the tree into the wagon. There were bells attached to the harnesses on the horses. They sang carols together to the jingling bells as the horses trotted back to the ranch. The temperature was dropping, and it felt like snow was coming.

Back at the ranch, Clark attached the tree to a stand, and positioned it in the family room. Steven got the lights and strung them around the tree as Roy carried the ornaments from the attic. The boys had fun laughing at all the childhood ornaments they had forgotten about from the years before. Once the tree was decorated, they turned on the lights and viewed their masterpiece. Roy, thoroughly enjoying spoiling the boys, put out some bowls of soup and sandwiches, and they all sat down for lunch.

That evening after supper they walked down to the ranch chapel. The chapel was nestled within a grove of pine trees south of the ranch. Inside the chapel, they lit candles for Jesus, and all their family that they missed, and wished them Christmas joy. They sang "Silent Night", "Jingle Bells", and "We wish you a Merry Christmas". As they walked back to the house, big snowflakes started to fall.

Christmas morning was full of laughter, presents, and family stories. Roy smiled as he watched his nephews enjoy themselves. After they opened most of the presents, there were a few left tucked under the tree.

"Uncle Roy, these are for Lilith," Clark said, looking at his uncle, and noticing the drop in his happy expression. "Sorry, Uncle Roy: I was selfish. I acted like a spoiled brat. It really would have been nice to meet her."

"Thanks for saying that. I'll make it up to her," Roy said. He planned to call Lilith later that day.

Lilith awoke to a bright, white day. She looked out her window, and saw a world covered with fresh snow. It was still lightly snowing. She smiled at the beauty. She climbed out of bed, stretched, and turned on the lights of her table Christmas tree.

Taking a deep breath in, she said, "Merry Christmas, Lord. I'm thankful for my blessings, and my learning. But I'm sad, and I know I have to work through the sadness even if it is Your birthday."

Lilith made coffee, and had some oatmeal. There were a few presents from friends under her tree, but she decided to open them later. She thought a walk, and then a run would feel good. She changed into her running clothes and put on her jacket, hat, and gloves. She locked her door on her way out.

The streets were quiet except for the crunch of her feet on the new snow. There were lights on in the houses, and Lilith could imagine families around their trees opening presents. She smiled at the memory of Christmas morning with her mom. She remembered the excitement. Even though it had been ten years since her mom had died, the memories were fresh and vivid. Lilith shook some snow from her hat, and started her run. She ran around the lake at the park near her house. There was a small area of lake that wasn't frozen and some ducks and geese were swimming.

All of a sudden Lilith was airborne. A patch of ice had been hidden by the snow. She landed on her left hip and elbow. She quickly looked around to see if anyone had seen her. But she was alone at the park. She sat up to assess for injuries and found that, other than some soreness, nothing was broken. Then she cried. She cried for her loneliness, her heartache, foiled plans, and her sore bottom and arm. Gingerly she got up. She slowly walked home.

Her ears buzzed and she heard, *We love you. Be gentle with yourself.* Lilith said out loud, "I know. I'm trying to barrel through everything. Fix my life, make plans. I need to relax, get through the holidays, give myself time to think, and not rush into anything."

Lilith took a slow breath in, and let it out slowly as she envisioned her sore muscles and tired shoulders relaxing. Lilith walked up to her door, and put the key in the lock. She heard a swoosh, and stopped to pay attention.

She heard, "Meow."

Surprised, Lilith looked around, and out from behind one of her bushes came a small, thin, black kitten. She leaned down quietly as the kitten approached.

She said, "Hi, Kitty. Are you lost?"

The kitten gave a "Meow." Then he jumped up on Lilith's shoulder, and settled into the fluffy collar of her jacket.

"Well. Make yourself at home." Lilith laughed. "Let's go inside where it's warm, and figure out what to do with you."

Lilith entered her house with the kitten still on her shoulder. She took off her coat and gently placed the kitten on the floor. She went into the kitchen and looked in the refrigerator. The kitten followed her.

"Well, I have some milk, but not much else for a kitten." She poured a small amount of milk in a saucer, and put it on the floor. The kitten drank eagerly. "You're hungry. Not many places are open on Christmas."

Lilith tried to think of any place that would be open. She remembered a convenience store near the hospital that was open twenty-four hours a day. Lilith noticed the kitten was a male. She got out some paper and a black marker, and wrote several signs that read, "Found Black Male Kitten", and she added her phone number.

She swooped up the kitten, and looked him in the face. "I'll call you Christmas until I find out who you really are. And you're coming with me to put out some signs to alert your owner that you're safe. Then we'll go get you some food." She placed the kitten on her shoulder.

Lilith drove to both ends of her street, and put up the signs on trees and posts so that anyone driving to or from her neighborhood would see them. She made a note to herself to call the local shelter and vet tomorrow to see if anyone was searching for a lost kitten. She drove the three miles to the 7-Eleven near her hospital. To her delight, it was open. She left the kitten in the car, and went inside.

As she entered the store a young female clerk with a Santa hat on said, "Merry Christmas!"

Lilith looked over at her, and said, "Merry Christmas to you! Do you have any cat supplies?"

"Well, yes. Aisle 4 on your left. Did you get a cat for Christmas?" the clerk asked.

"Well, we were gifted to each other," Lilith smiled.

She scanned the shelves, and found canned and dry kitten food, a litter box, some cat litter, and a few toys. Lilith realized she was having fun. After she paid and exited the store, she saw Christmas standing on the steering wheel. He was peering out the front window at her. It made her laugh.

Once home, Lilith set up the cat box. Christmas jumped right in, and did his business. "Smart kitty," Lilith said. "Or is this a sign that you do have a home? We better not get too attached, because someone might be missing you very much." Lilith bent down to stroke Christmas, and he jumped up onto her shoulder.

Lilith walked with the hitchhiker into the kitchen, and opened a can of kitten food. She heard "Meow" in her ear, and Christmas rubbed against her check. She put the food on a plate and placed it with a bowl of water on the floor. Christmas jumped down, and ate heartily. He then curled up on the couch, and licked himself clean.

Lilith laughed, "You sure are making yourself at home."

Lilith noticed that her answering machine was blinking. She touched the button and heard, "Hi Lilith, it's Roy. I wanted to wish you a Merry Christmas. So sorry about the change in plans. I'll try and call you another time."

Lilith looked at Christmas and said, "That Roy. He's sweet, but not very insightful!" She laughed at how good it felt to be pissed off.

Christmas, watching Lilith, jumped off the couch, and ran to her as she grabbed one of the string toys and whirled it around. They played and then Christmas curled up with her while she read her book on the couch. After dinner they watched TV together. *Miracle on 34th Street*, the original one, was playing. It was a nice way to end Christmas Day. After the movie, both Lilith and Christmas were yawning. She went into the bathroom to get ready for bed. Christmas followed her, and used his box which Lilith had placed in a corner. Lilith climbed into bed and Christmas jumped up and settled next to her. As Lilith stroked the kitten, they drifted off to sleep.

Lilith was dreaming of a bell ringing. She couldn't find the bell, and awoke to realize it was her phone.

She reached for the phone and answered. "Hello?"

She heard, "Lilith, this is Marsha. I know you didn't sign up for today to work, but would you be willing to come in? We have a special case that you have the expertise for."

Lilith yawned, thinking of Marsha with her head of black curls all about her determined face. She replied, "Actually, I did sign up, so I'll be in."

"Thanks Lilith. See you soon," Marsha replied, and hung up the phone.

Lilith stretched, crawled out of bed, and made her way to the kitchen to brew some coffee. She saw the sticky buns in the freezer, and frowned. Her heart ached.

She said to herself, *Oh, well.* She took out a roll, and put it in the microwave to heat.

Then she heard, "Meow."

"Good morning, Christmas. Do you want some breakfast?" Lilith said as she got a can of cat food out of the cabinet, and poured the contents onto a plate. She smiled as Christmas ate hungrily. She poured some dry kitten food in a bowl, and added water to soften it. "I will be at work all day so here is some food and plenty of water for later. You be a good little kitty." She leaned down, and stroked the soft black fur.

After she had a quick breakfast, and put on her scrubs, Lilith headed for the hospital. She parked her car, entered the hospital, and walked down the hall. She stopped at the chapel, dipped her fingers in the holy water, and made the sign of the cross.

Lilith said, "May I heal, and do no harm."

As she walked toward the ICU, her ears buzzed. She heard, *We like Christmas.*

I do too, she answered silently.

When Lilith entered the ICU she saw Marsha. Marsha approached Lilith with face flushed, and black curls flying.

"Lilith, we have a sad and unusual case. Cindy will give you report. You will have just one patient, because you will care for her and her unborn baby. She is a 25 year-old female who is 37 weeks pregnant, and had a cerebral bleed from an undiagnosed aneurysm that ruptured. I'm so glad you were able to work. You're the only one with obstetric experience. Those flight nurse days come in handy." Marsha gave a weak smile.

"I'll put away my purse, and get report. Thanks, Marsha," Lilith replied.

Lilith put her purse in her locker, and used the bathroom. She felt it was going to be busy and didn't know when she would get a chance again. She saw Cindy sitting outside ICU 10, and pulled up a chair next to her to get report.

"Hi, Cindy. Are you ready to give me report?" Lilith asked as she sat down.

Cindy's gray hair was pulled back tightly. Her shoulders were slumped forward as she looked at the computer screen. When she looked up at Lilith, Lilith could see the fatigue in her red eyes as she blinked, trying to focus.

"Oh, Lilith, I'm so glad to see you. I'm out of my league here. I haven't seen obstetric patients since nursing school, and that was thirty years ago." Cindy took a deep breath in, and let it out. Just then a tearful woman stepped out of ICU 10, and nodded at Cindy as she hurried out of the ICU. "That's Catherine, your patient's mom," Cindy said.

Cindy began, "OK, Jessica is a 25 year-old, gravida 1 para 0, female, 37 weeks gestation. Lilith, I know you're aware that means first pregnancy and no live children yet. I had to be reminded of that. The pregnancy has been uneventful. Reportedly, her mom was visiting due to the planned C-section next week. Jessica went to bed early last night stating she had a headache. Her mom, Catherine, went to check on her before she went to bed, and found her unresponsive and barely breathing. She called EMS, and when they arrived an airway was placed and fluids started. On arrival to the emergency room the patient was still unresponsive, pupils were fixed and dilated, blood pressure was slightly elevated, heart rhythm showed normal sinus, afebrile, a nurse from the OB department came to check the baby, and found normal heart rate for gestational age, membranes intact, patient was dilated 1 cm, no sign of contractions. Blood levels and urine are within normal range. Patient was taken to have a Cat Scan of her head. She has a cerebral hemorrhage from an undiagnosed aneurysm that ruptured. The blood is tamponading the vessel in her brain, so there is no more bleeding. An EEG was ordered to evaluate brain activity. It showed minimal brain activity. The Cat Scan showed damaged brain tissue. The vessel isn't in an operable area of the brain."

"What about the baby?" Lilith asked.

Cindy began again. "Jessica's mom was told by the neurologist and neurosurgeon that this was not a survivable injury for Jessica. When she goes into labor an emergency C-section will have to be performed to save the baby. There is a good chance that Jessica will not survive the C-section due to her injury. If Jessica goes into labor, Jessica's mother, Catherine, agrees with an emergency C-section to save the baby."

"Is the baby still doing OK? Any D cells?" Lilith asked.

"I don't know. The OB nurse comes every couple of hours to check. She hasn't said anything. Remind me what D cells are?" Cindy rubbed her temple.

"Oh, sure. It's a decrease in the baby's heart rate. It can be normal in labor as long as the heart rate comes up quickly after the contraction ends. It is abnormal during pregnancy with no contractions; baby is in distress." Lilith explained.

Cindy said, "Thanks." And then she added, "We're giving diuretics to help decrease brain swelling. The drugs don't cross the blood/brain barrier so are safe for baby. Oh, and the baby is a girl."

Lilith sighed. "Thanks, Cindy. Good work. I'm going in to check on Jessica and her baby girl."

"I have a little more charting. Let me know if you have any questions." Cindy said.

Lilith entered ICU 10. She was struck by the beautiful young woman with curly red hair, and a big gravida belly. Except for the tubes coming from her, she looked as if she were sleeping.

After washing her hands and putting on a pair of gloves, Lilith took Jessica's hand. "Jessica, my name is Lilith. I'm going to be the nurse caring for you, and your baby. I'm going to look in your eyes, check your reflexes, and listen to your heart, lungs, and belly. I'll be turning on the baby monitor so we can monitor your little baby girl's heart beat, and check to see if you're having any contractions. I'm going to check your cervix and membranes by inserting a speculum."

Lilith moved quickly and gently around Jessica, gathering information. Then she viewed the strip on the baby monitor. The baby had a nice strong heartbeat. There were no D cells signifying a drop in the baby's heart rate, and no contractions. Jessica was still unresponsive with fixed pupils; her heart rate and blood pressure were normal and her oxygen saturation was 100%. Lilith put her hands on Jessica's abdomen. The baby kicked her hand.

"Jessica, I think she's going to be a dancer. That's a strong kick. Her head is down. She looks like a good size. I am going to raise up your legs and place a speculum in your vagina to view your cervix and membranes." Lilith gently raised Jessica's legs and inserted the speculum. "Jessica, you're still only 1 cm dilated, and your membranes are intact."

Lilith cleaned Jessica, and repositioned her on her left side which she knew helped blood flow to the baby. "Jessica, I'm going to give you a back rub, and then a belly rub, and talk with your sweet baby."

Lilith warmed some lotion in a pan of hot water. She placed some warm lotion into her gloved hand. As she rubbed Jessica's back she hummed a lullaby.

She moved to Jessica's belly. "Hi, baby. My name is Lilith. I'm going to put some lotion on your mom's belly. I'll do it gently so as not to disturb you." Lilith rubbed Jessica's belly and hummed. She felt several kicks. "You're an active little girl, aren't you?" Lilith laughed.

Lilith's ears buzzed. She heard, *That's a lullaby that my mom sang to me.*

Lilith replied silently, *Are you Jessica?*

She heard, *Yes. What's happening?*

Jessica, you had a headache at home. Do you remember? Lilith asked silently as she rubbed Jessica's belly.

She heard, *Yes, I think so. So why am I here? How can you talk to me?*

Lilith responded silently, *I have a gift of hearing those who are in a coma.*

Am I dying? Is my baby OK? Jessica pleaded.

Lilith responded silently, *Jessica, your baby has a strong heart beat and kick. She's fine. You have had a bleed in your head. It is not something that we can operate on.*

Lilith heard, *Am I going to die?*

Lilith said silently, *Jessica, you can't survive this injury. I'm so sorry. We'll do everything we can for your baby girl.*

Lilith heard, *No... No....I can't die. I have a baby. What will happen to my baby? Mom can't care for her on her own. She's older, and raised me by herself when Dad died. Oh God, help my baby.*

Lilith asked silently, *What about the father of your baby?*

There's no father. I became pregnant from a sperm bank. I wanted a baby and to start a family, but I was not in a relationship. I had bad endometriosis all my life and was told I might not be able to have children, but if I wanted to, I should start sooner rather than later. There's no family except my mom.

Don't worry Jessica. I will work with your mom, Lilith said silently. Just then the baby kicked several times against Lilith's hands. "You are going to be a dancer. Sweet baby, your mom loves you very much, and wants to keep you safe and warm." Lilith started to hum *Brahms Lullaby.*

Lilith was startled to see Catherine standing just inside the door. "Oh, I didn't see you there. My name is Lilith. I'm Jessica and her baby's nurse."

"I can see that. You're very good with her." Then Catherine started to cry. "What am I going to do without my girl?"

Lilith went to Catherine and the older woman collapsed into her arms. "She's not going to get better. It happened so fast. Could I have done something to prevent it?" Catherine sobbed.

"You did just the right thing. You called 911. There was nothing more that you could have done." Lilith held Catherine tight, and then led her over to some chairs she had set up next to Jessica's bed.

"I love her so much. I can't lose her. Her baby needs her," Catherine wept.

Catherine sat down tentatively next to Jessica's bed. Lilith was watching her as she started to touch Jessica's hand, and then stopped.

Lilith sat down next to Catherine, and gently lifted Jessica's hand. She said, "You won't hurt her. Here, take her hand, and talk to her. I always believe that no matter how sick a person is, they can always hear you."

Catherine took Jessica's hand and cried. "She looks like she is sleeping and her hand is warm, but she doesn't react to my touch." Then she said, "Baby, I'm here. You get better. Your baby, and I need you."

Lilith heard, *I'm here, Mom. I love you. I want to get better. My baby! Who will take care of my baby?*

She loves you, Jessica. She just can't hear you. Don't worry. I'll work with your mom, Lilith said silently.

Catherine turned to Lilith. "Do you have any children?"

"No, not right now, but I want to someday," Lilith said as she touched Jessica's belly. The baby kicked. "Your granddaughter has quite a kick."

"I haven't felt her kick," Catherine said with surprise.

Lilith said, "May I?" Catherine nodded as Lilith took Catherine's hands, and placed them on her daughter's belly.

Lilith showed Catherine where the back of the baby was positioned. She told her that the head was down. And then Catherine felt a kick.

Lilith said, "That's right, baby girl. This is your grandma." Lilith smiled.

But Catherine's smile was bigger. "That's amazing. I had forgotten how wonderful the kick feels. It's a miracle. Those little tiny feet are powerful."

Lilith heard, *Lilith, you can raise my baby.*

Shocked, Lilith said silently, *Give your mom a chance. This is a big adjustment.*

Lilith got up, and checked Jessica's neurological status, lungs, and heart. She checked the baby's heartbeat, and saw no contractions. The baby monitor added noise to the beeping monitors in the room.

Catherine looked up. "I haven't heard that monitor before. What is it?"

Lilith looked over at Catherine. "It's the heart beat of your granddaughter."

"How's she doing?" Catherine asked.

"She has a strong, healthy heart beat. She's doing just fine." Lilith smiled.

"I'm going to get some supplies. I'll be right back." Lilith left the room.

When Lilith returned she saw Catherine leaning in, holding Jessica's hand, and talking to her. Lilith felt a twinge of sadness as she remembered her mom, and thought of the loss facing Catherine.

Throughout the day Catherine and Lilith chatted and got to know each other. Lilith monitored Jessica and her baby. Catherine became more comfortable being around all of the monitoring equipment. She combed Jessica's curly, shiny red hair.

"I love these curls. Jessica straightens her hair to go to work or out with friends. I love it when she's home, and lets her hair be curly." Catherine brushed a curl away from her daughter's closed eye.

Catherine asked, "Does your mom live in town?"

Lilith's breath caught as she responded, "No, she passed away ten years ago."

"I'm so sorry. Was it an expected death? I hope you don't mind me asking," Catherine said.

"No, it's OK. And no, it wasn't expected. She had a situation like Jessica's. We didn't even know she had an aneurysm. It happened very fast. I miss her terribly." Tears leaked from Lilith's eyes.

Catherine approached Lilith, and gave her a hug. "I'm so sorry for your loss."

Lilith hugged her tightly. "And I'm so sorry for yours."

Just then the baby monitor started beeping an alarm. Lilith went to the monitor and saw that Jessica was having contractions. The baby's heart rate elevated with the contractions, but recovered nicely.

Catherine asked, "What's wrong?"

Lilith had a buzz in her ears and heard, *Is my baby OK?*

Lilith said, "Jessica is having contractions. I need to check her, see if she is dilated, and if her membranes are intact."

Catherine asked, "What do you mean?"

Lilith said, "I need to see if her water has broken. That's the birth sac around the baby inside the uterus."

"Oh, that's right." Catherine looked down at her daughter and cried. "I have to say good-bye to my daughter."

"Yes, I'm afraid you do. Her water has broken, and the contractions are getting stronger. The baby's heart rate is now decreasing with these contractions. I need to call the team so we can do an emergency C-section," Lilith said with softness as she touched Catherine's shoulder and then left the room.

Lilith heard, *Save my baby!*

We will, Lilith answered.

Lilith called the obstetric team to prepare for their arrival, and also called the chaplain to come and be with Catherine. Catherine kissed her daughter on the forehead, and gently stroked the belly which held her granddaughter. One of Lilith's coworkers, Jeff, helped Lilith move Jessica's bed, and the monitoring devices to the operating room for the C-section.

Jessica's belly was prepped for surgery, the doctor performed a C-section, and a baby girl was delivered. She was cleaned, assessed, and weighed. She weighed six pounds. She was wrapped, and kept under the warming lights. Jessica's blood pressure was dropping, and her heart rate was rapid. She remained unresponsive, with fixed and dilated pupils.

One of the obstetrical nurses stepped outside the room, and spoke to a waiting Lilith. She told her it was time to get Jessica's mom. Lilith went to the waiting room to get Catherine.

When Catherine saw Lilith she said, "How's the baby?"

Lilith answered, "She's beautiful, and waiting to see you."

"And Jessica?" Catherine asked with tears welling in her eyes.

"It's time to say good-bye." Lilith put out her arms, and Catherine fell into her embrace.

They walked arm in arm to the operating room. As they entered, the operating staff stepped aside for Catherine to come near her daughter. Jessica was covered in clean linen and warm blankets. The monitor showed a now slow heart rate and low blood pressure. Fluid was being pumped into her veins, but her blood pressure continued to drop.

Catherine approached Jessica, and picked up her hand. "Sweetie, I love you so much. I'm going to miss you. We'll take good care of your baby."

Lilith's ears buzzed and she heard, *I love you, Mom. You and Lilith take good care of my baby. I'll be watching out for all of you.*

Be at peace, Jessica. We'll take good care of your baby, Lilith responded silently.

Just then, the monitor showed a slowing heart rate, and then a straight line. Catherine hugged her daughter, and cried. Through her sobbing she heard a small cry. She raised her head, and saw the isolette in the corner of the room. Lilith took Catherine's hand, and walked her over to the baby.

"Catherine, this is your granddaughter," Lilith said.

Lilith lifted the wrapped baby girl up out of the isolette, and handed her to Catherine. Catherine tenderly carried her over to Jessica.

"Honey, she is beautiful. You did a good job. I'll love her as I love you. And she'll be called Jessica after her brave Mom." Catherine kissed the infant's head.

Lilith helped take little Jessica to the nursery. She showed Catherine to a room near the nursery where she could stay while the baby was in the hospital. The two women stood side by side looking at the sleeping baby.

"I have to go home now. I'll come back in the morning," Lilith said with eyes still on little Jessica.

Catherine placed a hand on Lilith's. "I look forward to seeing you tomorrow. We have a lot to talk about."

Lilith hugged Catherine and said, "I know. You take care. I'm so sorry for the loss of your daughter. The chaplain is still waiting outside. She'll be with you as long as you need her."

Lilith went back to the ICU to finish charting, and get ready to return home. She stopped by the chapel on her way down the hall.

Lilith knelt in prayer. She said silently, *Lord, bless dear Jessica. May her soul rest in peace knowing that her daughter will be well cared for and loved. Bless Catherine and comfort her in her pain. And bless little Jessica. May she grow strong and healthy and feel the love all around her. Thank you, Lord, that I was able to be a part of this journey. Please guide me as I think about little Jessica. In the name of the Father, the Son, and the Holy Spirit. Amen.*

Lilith rose slowly, went to her car, and drove home. She entered her house, and Christmas met her at the door. She scooped him up, and placed him on her shoulder. He gladly snuggled against her neck. Lilith saw her answering machine light blinking.

She touched the button and heard, "Hi Lilith. This is Roy. I" She hit the delete button without letting the message finish. She wasn't really mad at Roy, just not sure how she felt about continuing a relationship with him.

Lilith poured herself a glass of wine, and carried it into the bathroom. She set Christmas on the counter. She filled the tub with warm water and bubbles. After undressing and sinking under the warm bubbles, she started to relax. Christmas settled along the edge of the bathtub, batting at the bubbles.

Lilith's ears buzzed. *You did a great job today. We're proud of you, and send you love. You have exciting things ahead.*

Lilith answered, *Thanks, I love you too. Yes, lots to think about.*

Christmas looked up as if he heard her angels too, and he answered, "Meow."

Lilith smiled at Christmas. "You heard them too, didn't you, boy?"

Roy had slept fitfully. He rose early, and looked out at the snowy mountains as he drank his second cup of coffee. Lilith had not answered his calls. He had called her twice. She always returned his calls.

He thought to himself, *Maybe she is upset with me. Maybe we don't know each other as well as we thought.*

He went for a walk around the ranch. When he returned, he kicked the snow from his boots, and entered the house. The boys were up, and had made breakfast. It smelled great. There were pancakes, eggs, bacon, and freshly squeezed orange juice.

"Wow!" Roy exclaimed.

"We thought we would spoil you for a change. You always spoil us, and probably don't get enough thanks," Clark said.

"We do appreciate all you do for us," Steven added.

Roy, Clark, and Steven filled their plates. They sat down at the table and ate in silence.

"What do you want to do today?" Roy asked as he stared out the window.

"You OK, Uncle Roy?" Steven asked.

"Yeah. Well, I haven't heard from Lilith," Roy said. "I've called her twice."

"She's probably still pissed," Clark said.

"No, she wasn't mad. She said, she was sorry it didn't work out," Roy explained.

"That the holiday didn't work out, or that you guys didn't work out?" Steven asked.

"Oh, I'm sure she meant the holiday," Roy said, looking away, and rubbing his brow.

"Uncle, do you really like this lady?" Clark asked.

In surprise, Roy said, "Yes. I think I love her."

"Then you need to go to her. We could go too. We need to see if she's good enough for you." Steven laughed and Clark added, "Let's bring her dinner."

Lilith awoke and stretched. Christmas stood up from where he had been curled up next to her side. He stretched, and then came to stand on top of her chest, looking down into her face.

"So, are you hungry, boy?" Lilith asked.

"Meow," Christmas answered.

After feeding Christmas, eating breakfast, and dressing in some jeans and a sweater, Lilith headed for the hospital to see Catherine and little Jessica. It was a nice way to spend her day off. She was anxious to see them. She knew Catherine wanted to talk with her about the baby. Lilith thought it was just going to be a matter of time before Catherine realized she could raise her granddaughter herself. Lilith's mind was whirling.

Lilith entered the nursery. She found Catherine holding little Jessica, and feeding her from a bottle. She looked up, and smiled at Lilith.

"She's a good eater. I've already changed a wet, and a poopy diaper," Catherine announced with pride.

"Good for you. You look like a natural." Lilith pulled up a chair, and sat down next to Catherine.

"Would you like to hold her?" Catherine took the now empty bottle from little Jessica, and handed the baby to Lilith.

Lilith took little Jessica. She placed her across her shoulder and gently patted her back. The baby let out a burp. Laughing, Lilith said, "She's doing very well."

Lilith closed her eyes, and breathed in the baby smell. She felt the warm snuggly body against her. It felt like heaven.

"Lilith, you're a natural. Little Jessica deserves to have a young mom. But I still want to be her grandma. Will you think about it, please?" Catherine touched Lilith's arm tenderly.

Lilith sighed. "Catherine, you can do this. It will take some getting use to, but you can be everything little Jessica needs."

Catherine leaned in close to Lilith, and squeezed her arm. "Lilith, you should be little Jessica's mom. I want to be the best grandma ever! Please, think about it!"

Lilith returned home exhausted. Her days had been charged with emotion. She decided to go for a walk around the lake. The fresh air felt good, and she picked up her stride. A few times around the lake, and she was feeling better. She headed home. She had so much to think about. When she got inside her house she showered, and changed clothes.

Lilith put on some country music. She scooped up Christmas, and danced around the house with him. "What should we make for dinner?"

Just then, the doorbell rang. Lilith went over to the door, and looked through the peep hole. It was Roy. She looked at Christmas and frowned.

She whispered to Christmas, "What's he doing here?"

Christmas hissed.

Lilith looked through the peep hole again and said to herself, *How would you know that I was home!*

Then she heard, "Lilith, I know you are there. Remember I can hear thoughts you direct to me. I took a chance that you would be home; otherwise I would have waited until you got off work. Please let me talk to you. I made a mistake," Roy pleaded.

Roy looked over at his car where Clark and Steven sat watching. He shrugged his shoulders, and put up his arms in defeat. The boys quickly climbed out of the car, and joined their Uncle on Lilith's porch.

Lilith was embarrassed at her behavior. She opened the door just as two young men joined Roy. She said, "Hi Roy. This is a surprise."

With a smile Roy said, "Hi Lilith. I want you to meet my nephews."

"Hi, I'm Clark. Nice to meet you, Lilith," Clark shook Lilith's hand.

Next Steven stepped forward, and said as he extended his hand to Lilith, "Hi, I'm Steven. It's nice to meet you."

Clark and Steven held up two baskets. "We brought dinner," Steven said.

Lilith invited them into her house. She looked up into Roy's sad eyes, and said silently, *We have a lot to talk about!*

Roy nodded as he gently took her hand, and kissed her check. "I brought presents."

Choices and Compromises

ONCE ROY AND HIS NEPHEWS WERE seated in Lilith's house with drinks in hand, she excused herself to the bedroom, and changed into a more festive outfit. Viewing herself in the mirror, she saw a change, a confidence. She felt sure of herself and her goals. But she wondered how the lovely man in the next room would fit with her now.

When Lilith came out of her bedroom she saw Christmas peeking into the baskets of food the boys had set on the counter.

"Christmas, you must smell something delicious!" she said with a smile as she set the kitten down on the floor.

Lilith took out plates and Roy joined her setting the table. He touched her waist as he passed behind her, and she felt the familiar warmth.

Her ears buzzed, and she said silently to her angels, *This will be tough.*

The four filled their plates with delicious ham, smoked turkey, cheesy potatoes, green beans, and salad. Lilith had taken some dinner rolls from the freezer and had heated them in the microwave. They all sat in silence as Roy said a blessing, and then they started eating. Lilith asked the boys about their vacation in Hawaii, and what they did over Christmas. Roy talked about working on his book, and Lilith shared some of the busy times at work and how Christmas had joined her family.

After dessert, the boys said they wanted to go into town and ice skate. Both Lilith and Roy knew it was a ploy to leave them together for a while.

Clark asked, "We'll be back in a couple of hours. Is that OK?" He gave a wink to Roy.

Roy smiled. "Sure. Why don't you call when you get close, and I'll meet you outside."

Steven chimed in, "Great. And Lilith, it was great meeting you."

Lilith hugged the boys, "It was great meeting you both, too. And thanks for bringing the delicious food."

The door closed, and Roy and Lilith faced each other, an uneasiness passed between them.

"I'll just box up the leftovers for you, and put the dishes in the sink to soak. Would you like a glass of wine?" Lilith said as she turned to hurry into the kitchen.

Roy reached out, took Lilith by the shoulders, and stopped her. He gently turned her to face him. "I'm so sorry for how I handled our Christmas plans. I really messed up. Can you forgive me, and give me another chance?" Roy looked deep into Lilith's eyes searching for hope.

Lilith relaxed in his grasp, and smiled up into his sad eyes. "I've forgiven you. I know that your boys are your priority. Staying home and working during the holiday has given me time to look at my life, and realize what is really important to me." Lilith took Roy's hand and led him to the couch. "Let's sit down. The food can wait for a while." Roy followed Lilith, and they sat down together. Lilith began, "I want to tell you about a patient I took care of in the ICU." Lilith described the situation with Jessica, the bonding with Catherine, the birth of little Jessica, and the death of mom Jessica.

Roy sat back against the couch, and let out a big sigh. "That must have been terrible. I can't even imagine. How is, uh, Catherine doing, and the baby?"

Lilith answered, "Catherine's grief is eased by her sitting, watching, and caring for little Jessica." Lilith sighed, "There's more."

Roy looked at Lilith, "Go on, I'm listening."

Lilith began again, "Jessica, the mom, asked me before she died and when she was in a coma, if I would adopt her baby. Catherine wants to be a grandmother. She feels too old to be a mother so she also wants me to adopt little Jessica." Lilith paused, and waited for Roy to absorb what she'd said.

Roy shook his head. "I know how close you get with your patients and their families, but it isn't your responsibility to adopt the baby. You said you wanted children of your own." Roy looked questioningly at Lilith.

Lilith began, "I do want to have children of my own, but I am strongly drawn to this baby and family. I'm considering the adoption." Lilith felt relieved that she had spoken the words, and realized that she wasn't just considering; she'd made her decision.

Roy sat forward then back, and held his head in both his hands. "Wow. A lot has happened while we've been apart. I was just coming around to the idea of having a baby with you, but adopting too? Wow!" Roy paused a moment, took in a slow breath, and let it out. "Please don't take this the wrong way, but aren't you being impulsive?" Roy asked.

Lilith's skin flushed red, and her anger boiled to the surface. She shot a look at Roy that was thick with emotion, and sliced through the silence. Roy grabbed for Lilith's hand, but she pulled away, and started to rise from the couch. Roy grabbed her hand again, and pulled her into his lap. She fought briefly, and then the two held each other and cried.

With tears of sadness wetting her face, Lilith said, "I believe I do love you, Roy, but I have dreams that don't seem to work with you."

Roy touched Lilith's cheek. "I do love you, Lilith, but I don't know if I am ready for this. I don't want to lose you, but I need some time to think."

Lilith replied, "I appreciate your honesty. I'm going to talk with Catherine tomorrow, and make a decision."

Roy said, "I'm going to help you clean up, and wait for the boys to return. I hope we can talk in a week or two. The boys go back to school the middle of January."

Roy and Lilith rose, and went into the kitchen. Lilith rinsed the plates, glasses, and silverware, and placed them in the dishwasher. The task was a partial relief from the tension.

Roy asked, "Would you like to keep some of the food?"

Lilith replied, "Thanks, but I have some leftovers I need to eat up. You take them home. I'm sure your nephews would love the food." She tried a smile.

Roy took Lilith in his arms. "Lilith, this is not how I wanted this evening to play out."

Lilith looked up at Roy. "I know. Life is more complicated than I ever dreamed when I was younger. There are so many variables, and so many other people who have to be considered."

Roy shook his head, and waved his hands in the air. "Lilith, don't give up on me. Please give me time, even if you are making big decisions for yourself. Please don't shut the door on me."

"I won't. I'll keep in touch," Lilith promised.

Roy kissed Lilith with a sweetness of goodbye, and an urgency and panic of loss. He had so much longing, and desire for Lilith. Lilith returned Roy's kiss with the sadness of "what-ifs", and hopes of things unimagined. Roy's phone rang. It was the boys. They were waiting outside. Roy hugged Lilith one last time. He quietly gathered the baskets, and closed the door as he left.

As Roy joined his nephews, they excitedly asked if he was back in Lilith's good graces. Roy replied, "I don't know how this is going to work out. She has some wild ideas about how she wants her life. I just don't know. It's so complicated. My head hurts." Roy climbed into the car, and rubbed his temple.

Lilith plopped down on the couch, tears near the surface, but she was too tired to let them fall. Christmas joined her, and the two hugged. Lilith stroked his soft fur as he purred contently, curled up in her lap. She noticed the unopened presents under the tree. She would send the boys theirs, but Roy's would have to be a "wait and see". She wondered what Roy had brought for her. But she didn't want to open it, and find out.

As the distant church bell rang at 11 p.m., Lilith and Christmas got up, and went to bed. Lilith slept fitfully. In the morning she rose, dressed, fed Christmas, ate her oatmeal, and headed for the hospital to see Catherine and baby Jessica.

Moving Forward

❧❖❧

LILITH SAT NEXT TO CATHERINE AS she rocked baby Jessica. There was a warmth and comfort that passed between the two women.

"Have you made a decision, Lilith?" Catherine smiled hopefully.

"I want to be sure you know what you're asking of me." Lilith turned her chair to face Catherine.

Catherine gently passed the sleeping Jessica to Lilith. Lilith leaned back in the chair and rocked. "Now, that's a picture of a mom and child," Catherine said as she clapped her hands together and smiled through tears.

Lilith looked deep into Catherine's eyes. "Are you sure?"

"I'm so very sure." Catherine hugged Lilith and Jessica.

Lilith heard a buzz in her ears. She heard, *You are a family.*

Lilith answered back silently as her eyes filled with tears, *I know.*

Jessica remained in the hospital for two more days. Lilith took twelve weeks of maternity leave, turned one guest room into a nursery, got supplies, and set up her other guest room for Catherine.

Catherine planned to move to Denver to be near her granddaughter. She happily accepted Lilith's invitation to stay with her until she found a place to live nearby. She offered to babysit Jessica when Lilith worked.

Lilith and Catherine brought Jessica home on a beautiful, sunny, crisp, cool day in January. The roads and sidewalks were cleared of snow. It was a safe passage home. As they turned the corner to Lilith's street, they saw a crowd in front of the house. Several of Lilith's friends including Michele and one of Catherine's from Florida had come with baskets of food, and presents to welcome the new family home. It was a wonderful celebration that Jessica slept peacefully through. The friends quietly peeked at the sleeping angel in the bassinette.

It took a couple of weeks to draw up the papers, and go to court to make the adoption legal. Lilith adopted Jessica Lily Montgomery as her daughter. Catherine, Lilith, and Jessica Lily had a celebratory lunch.

The new family was transitioning well. Lilith, who had always lived by herself, now had a baby, and the grandmother living with her. But things were running smoothly. Both women respected each other's privacy, and loved doting on little Jessica Lily. Lilith found she wasn't always at her best behavior when sleep deprived. Catherine intuitively understood, and swept Jessica Lily away so that Lilith could rest. It was a great arrangement, and a growing friendship.

Lilith could not believe the love she felt in her heart for this little baby girl. One day she sat in the rocking chair watching Jessica Lily sleep. She loved her baby smell, the soft rhythm of her breathing, and the sweet noises she made.

Her ears buzzed and she heard, *She is so beautiful.*

Lilith asked out loud, "Is that you, Jessica?"

She heard, *Yes, I came to see my baby girl. I'm so glad you adopted her, and welcomed Mom into your life.*

Lilith answered out loud, "You have a great mom and she's a wonderful grandmother."

Lilith heard, *Please tell her I love and miss her.*

The door opened quietly, and Catherine peeked in. "I heard voices so I thought Jessica Lily was awake." Catherine joined Lilith as they stared down at the sleeping baby. "What an angel!" Catherine sighed. "I feel so close to my daughter when I'm with her baby. Sometimes I feel my daughter is right here."

Lilith heard, *Lilith, tell her I'm here. She'll understand. She believes in spirits.*

Lilith answered silently, *I'll try.*

Before Lilith could speak, Catherine said, "Lilith, do you believe that people who have died can come back, and watch over their loved ones?"

Lilith let out a slow breath. "Yes, I do." Lilith took Catherine's hand. "Catherine, I have the gift of clairaudience."

Catherine interrupted, "I've heard of that. Let's see, that's where you can hear spirits, and talk to them. Is that right?"

Lilith began again, "Yes; that's right. I can talk with those who have died, and also talk with them when they are in a coma."

Catherine spoke louder than she meant to, "Does that mean you have spoken to my daughter? Did you talk to her before she died?" Catherine started to cry.

"Catherine, I didn't mean to upset you." Lilith squeezed Catherine's hand.

"No, no, you didn't upset me. I just have so much I want to say to Jessica." Catherine wiped her tears.

"She's with us now, and can hear all that you are saying. She wants you to know that she loves and misses you," Lilith said.

"Oh, Jessica! I love you so much. You should be here with your baby. I'm so sorry." Catherine cried.

Lilith heard, *Tell Mom that I'm in a good place. Little Jessica Lily is right where she belongs, with the two of you.*

Lilith told Catherine what Jessica had said, and she spent almost an hour sharing Jessica's words with her. Baby Jessica Lily started to stir in her bassinette. It was time for a diaper change and feeding.

Lilith heard, *Give our baby a kiss from me.*

Lilith answered out loud, "We will. Love you, Jessica. We'll tell your baby about you, and give her your love." Lilith wiped a tear from her cheek as she leaned down, and picked up the child they all loved.

The next day, Lilith saw Catherine in the living room rocking Jessica Lily and crying. She quietly went into her bedroom and closed the door. She suspected that Catherine was thinking of her daughter.

Lilith heard the baby monitor turn on and knew that Catherine had put Jessica Lily down for a nap. She came out of her room, and saw Catherine in the kitchen.

Lilith walked into the kitchen, and stood close to Catherine and said, "You OK?"

Catherine turned to look at Lilith as she wiped tears from her red eyes. "I'm just missing Jessica. She should be here with her baby."

Lilith hugged Catherine as tears rolled down her checks. Catherine pushed away and looked at Lilith. She said, "Please know, I'm so grateful that Jessica Lily is with you."

Lilith said, "You don't have to explain. It's OK."

The weeks flew by, and one morning Lilith remembered that Roy's nephews were probably back at school. She hadn't spoken to Roy since he'd left her house; it had been a night of gut-wrenching honesty. She wondered what he was thinking and feeling.

Jessica Lily stirred in her arms. Lilith nuzzled into the soft red curls, and breathed in the beautiful baby smell. She gently placed Jessica into the bassinette. She closed the nursery door, and went into her bedroom. After turning on the baby monitor she reached for her phone.

Lilith dialed Roy's number and waited. Roy, who was reading, reached for his ringing phone. "Hello?" Roy answered.

"Roy, it's Lilith. How are you?" Lilith asked hesitantly.

Surprised, Roy said, "Oh, hi Lilith. I'm fine. How are you?"

"I'm very well, thank you." Lilith was embarrassed that they were so awkward with each other. Forgetting about Roy's gift of telepathy, Lilith thought to herself, *What a shame we are so uncomfortable with each other.*

Roy said, "I don't want to be uncomfortable with you, Lilith."

Embarrassed again, and realizing that Roy had heard her thoughts, she said, "Roy, I don't want to be uncomfortable with you either."

Roy said, "Let me start again. Hi, Lilith, tell me about your new baby."

Surprised and pleased, Lilith said, "She's beautiful. Her name is Jessica Lily Montgomery. Catherine is staying with me until she finds a place of her own. We're both enjoying spoiling her. I took twelve weeks off from work to get to know little Jessica Lily. It's amazing, Roy." Lilith realized that she was talking very fast. "Sorry for blurting so much out. I'm just so excited."

"I can hear it in your voice. I'm so happy for you. Well, I've to get back to work. It was nice talking with you, Lilith," Roy said.

"Please call me sometime. I want to hear about you. Bye for now." Lilith hung up the phone.

Lilith sat in silence. She thought about how her relationship with Roy had changed. She was sad, but her love and priority was Jessica Lily. If Roy didn't want to be a part of her life now, then it wasn't meant to be. She heard Jessica Lily cooing on the monitor. She shook off the sadness of Roy, skipped out of her room, and went to embrace her daughter.

Roy sat back hard in his chair. He didn't really have to get back to work. The staff were busy with the guests, checking them in for the hunting season. He just didn't have anything else to say to Lilith. He wondered why the two women in his life both took directions away from him. How could he have been so wrong about Lilith, and Jane, his former fiancée? Lilith just went boldly on with her life.

Roy said out loud, "That really pisses me off." He let out an angry sigh. "She's impulsive and irrational. She has no idea what she is getting herself into." He threw his arms up in the air as he stood. "Well, good luck, and good riddance!"

Roy grabbed his coat and headed for the stable. He saddled his favorite horse, Warrior, and took off on a ride. Warrior sensed Roy's mood, and moved quickly down the road, and up the mountain as if man and horse shared the same urgency. Roy remembered his nephews' surprise at Lilith wanting to adopt her patient's baby. They seemed to understand his feelings of hurt, and insignificance when Lilith was making big decisions without him. Roy squeezed his legs around Warrior, and they continued at a gallop. When they reached the clearing, Roy pulled Warrior to a stop on the hill that overlooked the property. He and Warrior were both breathing heavily.

He patted the damp softness of Warrior's neck and said, "Sorry boy, I was upset. It didn't have anything to do with you. I'm sorry I rode you so hard up the hill."

Roy found he was weeping. He wondered how things had changed so fast with Lilith. He wiped his tears with the back of his glove.

Looking up at the sky, he yelled, "I love her, and I miss her. What am I supposed to do now?"

When no answer came, he turned Warrior toward home, and they slowly walked as Roy tried to clear his thoughts. He welcomed the busy hunting season. It would distract him. Fresh air, tracking, and hunting would bring him back to his reality.

The twelve weeks had flown by, and Lilith was not ready to leave Jessica Lily, and go back to work. Jessica had grown so much. She was sleeping and eating well. The days were still cold so they had to bundle up even for short walks around the neighborhood. The movement of the stroller would put Jessica to sleep. Christmas liked walking with them.

Christmas had been curious about baby Jessica Lily when she came home. He would climb in the bassinette when the baby was out of it for changing and feeding. He would follow Lilith and Catherine around. He seemed very happy with the growing family.

Catherine had found a condo a half-mile from Lilith's house. She could easily walk over to visit, and play with Jessica Lily. She babysat when Lilith ran errands, or went for a run.

Lilith looked out the window as the sun melted snow from the sidewalk. She rubbed her hands, not because they were cold, but because she was anxious.

She thought to herself, *How can I leave Jessica Lily?*

Her ears buzzed, *She will be looked after.*

Catherine noticed Lilith by the window, and joined her. "I know this is hard. I remember having to leave my daughter to go back to work. I'll take good care of her. You need to go back to some of the things in your life. What about that nice man you told me about?"

Taken by surprise that Catherine had remembered, Lilith said, "Oh, Roy. I haven't talked with him in a couple of months. I don't think there's anything for us to talk about. He didn't want a family, and was less than supportive of my adopting Jessica Lily. He's just a nice memory."

"I can tell you cared about him," Catherine added.

Lilith sighed, "Yes, I cared very much for him."

Catherine put her arm around Lilith's shoulder, and squeezed. "Your patients will be glad to have you back at work."

Lilith leaned into Catherine. "I'm so lucky you're here. What would I do without you?"

Catherine smiled. "I'm the lucky one."

That night, Lilith rocked Jessica Lily to sleep, and told her in whispers that she'd miss her when she went to work. Catherine was in the guest room, and she would be available if Jessica Lily woke in the night. Lilith needed to sleep before going into work.

Lilith stretched and rose after her alarm clock sounded. She peeked into Jessica Lily's room, and saw she was still sleeping. She blew her a kiss, and quietly closed the door. After dressing, feeding

Christmas, and eating a bowl of oatmeal, Lilith headed out the door to work.

It was a busy day. It felt good to return to the work that she loved. Her patients in body, and spirit were glad she was there. Lilith called home only three times to check on her baby. As she drove home she thought of Roy. She sent him wishes of happiness.

It had been two months since Roy had talked to Lilith. He thought that she was probably back at work. He sat in semi-darkness, inside the glow from his desk lamp. The ranch was full of hunters. He was getting a lot of exercise outside, and eating well. But his evenings and nights were lonely. He was trying to work on his book, but he just wasn't motivated.

He said aloud to the darkness, "I'd like to hear her voice. I wonder if she's thinking of me. But, what would be the point?" He turned off his light, and went to bed.

The end of March brought occasional days of warmth, and a hint of spring. Lilith, Catherine, and a sleeping Jessica Lily in the stroller had just entered the house after a walk. Lilith was unstrapping Jessica when the phone rang.

Catherine said, "I'll get the phone."

She reached for Lilith's phone and said, "Hello?" Then Catherine said, "Yes, I'll see if she can come to the phone."

Lilith looked up as Catherine whispered, "It's Roy. Do you want to take it?"

Lilith nodded as she took the sleeping baby to the nursery, and placed her in the crib. Jessica Lily had outgrown the bassinette, and was sleeping in her crib now. Lilith turned on her lullaby music, and tiptoed out of the room.

Picking up the phone, and raising her brow at Catherine, Lilith went into her room and closed the door. She sat on her bed to answer the call. "Hello?"

"Lilith, it's Roy. How are you?" Roy said hesitantly.

"I'm fine. How are you?" Lilith responded, frowning at herself in the mirror.

"It's a busy hunting season. The guests are happy, the weather has been great, and blah, blah, blah." Roy paused and then said, "I'm not great. I miss you."

Surprised, Lilith was silent for a moment and then said, "I've missed you, too."

Roy was silent, but Lilith could hear his breathing. He then said, "Would you like to go out Saturday night? I could come up, and take you to dinner!"

Surprised again, Lilith answered, "I'll have to check with Catherine. Can I give you a call back?"

Roy responded, "Sure. I have to go now. I'll talk to you soon. Bye, Lilith."

"Thanks for calling. Bye, Roy." Lilith hung up the phone.

Lilith took a slow breath in, and let it out. She looked again at her perplexed reflection in the mirror. The phone call was a surprise. Her heart was pounding, but she wasn't sure what she was feeling.

Lilith's ears buzzed and she heard, *Trust your heart.*

Lilith answered back silently, *Oh boy, I don't know what to do.*

Lilith heard, *You will know.*

Lilith sighed deeply. She slowly got up, and went out into the living room. Catherine was reading a book by the window, and looked up as Lilith approached. She patted the cushion next to her. Lilith sat down with a thud.

"You OK?" Catherine asked.

Lilith sighed. "I don't know what I am."

"What did he say?" Catherine inquired.

"He asked me out for dinner Saturday night," Lilith answered.

"That's good, isn't it?" Catherine asked.

Lilith took some more deep breaths in and out. "I don't know. Just when I get used to the idea that we're over, he appears."

"He must still care about you," Catherine added.

Lilith looked out the window. "We both care about each other. But I don't think we want the same things in life."

Catherine touched Lilith's hand. "Well, he seems to be reaching out to you."

Lilith squeezed Catherine's hand. "Perhaps. I know we should talk. Are you available to babysit on Saturday?"

"Of course," Catherine responded excitedly.

The next day Lilith phoned Roy, and told him she could go out with him. They decided to meet at a restaurant south of Denver so Roy didn't have to drive in so far. Lilith didn't want him coming to the house, at least not until she knew what was happening between them.

The days were busy with work, and playing with Jessica Lily. Then it was Saturday. Lilith was surprised that she was nervous. Catherine walked by her room, and saw her looking at various dresses.

"Need some help?" Catherine smiled.

Lilith looked up at Catherine, and gave a grateful smile. "Yes!" Lilith turned back to the dresses. "I'm acting like a school girl. I don't know what to wear."

Looking at the dresses on the bed, Catherine offered, "Well, they're all pretty. What kind of message do you want to give?"

Lilith laughed, "Message? Well, how about – yes, I'm a mom, but I'm still hot!"

Catherine laughed hard holding her belly. "How about pants, a flirty top, and heels?"

Lilith smiled and said, "You're good at this."

Catherine answered, "Well, thank you. But seriously, I just want you to have some fun. Just because you're a mom now, doesn't mean you can't have a life."

Lilith hugged Catherine. "You're the best." And Catherine hugged her back.

Roy was rushing through his day so he could shower, and get ready. He was glad that Lilith had agreed to go out, but he was nervous about the evening. He wondered if she still felt the same about him, and wondered if he still felt the same way about her.

Lilith and Roy met in the lobby of the remodeled Grand Hotel with its authentic southwestern dining. Roy had arrived first, and was pacing. He looked up, and saw Lilith enter. He watched her as she glanced around the lobby looking for him. When their eyes met they both smiled. There was a noticeable relaxing of shoulders, and breathing for both of them. They approached each other, and Roy kissed her cheek. He breathed in the smell of her, and his body flushed warm. Lilith smelled his familiar smell too and smiled.

Looking up into Roy's eyes she said, "Nice to see you, Roy. I'm glad you suggested we get together."

Roy smiled. "I'm glad you agreed to meet me. Why don't we see if the restaurant is ready to seat us?" He put his hand out, and Lilith accepted it. They strolled into the restaurant.

The restaurant was dimly lit with candles and lamplight that warmed the burgundy, brown, and bronze colors of the room. Lilith and Roy were shown to a table in a quiet corner upstairs that overlooked a dance floor and stage where musicians were tuning their instruments. The band wore cowboy boots and hats.

Roy asked, "Would you like a glass of wine?"

Lilith thought a moment and answered, "I'd like a mimosa, please."

When the waiter came, Roy ordered the drinks. Lilith and Roy sat silently studying their menus, and were ready to order when the waiter arrived with their drinks. Lilith ordered a Caesar salad with smoked salmon, and Roy ordered a Caesar with braised steak. They laughed at the similarities of their orders.

While waiting for their food, they chatted. Roy told a funny story about one of the hunting trips where an inexperienced hunter got so excited when he saw his buck that he backed up, falling into the brush, and scaring the buck off to safety. Lilith enjoyed the ease Roy showed as he laughed, telling the story. She laughed right along with him.

Lilith told Roy about one of her young patients who was gravely ill, and how hard they all worked to save him. Finally the patient responded to treatment and his prognosis improved. She sighed deeply showing the stress and relief she felt, and Roy reached over, and squeezed her hand.

Lilith said silently, *This is nice being together.*

Roy heard her thought and smiled. "Yes, this is nice." Lilith squeezed his hand and smiled up into his face.

When their food arrived the band started playing. The music, which was loud, was country rock. Both Roy and Lilith found it hard to hear each other so they listened to the music and ate. They stole looks at each other, smiled, and sometimes laughed. They both felt the tension easing between them.

As the waiter cleared their empty plates, Roy stood and put out his hand to Lilith. He motioned toward the dance floor. She nodded, rose, and took his hand. They walked down to the floor as the band was finishing one number, and beginning another. It was a slow waltz. Roy took Lilith into his arms, and waltzed her around the dance floor. She found that she was leaning into him, breathing in his familiar smells of horse, aftershave, and man.

Roy felt the warmth of her now against him, and found he was blissfully happy.

They danced through three songs, and then climbed the stairs hand in hand to sit at their table. The band took a break, leaving them sitting in quiet.

Roy looked at Lilith. "Lilith, there's so much I want to tell you about myself, and what I've been going through, but for tonight I just want to be together. Can we go out again sometime to a quiet place and talk?"

Lilith smiled, and gave a sigh of relief. "I agree. This is really nice being together. Yes, I would like to go out another time, and we can talk."

They danced a few more times, and then Roy walked Lilith to her car. At her car she turned to him, and he lightly kissed her lips. Lilith leaned into him breathing in his energy. As she got in her car she felt a bit light-headed and flushed. Roy leaned through the open window and touched her check.

"Be careful driving home. I sure had fun tonight. I'll call you next week." Roy touched her blond curls before stepping away from the car.

"I had a great time too. I look forward to hearing from you. Goodnight." Lilith gave Roy a smile as she slowly drove out of the parking lot.

Lilith looked in her rearview mirror as her car started the turn onto the street toward home. She saw the warm smile of Roy as he waved. She wondered how he knew she would look back. She gave him a wave outside her window. Lilith smiled to herself thinking about their evening. She thought how good they were together, especially if they didn't talk about anything heavy. She really didn't want to think about the complications. She just wanted to feel the evening.

Roy felt a huge tug at his heart as Lilith drove away. He waved, hoping she would look back, and see him. He was elated when she waved back. He felt this was a good first step toward each other again.

When Lilith arrived home, her house was dark. She suspected Catherine had decided to go to bed, and not return to her place so late at night. After quietly letting herself in she saw a note on the dining room table confirming her thoughts. Catherine had also written that she hoped the evening went well, and added a big smiley face. Lilith smiled to herself as she went to check on her baby. She found Christmas curled up in the rocking chair next to Jessica Lily's crib. He looked up, and was about to meow when Lilith quickly picked him up. The two peeked at the beautiful sleeping baby girl.

Lilith whispered, "Hi, baby. Your mom had a good time tonight. We'll see."

Lilith's ears buzzed, and she heard love and encouragement from her angels.

Hugging Christmas she tiptoed to her room. She set Christmas down, undressed, washed her face, brushed her teeth, and went to bed. Lilith and Christmas fell fast asleep.

Lilith and Roy talked every week, and finally got together again in the middle of April. Roy was staying in a hotel in downtown Denver where he met with his editor. Lilith drove to the hotel to meet him. They sat in the hotel lounge at a booth in the far corner of the dimly lit room. It was very private, and almost empty, because it was the hour between lunch and dinner. They sat close to each other, and ordered coffee.

Roy took Lilith's hand in his and began. "I'm so glad to see you. I want to be brave and tell you about my feelings." Roy took in a deep slow breath, and let it out.

Lilith said silently, *You can tell me anything. I care very much for you.*

Hearing her thoughts, Roy smiled and continued, "I've had a lot of loss in my life. I lost my family, and then my job, and then my fiancée, who didn't want to come with me to the ranch." Roy paused as if reflecting, and began again as Lilith listened patiently. Roy looked deep into Lilith's eyes. "As you know, when I took on the responsibility of raising my nephews, they were my first priority. I came last. So I thought that once they were grown and took over the ranch, then I would be in control of my life. I realize that can be true to a point, especially if I want to remain single. But if I want to have a partner there has to be compromise with give and take. I'm embarrassed to say that I was angry that you had dreams different from my own." Roy looked away for a moment, and then looked back at Lilith as she softly squeezed his hands. "I was even angrier that you took the big step to adopt a baby."

Lilith was not surprised. She had been waiting for him to admit to his feelings. She was anxious to hear where they might go from here.

Roy, sensing her anxiety, pulled her close, and continued. "During our time apart, I realized that I was free to do anything in my life, but there would be no you. I want you in my life." Roy's eyes welled with tears.

Lilith took Roy's face in her hands, and wiped a tear that had escaped from his eye. "I come as a package now." Lilith looked up questioningly into Roy's face.

Roy hugged Lilith, and spoke into her ear. "I know. Will you let me try to be a part of your package?"

Lilith was touched by Roy's honesty, and told him so. She invited him over for the afternoon, and dinner the next Saturday. He said he could be there about 3 p.m. Lilith knew that would work out well, since Jessica Lily would be waking up from her nap.

Lilith and Roy talked every day or two until Saturday arrived. Lilith had prepared dinner while Jessica Lily was sleeping. The house was filled with wonderful smells. Catherine had stopped by to check on her favorite girls, and was helping Lilith tidy up the house.

"Do you want to stay for dinner?" Lilith asked Catherine.

"I don't think you need a buffer. You'll be fine. But I'll stay to briefly meet this mystery man. I want to see if I approve." Catherine laughed, and gave Lilith a hug.

The doorbell rang at 3 p.m. Lilith was getting Jessica Lily changed so Catherine answered the door.

Roy tried to hide his surprise at seeing a short, fine-boned woman with curly gray hair smiling at him. "Hi, I'm Roy. You must be Catherine." He extended his hand to Catherine.

Taking his hand, and giving it a hearty shake, Catherine answered, "Yes, I am. It's nice to finally meet you, Roy. I've heard a lot about you." She smiled, released his hand, and stepped aside to allow Roy to enter.

Lilith came into the room carrying her baby, and saw Roy. "Hi. I guess you met Catherine. And this is Jessica Lily." Lilith approached Roy, and gave him a kiss on the cheek.

"I'll head on home now," Catherine said, smiling as she stood behind Roy. She gave an approving nod to Lilith, and headed for the door.

"Thanks, Catherine, for all the help. I'll see you tomorrow," Lilith called out to her.

Roy turned and said, "Nice to meet you, Catherine."

Catherine answered, "Nice to meet you, too. You youngsters have fun." Catherine quietly shut the door behind her.

Lilith placed Jessica Lily in a swing in the living room.

Roy glanced around and saw the difference in Lilith's home. There were toys, and baby equipment all about. Furniture was moved back to allow for a quilt that was scattered with toys, and covering the soft rug.

Lilith noticed Roy looking around. "Place looks different, doesn't it?"

Roy answered, "Yes. I can see a family lives here."

Lilith asked, "Would you like some lemonade?"

"Yes, that would be nice," Roy answered.

Lilith stirred the dinner in the slow cooker, and checked the pie in the oven. After pouring a couple of glasses of lemonade, she handed one to Roy, and placed the other on the side table. Gathering Jessica Lily out of the swing, and picking up a toy set of keys, she joined Roy on the couch.

"Something smells delicious," Roy said.

"I hope you'll like it. I feed Jessica Lily at 5, so I thought we could eat at 5:30," Lilith said.

"Sounds great." Roy looked over at Jessica Lily. "Now, it's been a long time since I've been around babies. Tell me what to do."

"Just be yourself," Lilith responded.

Lilith sat back, and laid Jessica Lily on the couch between them. Lilith leaned down, and blew raspberry kisses on Jessica's belly which caused her to laugh. Lilith laughed, and did it again. Soon everyone was laughing. Jessica looked from Lilith to Roy.

Lilith said, "She hasn't heard a deep male voice, and she's curious."

Roy watched Lilith play with Jessica Lily. He could see the love between the two. He felt love like that with Clark and Steven. He found himself loving Lilith even more.

After a while Lilith rose from the couch with Jessica on her hip to check on dinner.

Roy asked, "Can I hold her?"

Surprised, Lilith answered, "Sure, but don't be offended if she cries. She is suspicious of new people." Lilith sat back down on the couch with Jessica Lily and leaned into Roy. "Baby, my special friend wants to hold you while I check on dinner." Lilith gave Roy the toy keys and he shook them. Jessica looked at the toy, and then at Roy.

"Come play with me a while." Roy put his arms out.

Lilith placed Jessica Lily in Roy's arms, and gave her raspberry kisses on her neck, making her laugh. Then she gave Roy raspberry kisses on his neck, surprising him and making him laugh. Jessica Lily started laughing again in response to Roy's laugh, and Lilith gave her more kisses. Lilith stood up as Roy was giving Jessica Lily kisses, and they were laughing together. Lilith checked on the dinner, and looked over at her baby and Roy laughing. It warmed her heart.

At dinner Jessica Lily managed to get most of her dinner in her mouth, and some on her clothes. She was very distracted by Roy. She kept turning her head to look at him. He was making funny faces at her. Then Jessica Lily played in her swing as Roy and Lilith ate. They chatted easily together.

Roy smiled and said, "This is the best stew I've ever had."

Lilith laughed. "I think you just worked up an appetite so anything would taste good."

Roy tossed a roll at Lilith and she caught it. "That's not true. You're a fabulous cook."

The evening was busy, and full of laughter. After dinner, Lilith and Roy gave Jessica Lily a bath, and Roy got all wet from the splashing water. After Jessica Lily was fast asleep in her crib, Roy and Lilith looked at the sleeping baby girl.

"She's beautiful, Lilith," Roy said. He watched the baby making cooing noises, opening and closing her little hands as she slept.

"I'm glad you got to meet her." Lilith put her hand on Roy's shoulder. The two walked out of the nursery, and quietly closed the door.

Roy put an arm around Lilith, and squeezed her to him. He then reached down, touched her check, leaned in, and kissed her lips. Their bodies turned toward each other as Roy moved her against the wall, and leaned into her. They were hungry for each other. Lilith put her arms around Roy's neck, and he lifted her up. She hugged his waist with her legs. Roy walked them into the bedroom as their lips were exploring each other's necks, ears, and mouths. Roy gently placed Lilith on the bed, and climbed in next to her. They began to love each other all over again.

The relationship blossomed as the spring flowers. They traveled back and forth to see each other, and had family outings which included Catherine and Jessica. In June, when the boys were back from school and working at the ranch, Lilith, Jessica Lily, and Catherine came out for a week. An August trip to the ranch included horseback riding. Jessica Lily sat in the saddle in front of her mom. Both Clark and Steven were warming to Lilith, Jessica Lily, and Catherine. They teased their uncle, and showed how happy they were for him.

Roy, Clark, Steven, Catherine, and Jessica Lily were all at Lilith's for Thanksgiving. Lilith was at work. Roy and Catherine did the cooking while Clark and Steven played with Jessica Lily. When Lilith returned home she found a house filled with the smells of turkey, gravy, potatoes, vegetables, and rolls. Roy and Catherine were in the kitchen and waved. Jessica Lily squealed when she saw her mom. She had already eaten, and was taking steps, holding onto the furniture between Clark and Steven.

Before eating dinner, the family held hands around the table to give thanks for the blessings in their lives. Roy spoke last and he squeezed Lilith's hand as he talked about family and the blessing of having Lilith, Jessica Lily, and Catherine in his family circle.

Roy got down on one knee and faced Lilith. "You and Jessica Lily are a blessing in my life. Will you marry me?"

Tears welled in Lilith's eyes. While holding Jessica Lily, Lilith got down on her knees and said, "We will!"

And the three hugged each other as Steven, Clark, and Catherine clapped. Roy opened a small velvet box. Lilith looked inside and saw a beautiful canary diamond.

"To match your curls," Roy said with a smile.

"It's beautiful," Lilith exclaimed. She and Jessica Lily hugged him tight.

At Christmas the whole family gathered at the ranch for the holidays, and a family wedding with friends. All enjoyed the fun, preparations, celebrations, and great love.

One Year Later

LILITH CLOSED HER EYES, AND TIPPED her face toward the warming sun. She breathed in the fresh morning air filled with pine, fresh snow, and baby. Her hand rested on the sleeping bundle in the snuggly carrier attached to her chest. Dipping her chin, she kissed the soft baby head. Baby John was named after Lilith's father.

She thought about how her life had changed. Yawning, she stretched. She felt the delicious tiredness of motherhood. Now she had her family, and happiness enveloped her.

Roy's voice interrupted Lilith's thoughts. "You tired, babe?" her love asked.

Lilith leaned into him as she touched the snuggly that held her sleeping baby John. She answered, "What new parents aren't?" She smiled up into Roy's beaming face as he kissed her.

Just then Lilith felt a tug at the back of her head. Her hand brushed, and caught the fingers playing in her blond curls.

Lilith looked back and said, "Someday, my darling, someone will play in your beautiful red curls." She smiled at little Jessica Lily who hung out over the child carrier on her dad's back.

Lilith leaned against Roy, and shut her eyes, basking in the warmth of the sun. It had been a long journey to get them to this point. Lilith remembered Roy's pleading after Christmas to give him another chance, and then his abrupt turn about when she told him she was going to adopt little Jessica Lily. It looked as if they were at an impasse. It took a year of back and forth to realize that they had enough love and understanding to weave their lives together. They became a family from which Roy could not stay away.

As he snuggled with his family, Roy also thought back to the past two years. Clark and Steven liked Lilith right away, and were supportive of his relationship with her. But when Lilith adopted Jessica Lily, he felt as if his feet had been kicked out from under him. He ran at first. He then thought of the things that brought them both together in the first place. Roy found that the emotions and back and forth of the relationship proved to be all worth the journey. He was building his family.

Their wedding took place at their favorite vantage point on the mountain overlooking the ranch. The wedding party and some close friends traveled, covered in blankets, in the wagon that took them up to the ceremonial spot. The wagon and the two horses' harnesses were decorated with white bows, bells, and flowers. It was not bitterly cold due to low clouds. Snow was lightly falling. Lilith and Jessica Lily both had long white velvet coats with hoods. It was a beautiful ceremony.

Little baby John was born ten months later. Jessica Lily embraced her new brother. She enjoyed singing and dancing for him. Between naps, John would try to focus on Jessica Lily as she twirled around the room.

Lilith and Roy looked out over the ranch from the spot that marked their beginning. Down below in a utility cart, Clark and Steven waved up at them. Christmas was sitting in Clark's lap with his paws on the steering wheel. Behind them in the back seat was Grandma Catherine, smiling and waving as she held on to the roll bar.

"We have a wonderful family. And I'm so proud of the boys, and how they have taken over the reins of the ranch." Roy smiled at his beautiful wife as he held onto Jessica Lily's swinging snow boots that were constantly dancing even in the child carrier.

"This is a beautiful place to raise our family." Lilith put her arm around her man, and felt the love of her family.

Lilith's ears buzzed with whispers, and she heard her angels, *clapping, cheering and wings a-flapping.*

Lilith answered back silently to her angels, *I love you, too.*

I wonder what adventures are waiting for us? Lilith asked silently to her angels, and to her husband, who was also listening.

ABOUT THE AUTHOR

KAREN JOHNSON STEUR IS A NURSE who holds a master's degree in Nursing and certification in critical care. She has published several poems and stories in Palimpsest and Stepping Stone Magazine, and is currently pursuing a master's degree in Creative Writing. Karen lives, plays, and rides her horse in Boulder County, Colorado.